Adam's Franchise
by
Lawrence Gray

In the land of Daoistan, freedom has arrived at last. The revolution liberated all, then enslaved everyone, and now it was liberating them again by allowing people to own credit cards. And a man with credit is a man who has the world at his fingertips, or at least a trip into town where the temptations are pretty much as they have always been, only more people can afford them.

ADAM'S FRANCHISE is a story about Adam and his Franchise. He is not quite sure what that means, but he is a modern man, embracing the economic miracle and taking up a gift shop franchise at a new hotel. There he will sell much the same things that he always sold: baskets, pots, cultural artefacts of various kinds, except at a modern price to foreigners, should they ever care to come to the hotel. The desert that he lives in is not the most beautiful of places, policed by Omar who has to learn how to get out of his hammock, fuelled by Castrol who just loves the smell of petrol and the visions it gives him, and terrorised by nomads and Adam's volatile brothers-in-law. But if it ever rids itself of the last vestiges of barbarism, both pre-revolutionary and revolutionary, as epitomised by Adam's indolent, lustful, embittered, rapacious, cynical, superstitious father, Saleem, then harmony – both spiritual and economic –might assert itself. Or maybe, just air-conditioning.

Daoistan exists everywhere, or has done at some time or other. And there have been many Adams.

LAWRENCE GRAY was born and educated in the UK and took BA honours in Economics and Politics from Leeds University. He lived in Hong Kong for twenty four years and in 2015 moved to Johor Bahru, Malaysia. He is a professional screenwriter and director and has written many episodes of UK and Singapore TV dramas and written, produced and directed a number of films in English and Cantonese. He directed the feature film "Lust $ Found", which he describes as an eccentric English gangster movie set in Hong Kong. He has also edited and "doctored" many feature scripts from around Asia and Australia.

Gray's collection of short stories, *Odds and Sods*, was published in 2014 as a Proverse Prize Publication. It features stories that meld French farce, Chinese Opera, religious mysticism, Hollywood and Hong Kong movies in a kaleidoscopic tour de force.

His novel *Cop Show Heaven*, also published by Proverse Press, is a parody of parodies, set in a part of Hell rented by Heaven for the purpose of allowing dead film directors to continue making movies. It is a Pirandelloesque topsy-turvy concoction of Hollywood plotting and stories of actors desperate for roles in bad movies that strangely echo the world of Hong Kong during the 1997 return to China.

In London he was a founder of the London Screenwriters' Workshop and in Hong Kong he founded the Hong Kong Writers' Circle and chaired the group for twenty years, publishing many collections of stories from a wide variety of Hong Kong writers.

Gray has taught screenwriting in various cities around the world, and was one of the first to professionalise the industry. In 1996, he won the first Public Awareness of Science drama award (PAWS) and the Hong Kong Asia Film Financing Forum's (HAF) award for best Hong Kong Film project of the year 2006.

Adam's Franchise

Lawrence Gray

Winner of the Proverse Prize 2015

Proverse Hong Kong

Adam's Franchise
by Lawrence Gray.
Copyright © Lawrence Gray 22 November 2016.
1st published in Hong Kong by Proverse Hong Kong,
22 November 2016, under sole and exclusive right and licence.
ISBN 978-988-8228-51-5

Distribution (Hong Kong and worldwide):
The Chinese University Press of Hong Kong, The Chinese University of Hong Kong,
Shatin, New Territories, Hong Kong SAR.
E-mail: cup-bus@cuhk.edu.hk Web site: www.chineseupress.com
Tel: [INT+852] 3943-9800; Fax: [INT+852] 2603-7355.

Distribution (United Kingdom): Christine Penney, Stratford-upon-Avon, Warwickshire
CV37 6DN, England.
Email: chrisp@proversepublishing.com

Also available from https://www.createspace.com/6263009

Enquiries to: Proverse Hong Kong, P. O. Box 259, Tung Chung Post Office, Tung
Chung, Lantau Island, NT, Hong Kong SAR, China.
E-mail: proverse@netvigator.com; Web: www.proversepublishing.com

Cover design by Lawrence Gray and Artist Hong Kong.
Page design by Proverse Hong Kong.

British Library Cataloguing in Publication Data.
A catalogue record for this book is available
from the British Library.

"The people of Daoistan had their revolution in the hope that, being free would liberate their imagination, allow new arts and new achievements, and thus create a new society. They destroyed everything that could possibly imprison their thoughts and actions and left themselves with a blank slate. But dreams echo the experience of life. From those dreams all creation stems. With history destroyed, traditions suppressed, marriages, births and deaths became mere ticks in a register, and only the mundane, unnoticed, uncared for facts of people's lives governed their fate and inspired little."

Post Colonial Developments in Daoistani Culture
by Dr Reginald Farthing.
Published 1989, Stodder and Houghton, £12.95.

CHAPTER ONE

Saleem lived in Waihlahm, a sand-dune encroached village named by the Keffs who once settled on the edge of the Great Shan desert. The nearest town was too new to be given any more than the name No. 3 New Town, though Saleem rarely even bothered naming it that much. For him the town was, "the town," the village, "the village," and there was not much else besides the camels and shifting sands to attract his attention.

Since his wife, Jamilla, had been run down and killed by a passing truck, Saleem's favourite pastime, apart from spitting, was to sit stroking his grey unshaven chin, and watch his house succumb to the movement of the desert.

While he pissed up against the decayed front wall, his mind blank, his time his own, all jealousies negated, and all calls to serve the motherland forgotten, Saleem noticed that before him was a painted frieze depicting the story of a blue god and his sexual exploits.

"Most obscene," muttered Saleem, when he worked out what one figure was up to with another.

For all of the thirty odd years that he had been living there, he had never seen this. Had it been covered over by plaster before? Saleem inspected the picture. The design contained scenes of what he supposed were Daoistani life. Some revolutionary guard must have attempted to make the whole thing more acceptable to the new regime. They had painted in heroic workers driving their motorcars, aeroplanes and railway trains, all of which, as far as Saleem was concerned, had done to Daoistan much the same as the blue god was doing to everyone else.

"Most boring," said Saleem pulling off another hand full of plaster to reveal further sexual exploits. "Most dull," he said about the revolutionary additions. Then placed his hand over his mouth and turned away from the images shocked at his own opinions.

7

He was above such things, he told himself. As a true son of the revolution, he was indifferent to pain, to beauty, to all but the most useful things, but he was long tired of the intellectual effort required for discerning what was truly useful and what was unnecessary. So it was better not to have any opinions at all, least of all suspiciously critical ones.

Water, however, was necessary. There was no controversy about that. Not that he cared much about water, or cared much about anything. Life consisted of eating, drinking, sleeping, waking, pissing against the wall and shitting in a hole. So long as one did not fall over in-between these points of interest, nothing else need be of concern. Today, however, was a reminder that the threat of falling over was ever present. It was the day Saleem waited for his son to bring his supply of water. The last summer's sandstorms had filled in the well and now, after several not particularly energetic attempts to dig it out, the amount of water Saleem could find no longer warranted the amount of work. He had contemplated letting nature take its course. If he was not meant to die of thirst, then why had the well dried up? Even so, he had sent a message to his son because it only seemed right that Saleem should become a burden. It served the boy right, though for what crime, Saleem did not know. He only knew that Adam irritated him and it was only fair that Saleem irritate him back.

Adam ran a shop in town and made a respectable living supplying gifts to the tourists. How he managed this, Saleem could never understand. He assumed that his son must have been doing something illegal somewhere. Indeed he was doing something that would have been illegal a few years ago. But now the government's reforms allowed all sorts of things to happen. Somehow, Saleem was sure this was a backward step. To allow what had been banned, made Saleem wonder why they had been banned in the first place? What could those great minds that created the revolution have been thinking?

Saleem heard a sound like a bag of walnuts bursting over a tin shack's roof. The thought amazed him. He could remember when he was a child how his grandfather stored freshly picked walnuts on the roof and how some would roll down the slates. The rattling became more insistent and Saleem saw the dust cloud kicked up by Adam's struggling truck.

"If he's doing as well as he says," thought Saleem, "why doesn't he buy a new one?"

Saleem walked to the gate and waited for Adam. He rolled himself a cigarette. In his life there had never been much and he had not asked for much, except for the respect of his wife, his son, and a good supply of decent tobacco. Even this meagre amount of desire he suspected of being frowned upon by the authorities.

The truck stopped, belched exhaust and Adam jumped out. He looked like his wiry little father but he had given up pyjamas for a T-shirt and Jeans.

"This looks so bad," he said, "a rich man like me having his father living in these conditions! And look at the way you dress. Who dresses like that nowadays? Look at me. These are real Levis. Authentic. It says so on the label. That is what you should be wearing. Some decent clothes. Instead of making us all look backwards. So why don't you come and live with me in town? You could find a much better job there. You would look better. You would feel better. Instead of this."

"And what would the government say?" asked Saleem, pointedly lighting up the roll of paper in his hand, then trying to drag a few puffs of tobacco smoke from it. "They appointed me caretaker and caretaker is what I am."

"The place is falling down," said Adam, "So what exactly are you taking care of?"

Saleem ignored his son. His job was to oversee the process of decay. That was all. He searched through his mind for a few suitable words: unify thought, unify action, unify the nation, eliminate ideological impurities, learn and dig! He had learnt to dig instead of learning to read or write. And now he watched his son as if watching an alien being from another planet. Just where had this person come from? Surely Saleem's blood could not run through this person's veins?

Adam sagged under the weight of the red plastic canister and staggered towards the rusty water tank. He slopped the water into it and Saleem bent over the edge to watch as the level rose. Scum floated on the surface.

"Is that it?" asked Saleem.

"There's another load to go in," said Adam, "Don't you worry."

Saleem was not worried but he was not that impressed by the quantity. He wanted more and was horrified to have to admit it to himself.

"If you lived with us," said Adam, "There would be no need for this."

"I stick to my post," said Saleem, wandering away from Adam, hoping that he would avoid one of Adam's long suffering stares that said how Saleem should at least give him a hand humping the water canisters. That boy, thought Saleem, forgets my age.

Saleem lit himself a mostly paper cigarette and walked out of the gate. He looked down the ruined street towards the desert and found, playing on the edge of the village, the dark skinned children of the desert nomads. Saleem watched one of them walking towards him. She wore a crimson sari that blew in the wind.

"What are you doing here?" he shouted at her.

She continued to approach and looked him in the eye until he nervously looked away. Judging by the bracelets around her ankles and the silver rings through her black nose, Saleem recognised her as a dancer and wondered whether he should be speaking to her at all. The girl pulled out a package from her sari, unwrapped it, and offered him some sweet meat.

"Who are you?" he asked and glanced about to see if anyone was watching him.

One of the ruined houses further into the village seemed to shimmer with the heat of fires.

"What's your name?" Saleem asked the girl.

"Amina," she said, with a giggle.

Saleem, turned away, showing her the correct degree of contempt, and headed back for his house. He could see that his job as caretaker was going to take on more importance. A vision of him fighting off these gypsies came into his mind.

Amina followed Saleem into the courtyard. Her brown kohl rimmed eyes opened wide as she looked up at the frieze and saw beneath the soot, the blue god and his dancers.

"Ah, my people have been here before."

A gust of wind unravelled her veil to reveal her long black hair. She stomped her feet and set her jewellery jangling, then stopped, flashed her eyes at Saleem and grinned.

"And now we're here again!"

A typical gypsy, thought Saleem, she'll most likely steal everything from me and die in a brothel.

Saleem sucked in a nicotine-rich lung full of fumes and thought about his dead wife. She had been very respectable. He took a final drag on his cigarette, reducing it to barely enough to hang on his bottom lip, and stared hard at Amina, who grinned, holding her veil up to cover her mouth.

"Go on! Go away now. I'm busy," he said. "Go on! Go and play."

Saleem could hear Adam trying to clear some blockage in the water tank with a rusty metal rod and watched Amina walk out of the compound. Every movement was in harmony. Even the wind blowing her sari fell in with the rhythm of her prowling walk. Saleem shuddered. He had not felt like that for a long time.

"I've finished," shouted Adam. "But you think about what I said. This can't go on, you know. No-one else lives in the village anymore. They are more sensible. At your age you could do with some modern comforts couldn't you?"

"I have the bounty of the desert," said Saleem, spitting bits of loose tobacco, "What more do I need?"

***

"That old fool," said Sufiya, Adam's wife, "He would rather have you running after him all the time than attending to your work."

In the dusty town of mud brick buildings, Sufiya too had her work. She ran the shop and cooked the meals while Adam dealt with the stock. She was plump and, being plump, she wore the local clothes feeling them to be much more flattering than western ones. Even the often banned, often revived, veil was to her liking. She found it convenient when she needed to hide from the view of leering men. This convenience declared her a modest woman and, since government policy presently favoured it as a symbol of cultural independence, declared her a patriot. To be anonymous and a patriot was all that was required of any respectable person.

However, her striving to be anonymous, did not seem to be working. Every day she would look out of the shop window and see Omar, the local policeman, parked outside in his dust spattered Paddy 12 - People's Automobile Design No. 12. He always seemed

11

to be reading a newspaper or chewing on a chapati but she knew he was watching her.

"That is not a friendly wave!" she declared to Adam when she yet again pointed Omar out to him. "Why does he always come and sit there? If he wishes to read his paper and eat his lunch why doesn't he go to his office?"

"Maybe it is because your brother has been arrested," said Adam, secretly cursing Sufiya's family for agitating her so much that pregnancy seemed nigh on impossible. She was supposed to be the calm one and he was supposed to be the nervy one, but they always seemed to take their turns in this. How could they ever conceive when one or the other of them always had their minds on other things? And presently it was the trouble with her brother.

"No," said Sufiya, "Omar has been doing that for longer."

Adam tentatively looked through the window in case he could tell whether or not the brother's smuggling had anything to do with this. No, he could not tell.

"Shoo!" said Sufiya rapping on the window and waving at Omar to leave. "Don't grin at me you fat oaf!"

"You should not speak like that."

"He cannot hear me," she said, waving her hands again. "Go away and take a bath and a shave and cut your greasy hair and wipe your hands you smelly man."

"You cannot smell him from here," said Adam, reasonably. "But he might be able to read your lips."

Adam pulled Sufiya back from the window into the darkness of the souvenir shop. She shivered at the audacity of Omar leering at her, then went behind the counter looking for a means to busy herself and forget the indignation.

"He was not leering," said Adam. "He always looks like that. He even looks like that at me. So where is the leer?"

"He is just the sort who would even leer at you," replied Sufiya, hammering the old till on the counter. The drawer popped out with a ting of the bell and gave Sufiya's comment a timely punctuation. "One day he will be trouble," she said. "If they had not illegally imprisoned my innocent brother, I would be telling him to come down here right away. He would know what to do about it."

"Yes," said Adam, the image of her fierce father and hot headed brother flashed through his mind like a mountain tribe

12

raiding an enemy village. "A policeman dangling by his entrails from our roof would be just the thing to help build business confidence in our little enterprise. I would never get a credit card then, would I?"

***

The week went by with the usual activities. Sufiya served in the shop, cooked the meals, cleaned the house, and visited the market while Adam, when not declaring his great hopes for the future, his great ambition, his desire for "something better," made the occasional tour of the workshops and back yards of friends and suppliers. With them he would talk, drink tea, play chess, sometimes discuss a new line in trinkets, shake on a deal, and promise to pay. As Adam supplied the dreams and the contacts, it seemed only fair that Sufiya supplied the work.

Frequently Adam would pull his truck into Castrol's Garage for petrol and a glimpse of Castrol's satellite TV. The garage was the oldest building in the town. It had been there before the town became a town, when it was only a village and was called Choudeih: another Keff name. None liked to talk too much about what happened to the local Keff population, but whatever injustices had befallen them in the desert, they seemed not to have been stopped in becoming the country's star economic performers.

"Look at that Keff!" said Castrol, his hair slicked with oil, his grubby overalls bearing the name that became his, a rag soaked in petrol in his back pocket.

Castrol was standing before a group of lorry drivers pointing at the screen of his TV. The machine was set up in his courtyard, the satellite dish displayed to attract custom.

"See that Keff," he said, tapping the screen. "He was nothing. He was in re-education camp for twenty years and all but forgotten. But look at him now. Importing Mercedes. That's where the money is. At the top end of the market. Not here, dealing with you lot. But dealing with them at the top. You serve the rich and they make sure you become one of them. You serve the poor and you stay poor."

The gathered drivers, nylon shirts soaked in sweat, open at the neck to show gold chains and the occasional tattoo, all nodded in agreement with Castrol's undoubted wisdom.

13

"That's not the case," said Adam who always took Castrol's pronouncements with a pinch of salt. Adam considered Castrol not a little crazy. The man lived alone, was Omar's only approximation to a friend, and was notorious for never having been further out of the town than the rail pickup. Further, Castrol's father had been crazy and acted as the local priest: telling fortunes, presiding over burials, naming ceremonies, marriages and the raising of the dead. People said the reason he was crazy was because he had been tortured during the revolution but Adam, as he recalled him, thought he was just crazy and Saleem had once said that Castrol's father had made up his ceremonies as he went along. The man always declared that he believed in only what the state allowed, and no more, but Saleem could find no religion, state sanctioned or otherwise, that bore any resemblance to that professed by Castrol's father. Still, people, especially Adam's mother, Jamilla, had put up with him until he died. She made frequent visits to hear him reciting his dreams, foretelling who was pregnant and who by, and predicting the downfall of the government - one of the many things he got wrong - and now his son preached the value of watching TV.

"And are you a rich man, Adam?" asked Castrol. "Are they making TV documentaries about you?"

"They will be," said Adam, not really sure how to answer him.

Castrol took a sniff of his petrol rag and wiped his hands clean with it. Adam could not tell what he was doing but he watched as Castrol walked around, looking him up and down, stroking his chin, humming and hahing. The other drivers, cigarettes smouldering in their mouths as they stood beneath the "No Smoking - Petrol!" sign, began opening beer bottles, returning to their chess games and watching TV.

"Yes," declared Castrol, attracting the drivers' attentions again. "You want to know why you are not rich? It is not just that you do not deal with the rich. It is that you cannot deal with them. They will spot you a mile off as not a modern sort of person."

Adam gave Castrol a wry, modern sort of smile that could only say, "What are you talking about? Compared to all these oafs and idiots whose brains are in the forearms that wrestle their lorries over the potholed highways of our beloved country, I am a sophisticated man." And in case his smile was not read, he announced, "I am a sophisticated man!" Which provoked the drivers to jeer and hurl bottle caps at him.

14

"See," said Castrol, "They don't believe you. Because it is obvious that you have not got a lifestyle. And it does not take much TV watching to know that a man without a lifestyle is invisible. Money will just pass by you without a look."

Adam pulled out his wallet and flipped it open. A fat wad of notes revealed itself to all who cared to look.

"That is toilet paper," said Castrol, "This is real money nowadays."

Castrol pulled from his overalls the plastic credit card he used to pay for each shipment of petrol.

"I get "Lifestyle" points," he announced. "It says so on my account notice. And that means that I am part of the system and the system determines who will live and who will die. If you are not part of it, then tough luck. There is no place for you in this world."

"I am part of this, don't you worry," said Adam.

"You are small fry. You are a shopkeeper. That is it," said Castrol, "And soon the multinational franchise concerns will move in and you will not compete."

"Multi what? What is this you've been listening to? You know nothing. You think you know, but you don't know. But I know."

"And what is it that you know?" said Castrol stabbing his broken nailed forefinger in the air before him. "Nothing. Not as much as me. And I know little. But what I do know is that soon we will all eat hamburgers. We will all dress like cowboys. We will all buy from the same shops everywhere. The franchise boys! You cannot beat them. I can. No franchise boy can replace me. Nobody plugs a hole in an exhaust pipe like I can for the money I charge. Nobody! But shopkeepers, you will all become employees. And maybe you will do better that way, but never rich. That is what I know. I watch the skies. They tell me these things."

Adam could not answer Castrol and knew better not to even try. The man always had something up his sleeve in response and one never knew quite how seriously one was to take him.

"Franchise!" said Adam as he walked away from Castrol and his cronies, "There will be an Adam's franchise one day."

When Adam went home, he told Sufiya all about his encounter with Castrol. He went into elaborate detail about how crazy he thought Castrol was and how he had a shelf full of junk he had purchased from TV Telesales. He had abdominal muscle exercisers, pens that wrote under water, skin whiteners, teeth

15

whiteners, stain removers of all varieties, dog brushes, self-sharpening knives, and hair styling tools even though the man was somewhat lacking hair on top of his head.

"And he calls that his "Lifestyle!"" said Adam.

"He's a lonely man," said Sufiya as she counted out that morning's takings, her fingers expertly flipping over the abacus beads.

"He says prayers over his booty every morning," said Adam laughing at how outrageous the man was, "and he goes into his father's old temple, where he keeps the engine parts, and lights incense, and puts out fruit for the god of pistons. He has an old lorry engine with a red cloth on it and bits of engines with garlands draped over them. He's been sniffing that petrol just a bit too much, if you ask me."

"Maybe," said Sufiya, not missing a beat with her counting, "But he is right. You need to deal with more important people."

Adam did not want to listen to her telling him this. Sufiya had many good points but she did not understand business. She did not understand the subtle negotiations he had to perform, the subtle balancing act between being too grand and having no respect at all. No, Sufiya did not understand these things.

"The hotel manager," said Sufiya, "I read he is looking for people to run the shops within the new complex. They are expanding and want all sorts of people. Accommodation is being offered as well."

"We have accommodation!" spluttered Adam.

"I am just telling you the facts," said Sufiya, not looking up from her counting and sorting, "And I mentioned you and your father to the man, who is a very nice man, a handsome man . . ."

"Mentioned what to whom and how?"

Sufiya, still clicking on the abacus with one hand, picked up a newspaper with the other, showed Adam an advertisement detailing all that she had told him, and then tapped the top of their telephone with it.

"So you telephoned him," said Adam, "But how do you know he was handsome?"

"I went to see him. I caught the bus and went to the hotel complex and went to ..."

Adam paced about the room slapping the dangling "Authentic" wind chimes that hung from the ceiling with his hand. He wanted

16

them to make great clanging noises, but all they made were gentle tinklings.

"I did not want you to make a fool of yourself," said Sufiya, "So I went instead. I am a woman and am allowed to ask stupid questions. Now you can go and say how stupid I was and show how clever you are and how much you know about the whole situation. You can take your father there too. It will be all right. I have discovered this for you."

***

If he could have done so, Adam would have let Sufiya take the water to Waihlahm, but unfortunately she could not drive the truck. So Adam sighed as he drove the weekly supplies over to his father. He considered it a boring journey across a desert track to a destination without the usual distractions. No one was there with whom to drink a few cans of beer. No one was there to offer him a newly made "antique" for the shop. And there were no bored young girls looking for distraction from their pot cleaning and clothes mending to flirt with. Worse, he felt as if Sufiya had sent him on an errand. As the truck hit another spine damaging pot hole, Adam wrestled with the steering wheel and shouted out:

"Yes! She's right. She is always right, but just for once she could be wrong."

Along with the week's water, Adam took a fat clucking chicken to his father. It lay beside him on the passenger seat, glazed eyed and nervily twitching as if anticipating its fate. Adam had been thirteen when he saw his first chicken. One day, they started arriving by the crate-load in the schoolyard and the teachers told everyone they could take a pair home. He could remember all the excitement and the secret meetings of the adults discussing the change of policy. Everyone was to own their own chickens! Suddenly everyone had the one thing they had coveted for years: fresh chicken! Adam could remember being so excited, but he doubted merely having something would excite him anymore.

On arrival at the village, Adam found Saleem standing before the house looking bewildered. A couple of young tourists were waving their camera at him. They had backpacks, shorts, very red knees, and were snapping away. Adam pulled up beside them and put his best schoolboy English into action.

"Hallo," he shouted, "how are you? Come visit my shop. No3 Town. Just up the road. Business Unit Five! Hallo! Good souvenirs. Authentic. Many old antiques. Some new ones too as well also."

The tourists inexplicably laughed as Adam leapt down from his truck and immediately began shaking hands.

"Hallo hallo," he said, "All prices written down in good English. No bargaining. No hassle!"

Adam prided himself on having spotted the reluctance of Westerners to bargain and spotted how their ears pricked up at words like "Authentic" and "Antique". He often invented an old grandfather who supposedly spent his life making any article a tourist showed interest in. Sufiya never did that. She merely held up a piece of paper with the price on it and asked if they wanted to pay cash or credit. She claimed she sold as much as he ever did, but Adam thought that was only because she spent more time in the shop. "Five minutes with me," he told her, "And they will return with their friends for more. Five minutes with you, and they will just buy the first thing they pick up and leave." Adam had a theory that the Westerner travelled to escape efficiency and machinery and wanted to find "authentic" human beings with "human" virtues. The quickest way to a Western wallet was to stir the Western heart without provoking any moral dilemma.

"Where are you going? Where have you been?" continued Adam, "This is a good place. Newly discovered by tourists. And we are rediscovering our colonial heritage. We now know we learnt much from you people. Many of these fine buildings were inspired by Englishmen. And Frenchmen. Not the Spanish though. Germans were here too. They built the state brewery. We are very fond of the Germans. Ha? The French left us good coffee. The Germans left us good beer! And the English left us! Haa! Mark Twain! Good guy. George Bernard Shaw, another good Englishman! And yes. And Joseph Conrad! All True Blue English. Yes. Good. We learn all about England now. What a pity about Charles and Di! They need a jolly good spanking. Yes. And Margaret Thatcher. Beat the Argies! A good bashing. Yes. We get all the very latest news now. 2001! A new millennium."

The tourists smiled.

"You are Germans! I can tell."

The tourists shook their heads. They were Swedes.

"Ah, yes," said Adam searching his mind for the slightest piece of information he had about Sweden. "They did not colonise anywhere!" he said beaming and made the Swedes laugh. "But now you are coming to see what you were missing, ha?"

The Swedes explained how they had strayed off the road to explore. They had heard of this extraordinary village with its strange ornamented houses and the "magnificent" frieze had taken their fancy.

"Yes," said Adam, "It is magnificent."

He made a note of that word: magnificent. And looked around to try to find out exactly what it was they considered "magnificent."

"An authentic antique," he added.

The tourists took turns to stand beside Adam as the other took a photograph. Adam gave a cheesy grin and pointed to his father.

"Don't forget the old man," said Adam, "It is his livelihood. You must not forget that these people are very poor." Saleem smiled as the Swedes handed him a few coins and then, with Adam benignly smiling and shouting, "Don't forget to visit my shop!" They waved goodbye, climbed into their hired car and drove off. Immediately, Adam and Saleem's smiles dropped.

"See," said Adam, "by living here, you've become nothing but an exhibit in a museum."

"But it is you that have become the buffoon!" said Saleem counting the coins in the palm of his hand.

"You would have got nothing if it had not been for me!" grumbled Adam as he unloaded the back of the truck. "And also you would not get any water if it was not for me."

Adam glared at Saleem, grunted his disapproval, then, laden down, heavily plodded across the dried earthen squares of the long dead garden, and poured water into the metal tank at the back of the house. Fetching and carrying, he thought to himself, and sucking up to strangers for a few coins, that was the extent of his life so far. That would have to change. He was beyond that but he was not sure how far beyond it or what beyond it really meant. He shook the last drop of water from the red plastic canister and returned to his father staring up at the wall. Suddenly it all came into focus for Adam. There he saw the story of the blue god and dancing for the blue god was a black-faced dancer wearing little more than her ankle bracelets.

"Westerners are always interested in pornography," said Adam. "Obscenity is part of their everyday culture. The exploitation of one person for another's pleasure can be very lucrative."

Saleem puffed on his cigarette, filled the air before him with smoke and gave a shrug.

"Maybe you should clean it up," said Adam enthusiastically. "You could advertise and charge them. Then it would be worth your being caretaker and it would pay for my petrol and my time."

A cloud darkened the sun for a moment and the chicken, still trussed up and lying upon the hot passenger seat of the truck, started clucking as if enjoying the experience.

"Yes," said Adam, warming to his theme. "We clean it up. Add a few extra bits and pieces. The sort of thing the likes of those two find interesting and make some postcard pictures of it. I sell them in the shop and tell people where they can come and see the original. Then they can come to you and you can charge them a fee for taking photographs."

As he spoke, Adam strode about the courtyard, looking from one angle, then from another, attempting to assess which was the best from a photographic point of view.

"It does not take much of an expert to take a photograph of a wall," said Adam, "I'm sure it could be done."

Adam watched Saleem open the truck door, pick up his chicken by its feet and listen to its clucking.

"Well?" said Adam.

"Even the Chicken says you are stupid," replied Saleem. "If they have already bought pictures from you, why should they come here to take them themselves? When they already have them as postcard pictures, what is the purpose?"

"You know nothing of human nature," said Adam.

"I know they won't want your pictures," said Saleem, "They might want me! They probably think I painted this!"

"You know," said Adam, "I think you're right. They'll take your picture home and show their friends. Here's a picture of another monkey, they'll say. Except this time without his drum!"

As Adam burst out laughing, his father thrust the chicken under his nose and snapped its neck with a flick of his wrist. Adam pushed his father aside and shook his head.

"You're an evil old bastard," said Adam, "You have no sense of humour."

"What have I to laugh about? I have a son who does not give his old father the respect that is his right."

"Instead you have a son who comes here every week and makes sure you will live another. Instead you have a son who is so concerned about his father's welfare that he has been negotiating with some very tricky people to get him a decent place to live in."

"What are you talking about?" said Saleem, "What do you mean?"

"Ahaa!" said Adam, "You go and get some decent clothes on and I will show you."

"What are you on about?" demanded Saleem.

"I am going to take you somewhere very interesting."

"Where?"

"Go and get shaved. Get washed. And put on some clean clothes."

"Clean clothes?"

"Cleaner than those things. You look like you've not changed them since mother died. Come to think of it, I don't think you've changed them since I left home. I don't think you've ever changed them. And I don't think the man who wore them before you ever changed them!"

"What is the point of wearing out good clothes for no good purpose?"

"Well I have a good purpose for you," said Adam, climbing into his truck and switching on the radio. "I will wait until you are ready. But you better be ready in ten minutes otherwise I shall go and you shall never find out what I am talking about."

"I am not doing anything unless you tell me!"

Adam turned the radio up loud and began to sing along with the singer. "My love is like a big machine pumping power into all your parts..."

"Will you stop singing!"

"You have nine minutes left. Do not hesitate. These opportunities happen very few times. You cannot vegetate any longer."

"Vegetate? What sort of word is that?"

"You need a new Life Style."

"I do not!"

"You have eight minutes. That's not long to get ready. Go on. Go wash. You've plenty of water."

Adam turned his head and pretended to be engrossed in the song on the radio. In his mirror he could see his father deciding whether he should spit at the truck and curse Adam, or find out what the mysterious offer was. Saleem scuttled towards the door of the house with the twitching chicken in hand. He knew the old bastard would not be able to resist his invitation. If he had told him that it was just for a caretaking position, he would not have been so keen. But by implying it was a big deal, he hooked him.

Much to Adam's surprise he saw his father hurrying from the house, not particularly clean shaven, but hair parted and wearing a gleaming white pair of pyjamas, or at least gleaming in as much as they were not completely filthy.

"What has got into you?" asked Adam, admiring this vision of pristine rectitude and checking his watch: eight and a half minutes flat. This sort of hurrying was unheard of.

"Nothing!" said Saleem as he climbed in to the cab.

Adam felt that maybe the old man was not so bad after all. He just needed a bit of a push, like himself really, and most likely he also felt that change was in the air.

"Maybe with a new job, a new home, you'll get yourself a new wife," said Adam. "I'm sure my mother would understand. A new wife would sort you out."

"Like yours sorts you out," said Saleem, not meaning it to be any kind of compliment.

But Adam laughed and set the truck bouncing along the track, tailboard flapping, grit and dust churning, and horn blaring at the gypsies he saw now encamped amongst the ruins of the village.

"You've neighbours," said Adam, "No wonder you're all dressed up. Got to show them who's boss eh?"

"That's right," said Saleem, "Otherwise they'll steal everything."

"You haven't got anything."

"Just as well then."

Saleem clung on to the side strap as the truck sped out of the village across the desert. The dunes ran with loose sand as a hot wind blew in from the west. A mirage shimmered all around wherever one looked. Withered succulents provided homes for termites, shade for lizards and food for half-starved herds of goats

22

that bounced at the toot of a horn. The sooner it was tarmacked over, thought Adam, the better.

"So what's all this in aid of?" asked Saleem.

"The job," explained Adam, "Is that of night-watchman."

"What sort of job is that?"

"Much the same as the one you have now, only you get accommodation."

"I've got accommodation."

"Does your accommodation have air conditioning though?"

"I have all the air I need," said Saleem.

"Night-watchmen at the hotel," said Adam, as the steering wheel swung wildly in harmony with the holes in the road they had now joined, "Live better than I do myself!"

"Then you take the job," muttered Saleem.

"I am an entrepreneur," said Adam, "I wish to make a fortune whereas you need only to make a living."

Saleem sat up, rolled down the window, and spat out of it.

"At least you roll down the window nowadays," said Adam hitting the horn to pass the slow town bus and get out from under its black exhaust fumes.

Soon they were approaching the hotel complex, which sat in the desert like a moon station. The great domes, minarets, fountains and green gardens were separated from the dilapidated greyness of the surroundings by an electric fence. Adam crunched the gears of his truck as he slowed to meet speed bumps. The yellow and black striped barrier rose and a smartly uniformed guard beckoned Adam through.

"It is hard to know whether they want to keep people in or out," muttered Saleem. "It is like a prison."

"A very expensive prison," said Adam. "One that either of us should be so lucky to be thrown in."

After parking the truck, Adam mockingly held the door open for Saleem and waited for Saleem's reaction to the cupolas and minarets that rose up about them. These fellows who designed and built such palaces knew a thing or two, thought Adam. But Saleem grunted his disapproval and followed Adam through the gardens hissing with cicadas, rustling with snakes, and dripping with water coughed out of electronically controlled sprinklers.

"See," said Adam, "Here they have as much water as they like."

23

Saleem hesitated for a moment as if he had not noticed the water before Adam mentioned it. There was a look of horror on his face.

"It is real," added Adam, in case Saleem believed it to be some kind of hallucination.

Adam pushed Saleem forward and they walked across the large marble-floored foyer to the office of Rashid, the manager. Music gently twanged in the background. No particular tune could be made out. There was a little drumbeat, a little riff, maybe a human voice floating somewhere out amongst the cooling sounds of flowing water. There was a squawk of a macaw that drew Adam and Saleem's attention to the big red and blue bird shabbily sitting on a perch stretching out its ragged wings. And then in front of them, a man at least two feet taller than them and at least three feet wider, with pink face, shoulders and knees, strolled by in a pair of red, white and blue shorts, a towel dangling from his hand.

"He is an American I bet," said Adam, "They are much bigger than English people. Eat a lot of hamburgers."

Saleem nodded in agreement with this explanation.

"This place is dripping with money," said Adam feeling happy that he had had this magnificent idea. Not only did he have his father up for offer, but also he felt he could supply the Hotel's souvenir shop with cheaper and better goods. "Authentic," was the keyword he was planning to use on Rashid. He had practised his spiel with Sufiya who had hummed and haahed and thought he was over doing it a bit, but appreciated that enthusiasm was definitely something a man like Rashid might like.

"Stay here," said Adam, parking his father by Rashid's door. "Do not spit on the floor. Do not make a nuisance of yourself."

Saleem shook his head and muttered, "To be insulted is one thing, to have one's son do the insulting is another."

"I am not insulting you," said Adam, "I am merely pointing out some of the niceties of life here. And remember that all these Westerners have paid good money to be here. It is our job to relieve them of it as often as possible, and to do that, we must smile, and not spit."

Saleem muttered to himself and then wandered off towards the poolside.

"Don't go too far away," said Adam.

Saleem glared at the young bag boys in their smart uniforms as they indolently lounged on the lobby furniture. "Fetching and carrying," he shouted back to Adam, "Fetching and carrying: is that any alternative to smoking my cigarette and watching the desert? When the great prophets came out of the desert, they did not say, "Thou shalt fetch and carry!""

Saleem sniffed, making a fearsome noise in preparation for a good spit, but Adam quickly raised his finger and waved it, forbidding any such nonsense. For the moment Adam stood staring at his father. The noise of long brown fingers tapping a pot drum filled the air, like a fistful of coins falling. Saleem turned towards the sound and Adam followed him out of the hotel lobby towards the swimming pool, where at the far end boards had been lain down for Amina to dance. She was covered by a purple and saffron coloured veil and her black ankles jangled with bracelets. With all the gold and silver dangling about her, her blackness was made all the darker. She twirled on her knees as a turbaned old man beat on the drum.

"The whole bunch of them have taken over one of the houses in the village," explained Saleem.

Adam watched the girl dance. He calculated that she must have been about fifteen years old and from deep in the desert. She was also probably a slave, although no one called slaves "slaves" anymore, since it was illegal to have them. Or had the government's new reforms allowed slavery again? Either way, she would have been sold at an early age to the dance troupe. They would have trained her and led her around their circuit. By now, since she was getting older, they would be bringing men in for her. He felt a shudder of excitement at the thought.

"She's a mad woman," said Saleem. "Completely crazy."

"How do you know?" asked Adam.

"She thinks she's a camel and that's that," said Saleem lighting up another cigarette. "Go on. Go and see your manager. Let me watch this."

Adam took another look at Amina and then, feeling a little nervous, walked back into the foyer and knocked hard on Rashid's door. The voice inviting Adam in sounded not unfriendly, though it was definitely the sound of a man who was used to getting his own way.

Rashid, tall, friendly eyed, long nosed, stood up from behind his desk and offered his hand to Adam, who immediately noticed that Rashid wore a very expensive looking suit.

"Sit down," said Rashid, "Your wife has told me all about your ideas."

"She has?"

"Oh yes. A beautiful woman and a very intelligent one. I bet she's a handful. It takes a real man to deal with someone like her."

"Well, yes," said Adam, "She's a tough cookie. But putty in my hands. Devoted to me she is. I have no complaints. On the contrary. I think no-one has a better wife."

"I think you might well be right. Let's talk business eh? How can I be sure of taking delivery on a regular basis," asked Rashid, sitting upon his desk and looking down upon Adam slumped in the armchair. "How can quality be maintained, how can I be sure that the customers will like these goods?"

Adam looked up into those kindly eyes, so sincere, so concerned about the requirements of customers, so ... such an expensive suit! Where did this guy get such a thing in this part of the desert? How did this party cadre justify such an expense? Adam had seen even the highest officials on Castrol's TV set wearing crumpled old-fashioned suits with little woollen pullovers under the jacket and when standing besides Westerners looked shabby and second rate. Rashid though, could have been a world leader. Or better still, he could have been a film star!

"I wouldn't want you to commit yourself to something that you could not deliver, at the minuscule price that I can offer you," added Rashid, his eyes burning a hole through Adam's forehead.

Adam's hand stretched forward and brushed a speck of dust off the side pocket of Rashid's Suit. So stiff, so sharp, thought Adam. Rashid glared at Adam's hand. Adam withdrew it immediately.

"There was something crawling on your suit," explained Adam.

**

Inside Castrol's garage the flicker of the satellite TV beckoned. Omar played with the idea of doing what he usually did about this time of day. He could go there, sit and chat and drink with the truck drivers. Or maybe he should go and see that film everyone was talking about? It had good music. The trailer on TV was very sexy. He wished all lady bandits were like that. He wished any bandit were like that. Instead, he thought he would drive by Sufiya's shop and check up on her. This time was not going to be like the other times. This time he would make his presence felt.

Omar drove on past Castrol's garage and parked the car outside Adam's shop. He turned off the ignition and took a deep breath. Was his uniform irretrievably crumpled? Was the stain on his shirtfront too conspicuous? Did his breath smell too much? There was no way of telling but he felt reasonably assured that he was not completely beyond the pale. He had made a special effort to avoid spilling more than was necessary as he ate. He opened the car door, rocked his bulk in order to work up the momentum to swing himself free of the car and made a mental note to himself: either he go on a diet or get himself a new car. He opted for getting himself a new car if he could. But he had sent the official request to head office every month for the past five years without any luck so it was almost by way of a private joke with himself.

Omar looked across the road. He steeled himself. He was going to do something about his lust, his passion, no, his love - that was the term he preferred to use.

He crossed the road and peered into the shop window. There seemed to be no one there. He tried the shop door but it was locked. All that energy he had expelled for nothing. Omar was about to head back up the road to Castrol's place when he heard Sufiya singing. He stepped back and looked up towards the roof. She was most likely upstairs hanging out washing, which was about the only thing any of the local ladies did on the roof. He both loved her for her devotion to men, and hated her for her domesticity. Why could she not be a straightforward whore then he could indulge his fantasy without worry. He would be one of many and the guilt would be shared all round.

"Sufiya!" he called, looking up at the roof. This is insanity, he said to himself. "This is a friendly call," he shouted up to where he hoped she was listening. "I thought I would stop by and see if everything was all right. Especially with all your men away."

Omar did not like the way that sounded. Every woman's man was away at this time of day. So why should he pick her out for special treatment? But he had to make some sort of contact.

"That is," he continued, "As a policeman I am supposed to check these things. But I can also be friendly as well."

Omar did not like the way that came out either.

"That is," he went on trying to rescue the situation, "I am being a friend, but not anything improper, because it is also a duty."

That was better he thought but there was no reply. He listened a little more, but all was stillness. Even the desert wind had stopped picking up the dust. Somewhere in the distance he could hear a water pump chugging away but other than that there was not so much as the sound of footsteps on a staircase.

Omar walked back across the road and looked up at the roof trying to catch a glimpse. Maybe she was not there at all. Maybe all there was, was the flapping of some washing on a line. Perhaps that was just as well. Omar climbed back into his car and reversed it rapidly up the road, stopping it outside Castrol's garage.

Castrol stood by the red hand-driven petrol pump grinning and eating an orange. He peeled it with his teeth and spat the peel onto the floor.

"Perhaps you need, No Bald Patch: The Spray," said Castrol as Omar climbed out of his car.

"I am not bald!" said Omar, "But I am sure she is lonely."

Castrol pushed the nozzle of his petrol pump into the tank of the car and began hand cranking the machine.

"Ogling her is one thing," said Castrol, "But crying out to her like that, is another. Be careful."

"This is pure lust," said Omar mournfully. "I know there is no future in it. But I cannot help myself. Nothing happens here. What else have I got to prey on my mind?"

"You will make love to her and then there will be a feud," said Castrol sagely, "And then you will have a lot on your mind. Before the revolution the mere sight of a man ogling a married woman would have families wiping each other out in most hideous circumstances. Lucky for you we are civilised modern people nowadays."

Omar paid Castrol for the petrol knowing that Castrol's pump always showed at least a litre more than had gone in, but Omar reckoned that since Castrol performed the odd free repair they were most likely about even.

Sufiya's kitchen was sweltering when Adam entered. The gas rings were at full blaze and Sufiya was hacking and chopping everything in sight. She hurled scraps of meat, prawn slices, bean sprouts, rice noodles all atomised with her hefty chopper, into hissing black skillets that clanged like gongs as she whisked around the ingredients with a huge metal spoon.

"That Omar," she said, "He is a dangerous man. He is a mad rapist. He needs reporting, I'm telling you."

"What has that man done?"

"He has not done anything but he makes me think he will," said Sufiya as she turned up the flames of the oven and set the fat blazing for a few seconds.

"He is the police and so there is nothing I can do," said Adam pulling a can of lager from the fridge. "Besides he has not done anything. I cannot confront him about something he has not done."

"Talk to Rashid. He is a party member. He can do something," said Sufiya. "I take it you had a good meeting?"

"I think I should be more frightened of Rashid than Omar!" said Adam.

"Nonsense!"

"I am not so sure," said Adam. "You think much too highly of him."

"Well if you won't speak to him, I will!"

"Let me conclude my business negotiations before we start asking favours."

"This is not a favour. You mention Omar to him and he will report it to someone, without you asking him. That is the way they work. A party member only has to mention in passing and something is done."

"I don't think Rashid has that much power. He looks the part, dresses well, but why is he here? Why is a man like that working out here?"

"Because I tell you there is a lot of money coming into the region. That is why you must deal with him. He is going to be important. That is why he is here."

"He has some disgrace at the back of him. That is why he would be running a hotel out here and not running a ministry in the capital. That is why a smooth operator like him would be here. So don't you be saying anything to him. No more. Leave it to me. Let us play this shrewdly."

"You playing something shrewdly, means not playing it at all."

Sufiya turned her back on Adam and began assaulting more vegetables with her chopper. Adam watched a moment then closed in and began to put his arms round her.

"Don't you worry. I can play when I want to."

"I must get this ready," she said, shaking Adam off, "Otherwise you will not be eating tonight."

"Some things are worth going without food for!"

"Nothing is worth wasting food for!"

Sufiya pushed Adam away and left him wondering what to do next. With a deep sigh he peeled open his lager and headed for the stairs to the roof. That Omar had a lot to answer for, thought Adam as he climbed up to the roof. On the roof Adam sat on a dusty armchair that he had rescued from a fire at his father's village. Leaning back in the soft creaking springs, he looked up at the blue cloudless sky and thought how he envied the tourists sitting around the pool drinking and watching the dancer. They owned the world. They knew things. They built things. They had been to the moon. As a boy he had seen a documentary on the School's TV once and had been very impressed. By now, he mused, the moon must have a swimming pool, a hotel, and the locals would be dancing and selling carpets.

Adam sat drinking and musing and watching the shooting stars above the town's dusty graveyard of broken tombs, where his mother was buried. There he could see a flash of purple as the dance troupe walked their way to a performance in the marketplace. The drums still beat and the fiddle still played. The jet-black hair of Amina flicked across his vision. Around the crumbling tombstones she danced, picking her way over the broken rocks, her long thin fingers, hennaed and red nailed, snaking in the air.

These sorts of girls know things, thought Adam. They teach them things to please men. If the world ever lost such people, what pleasure in life would there ever be? A wife was one thing, but a girl like that, she was another. She did things no wife would ever do. She was beyond shame. She was there for others to take pleasure in. Love itself paled and faded into insignificance before - He tried to compose the right line to describe her. But words failed him. Before whatever she was, for the man he was, all else withered. If the world lost such creatures, he thought, it would lose its soul.

CHAPTER TWO

"**B**ut there is nothing in this house!" said Amina, as Saleem showed off where he lived.

He watched Amina prowling through the empty rooms; their light was golden, their shadows were black, their smell was dry and hot. The stone floors were cool. She clapped her hands and the noise echoed about the rooms. She stomped her feet and giggled, covering her blackened teeth with her veil.

"Crazy! See what I mean? Totally insane," Saleem whispered to his dead wife and wondered whether she approved of allowing gypsies into her home. There were some who would shoot them on sight, but Saleem could see little harm in most of them. People just envied the fact that they were free to come and go, no matter how often the government had tried to attach them to work units and get them settled down. On the whole they were poor and ignorant and if you made sure that everything was locked away from them, largely harmless and sometimes entertaining. He could remember his father telling him stories of his grandfather and the gypsy girls, two at a time! That was before the revolution though when people knew no better.

Amina ran from room to room, ululating. She came to a stop before one of the windows. Saleem could hear Adam's truck churning up the dust along the desert road and cursed his son's bad timing. Though what his son was interrupting he was not very clear in his mind. But he had his hopes, but only vague ones since such a thing was impossible for a man of his age with no money, no possible means of enticing a young girl. Besides, he could not remember the last time he actually did anything that could even approximate sexual activity. Jamilla, his wife, had long lost interest and he sort of went along with this, seeing it as the sign of the end of everything. Now was the time to make his peace, though with what he was not sure.

"The man on the roof," Amina said as she peered out of the window, and then turned and pushed passed Saleem. He reeled in a waft of sandalwood perfume. She must have stolen some soap from the hotel, he thought. And never had stolen goods been put to better usage.

Saleem followed Amina into the courtyard and watched Adam arriving with the weekly water delivery. So much for Adam's ability to pull strings, thought Saleem with contempt, a whole week and no news about any job. Not that Saleem wanted a job but he did like the idea of being able to belittle his son.

The hand brake creaked as it stopped the truck dead. The truck door swung open and Adam jumped down to the ground. Saleem watched Adam preening himself, obviously aware that he had an audience. The snotty nosed, barefooted children of the gypsies were running out of their encampments among the ruined houses and dancing about him. Also the dance troupes' manager, the fiddler, sidled over to Adam, scratching out a few musical notes on an instrument called a sarangi. Everybody's dirty little hands reached forward cupped to receive anything going.

"He's not going to pay you a cent!" shouted Saleem, annoyed at them for giving his son the honour of being begged from. "Go on, clear off. Leave him alone."

"I'm Ali," said the fiddler, lowering his sarangi, and giving his straggly beard a tug as if it would set his turban straight on his head.

"You don't need to give him your performance!" growled Saleem. "Save that for the tourists."

Adam ignored his father.

"Ali, do you make the sarangi yourself?" he asked. "Tell me how many can you make in a week?"

"Why would I want to make any more?" asked Ali.

"For cash," said Adam. "You could do with some cash couldn't you?"

"We have quicker ways of making money than making these," said Ali with a grin.

"Yes I bet you have ways," muttered Saleem as he lit up a cigarette and sent the grey lizards that clung to the wall beside him, darting for cover.

"Are you going to take up the fiddle?" Adam asked his father, "Or are you learning to dance?"

33

"If I did," said Saleem, "I would dance better than you."

Saleem then found Amina was standing beside him, hiding her face with her veil and giggling like an imbecile.

"And who's this?" asked Adam.

"You've seen her before," said Saleem through a cloud of smoke, "What is more to the point, is whether you are making your big deal still? Or was all that so much wind talking? A whole week has gone by and where's this job you talked about? Where are these strings you said you were pulling for me? You know what I think? I think you are all talk and no action. That is what I think."

"This old fool here," said Adam to Ali, "understands nothing. I could get him a decent job and a decent place to live, but he would much rather stay here and cause me all this bother."

"That is a lie," said Saleem. "I went with you. I did my bit. I was not lacking. You were."

"Don't worry," said Adam, putting his hand on his father's shoulder, "It's all being taken care off. Patience! Patience!"

Saleem shivered at this patronising attitude of his son and shook himself free of him. He could feel himself getting very angry because nobody was listening to him and he could see that Amina was smiling at Adam and Adam was all eyes for her and Ali was no doubt calculating how much he could charge Adam for ten minutes in bed with the girl.

"Are you a very important person?" Amina asked.

"Me?" Said Adam.

"No, idiot, me!" said Saleem.

"No," said Amina, "I was asking this man here."

Adam straightened his back and looked thoughtful.

"I am working on being an important person," said Adam.

"But as yet, like his father, he is of no consequence!" said Saleem.

Adam glared at him and Saleem took a long puff on his cigarette. Unfortunately this led to a choking fit and by the time he had composed himself, some of the children had begun tugging at Saleem's arms, yelling and screaming for him to join in their game.

"Shoo!" said Adam. "Be off with you. Go away! Aaak!"

The children took up the cry and ran off squawking like parrots.

"Don't do that!" said Saleem, "What other chances are there of me having children come around?"

34

"When I have time to sire them," Adam replied. "But in the mean time I am running after you and running a business."

The children returned and begged Saleem to join them. At first Saleem ignored their pleadings but he saw the look of distaste on Adam's face and so took a deep breath and staggered from one child to the next in an attempt to catch, and not to catch them, but most of all to annoy his son.

"Ali!" demanded Adam, "If you help us unload this lot, I'll give you a lift into town if you want."

Adam heaved up a big jerry can from the back of his truck and Ali, as if suddenly woken, did the same and followed him towards the water tank.

"For an old man, you've a strong arm," said Adam. "Whereas that breathless red faced fool cannot lift a thing."

Ali gave a toothless grin, every sinew taut with effort and carried the water to the tank and poured it in, mixing the scum of the surface, until there was something close to a clear clean tank full. Sweat dripped from Adam's nose as he scooped up a handful of the water and washed his face.

"Get in the truck," he said to Ali. Ali nodded and did what he was told.

Saleem pushed the screeching children aside and got close enough to speak with Adam. "Do not do whatever it is you are thinking of doing," he growled. "It is like that wall over there, one more crack and it will fall down and that sand dune will be up around your neck."

"Look at the state of you," said Adam, using his shirt to try to mop up the sweat that was dripping off his father's chin, "You are not a dignified person."

"I am not a fool," said Saleem, shaking Adam off him, "What you are thinking..."

"I am not thinking anything. It is you that is doing the thinking. And it is a shame you are only having these kinds of thoughts. If you were really thinking, you would not be forcing me to come out here every week."

"Why do you want me to live with you?" asked Saleem, "What happiness will that bring to either of us? Will it get me that job you speak of? And wasn't one of the benefits of this job, a room at the hotel? Why not wait until then? Why this idiotic idea of living with you temporarily?"

"You will see what I have made of myself. That is why."

"I can see now what you have made of yourself. So what further happiness can it bring?"

After that, Saleem bent over the water tank, cupped his hands and began scooping up the water and drinking it. He kept drinking until he could hear his son striding back towards his truck muttering how insufferable his father was, how he was just not trying, how the world was opening up and here was he, the man's son, offering him a chance to see something of it, a chance to reap some of the benefits, to have a taste of the riches life could offer. And it was all being thrown back in his face as if it did not matter.

"Why are you telling that scoundrel such lies about me!" shouted Saleem.

Ali smiled and then climbed into the seat beside Adam.

"What are you going into town for?" yelled Saleem. But Ali could not hear him shouting as the truck jolted into life and began its dusty journey back towards No 3 Town. Saleem could hear Amina giggling behind him, then she sidled past, wafting sandlewood through the air, and walked on down the road, every move a dance-step in itself.

***

Adam panicked as Sufiya hammered on the kitchen door. He had locked it while he removed his money from beneath a stone under the kitchen table. He had removed the lid from the cash box, prodded at the dirty crumpled notes and contemplated whether his wife would notice if any of the jewellery in the box was missing. But now she was hammering on the door yelling: "Put your money away! I know what you're doing!"

"Shut up!" shouted Adam. "People will hear."

He quickly slammed shut the lid and dropped the box into the hole.

"Come on," said Sufiya hammering. "I have work to do."

Adam quickly pocketed a couple of gold rings and when all looked in order, he calmly stood up and unlocked the kitchen door. Sufiya burst in.

"What are you looking at me like that for?" he said. "I have to know how much we have. I have to know the rate at which I bring in money. It is most important to know the rate at which you bring it in. That is the only way one can estimate how much one can afford to borrow. That is the way it is done."

"And how much have you added to it since yesterday, when you last counted it?"

"I am contemplating opening a bank account and I just don't know whether it is worth the journey as yet. After all, it takes such a long time and I don't know whether I can afford the time yet."

"Send your father," said Sufiya. "That would be something useful he could do."

Adam shook his head.

"It is too dangerous," he said. "There are bandits."

"But he would be a good disguise. No-one would think he had anything worth stealing."

Adam shook his head again.

"He would do something stupid," he said. "He would open the account in his name, or someone else's and forget who's."

Sufiya grunted her disapproval, began collecting pots and jars from the shelves, and started to grind the spices in a black mortar. She said no more, and neither smiled nor frowned as she busied herself with her routine. Adam knew this was her way of torturing him though he could not imagine what he had done to warrant such torture.

"I'll leave you to it," he said, retreating out through the kitchen door, knowing that whatever he did now put him in the wrong, and all the more in the wrong, because she would never complain, never shout, never mention whatever it was she felt he was in the wrong about.

Closing the door behind him, Adam looked out over his wife's vegetable patch towards the graveyard. A couple of vultures hopped about the broken stones like monstrous rag puppets. They would be eating a dog, thought Adam. Or a cat.

Adam clapped his hands and shooed the vultures as he scrambled over the dusty ruins of the gravestones. There would be some way of justifying what he was about to do, he thought.

After walking to his mother's last resting place, he began tidying it. He kicked a few stones off the surface, tried to balance the stone memorial back in place, with little success. For a moment he almost prayed. He knew his father spoke to his mother, but he always thought this a sign of senility. Now, what would she say if he asked her about this matter? He thought a moment, but could not

37

think of any way in which to put such a delicate question. Then he decided that if there was an after life, or a god, or anything, there was no need to try to form the question because such a being would know what was in his heart regardless of what he said.

Suddenly the doves rose in unison. Adam took this sound as the sound of life bursting forth. That was it, he thought, life was noisy, was full of misadventures, full of moments where one flew and fought and squabbled and that was the way it should be. This one thing he was about to do was going to break him out of his monotonous existence. It was going to turn him into the very person that he was sure Sufiya wanted him to be. It was going to make him the sort of person who could sire a child. This lack, this laziness, this essential smallness that he felt at heart, was about to be swept away. An adventure, he thought, just a little one, would make him irresistible. He began joining in with the noise.

"Whaaak!" he yelled. "Whaak! Whaak!"

He danced about the grave, kicking up the dust. He was going places, he thought and then sang out.

"I am wealthy with your love!" He had heard this song on his truck radio. "Let me feel inside your wallet!"

"What are you doing?" shouted Sufiya, waiting for him by the back door of the shop.

Adam stopped his dancing and looked back across the dusty ruins of the graveyard. Sufiya stood by the door with her yellow scarf blowing in the wind, the only colour to be seen. Sheepishly Adam grinned at her and put his hands in his pockets. He rolled a gold ring with a green stone between his fingers and told himself that he deserved a little treat.

***

Saleem was sitting amongst the dunes, his face glowing with the flickering light of a sputtering fire. He listened to the music and watched Amina whirling round and round, her skirt flaring out revealing her black legs. Somewhere in the darkness a hand rattled out a rhythm on a pot drum.

Besides Saleem sitting by the fire, a group of men from No. 3 New Town lay on Afghani carpets smoking. Children clambered amongst them lighting up their pipes. Besides Amina, were other girls wearing saffron and scarlet saris beating more drums and

38

singing. When Amina lost her balance, sprawling face down in the sand, the others began dancing in formation. Amina turned over onto her back and howled at the moon.

"Crazy, see what I mean?" said Saleem to Ali.

Saleem puffed at his pipe with one hand and Bar-B-Q'd a slab of mutton on a stick with the other. Then he saw Adam approaching over the dunes.

"And what are you doing here?" sneered Saleem.

"I was just passing," said Adam with a note of bewilderment. "When I heard all the commotion."

"Is that so?" said Saleem. "And you heard all the commotion above the din of that truck of yours. I didn't realise we were making so much noise."

"Noise can carry a long way in the desert," said Adam.

Amina stood up from where she lay hot and breathless from her dancing. Saleem watched as a man's hand closed over her ankle and began to smooth its way up her leg. With a flick of her heel she kicked the man off and walked down the slope to the fire.

"Some dance, huh?" she said to Adam, "It is supposed to be about pulling water in from the well."

"And then falling over," said Adam.

Amina laughed and hid her blackened teeth with her jewel-laden hand.

"She's a little jewel," shouted Ali. "A little jewel that I'm sure you'd like to hang around your finger."

Amina moved in closer to Adam.

"Relax," said Ali, holding a pipe up in his hand.

Adam took the pipe from him and sucked in the dry perfumed fumes. As he relaxed, Ali held out a gold tray for him. On the gold tray were a few sad and frayed bank notes, a couple of rings, and a can of lager.

"I paid for the lager," said Saleem.

"We are neighbours," said Ali by way of an explanation

Adam pulled the gold ring from his pocket, flicked it onto the tray and grabbed the notes.

"That is a fair price," said Adam.

Ali wobbled his head.

"You are a business man," said Ali. "You know these things."

"So you're staying," grumbled Saleem. "So you've nothing better to be doing?"

39

"It is easier to come here and see the dancing," said Adam "Than sitting in the hotel and paying their prices for drinks."

"Why are you paying with gold and not a few coins then? What is that worth?"

"It is tradition. And don't you worry. I know what is a fair price."

"A fair price for what though?"

Saleem gave what he hoped was a sneer of contempt and was disappointed that Adam did not see it because Amina was now prising open Adam's palm and closely examining it.

"This is the hand of a criminal," she said, and giggled.

"What's that?" said Saleem. "You can find no more money in there? Is that what you mean?"

"Read his palm," Adam said, pointing at his father. "See what evil and stupidity is in there!"

"I read his eyes," she replied. "And I can't tell you what I see."

"She can see through to my Grandfather," said Saleem, taking great delight in what he was about to tell them, "She can see what I saw at the old man's funeral. One of his wives being buried with him, alive."

"They didn't do that then," said Adam.

"I can remember it. I can remember seeing it. The hand still sticking up from the sand, still waving, like a flower. I can remember that," said Saleem screwing his eyes up trying to picture this half-recalled image from his childhood. "It was real," he added, "I'm not imagining it. I don't think it was my grandmother though. This girl was too young."

The fire crackled and hissed as Saleem struggled to bring the full memory back but he gave up and shook his head.

"She can see it though. It's in my soul!"

Saleem flashed his eyes at Amina.

Amina turned away from him and began a slow sinuous dance around the flames of the fire, her legs visible through the material of her sari.

One of their fellow guests stood up, drunkenly held his hands aloft and tried to copy her movements. His white stubbled chin framed a red wet-lipped smile as one of the other girls took his hand and led him away over the dune.

"What did you tell that wife of yours?" asked Saleem.

"What would you tell my mother?" asked Adam.

"She's dead," said Saleem with a grin. "She would understand. But I doubt that Sufiya would."

"She will never know."

"She will never know!" Saleem roared with laughter and almost fell off his stool. "She will never know!" he roared again. "My son," he said, "The great man! The big man! The man with all the answers says Sufiya will never know!"

"A good wife," said Ali, "Is one who never knows!"

Adam put his hand in his pocket and pulled out the keys to his truck. His manner suddenly changed and he became very brisk and business like.

"Must get on with my business," he kept saying, "I was only just passing. So I want no nonsense with Sufiya. Understand?"

Then as he turned to leave, he tripped over a pair of writhing bodies and became engulfed in legs and thighs lit by the flickering fire and hazy moonlight.

"I have a business to run!" shouted Adam, extricating himself from the bodies as Saleem watched him with mounting curiosity at just how much more absurd this son of his could behave.

"I don't know how much you've been smoking, but it is too much," said Adam, as he picked his way through the bodies up to the top of the dune.

"I haven't smoked enough," shouted Saleem. "But obviously for you, to even think about it is too much."

Adam stopped at the top of the dune and seemed to hesitate about leaving.

"Go on!" said Saleem, "Go! It is my duty to stay. And yours to go. That is the way it is."

"Shut up," said Adam, "Listen."

"I have listened all too long to..."

"No! Shut up," said Adam beginning to walk back down the dune.

Saleem gave a puff on his pipe, a smoke ring hovered in the air before his face. Then the ring of smoke gradually disintegrated and disappeared into nothingness.

"Did you hear that?" said Adam.

"You are an idiot," said Saleem.

He heard a low rumbling sound and all the camels of the village began groaning. Children began to run and yell and cheer as if something extraordinarily exciting was happening.

Adam ran towards the village. Reluctantly Saleem followed. When they arrived, they found a cloud of dust belching up the streets. Pushing through the dust, Saleem, heavily panting, watched the final assault of the sand dune upon his house. The back wall suddenly collapsed and the roof slid over and came to a halt, delicately propped up by the sand and rubble from the garden wall that had been swept up to it.

Saleem tried to get closer but Adam pulled him back.

"Let it settle first. See what else falls down."

With every crash, the children yelled excitedly. Then a pipe burst and the contents of the water tank spewed out.

***

Today, thought Omar, as he drove towards Sufiya's shop, he was going to be a policeman. He was going to be efficient, businesslike, and straight to the point. He quite liked the idea. Though when he did pluck up the courage to push open the door, he could not help noticing that Sufiya was already purple with rage at his presence.

"What do you want?" she yelled when he entered.

Her voice seemed to set all the wind chimes tinkling. With that and the stench of incense overpowering, Omar nearly fell back out through the door gasping for air.

"I've come to apologise for the last time I was here," he blurted out.

"Let bygones be bygones," said Sufiya, "Just apologise for your presence now and go."

Omar tried to puzzle out the meaning of that but thought it all too deep for him, so continued with the line of what he considered his reasoning.

"And, and," he spluttered, "Of course to ask you a few questions about your husband."

The expression on Sufiya's face betrayed nothing to Omar. He examined it hoping that there would be a glimmer of something that he could build on without having to explain everything from first principles. He began to sweat. He looked down upon the shirt he had so carefully swept free of crumbs that morning. Great stains were beginning to appear on it and it seemed to be pumping out malodorous fumes that no amount of incense could serve to disguise.

"Where is your husband?" asked Omar in his most policeman-like manner, hoping that Adam would not suddenly turn up. "It seems strange," he said before Sufiya could answer, "That your husband should disappear at a time like this."

"He has not disappeared," said Sufiya interposing the till between her and Omar, "What are you talking about? He is like everybody else, going about his business. Just as you should be going about yours and letting me go about mine!"

"I would not be so sure of that," said Omar taking a deep breath and trying to maintain a dignified bearing as a bead of sweat dripped off the end of his nose. Somehow, he thought, his brain told him to say one thing and his mouth managed to say something completely different. Why was the universe so constructed to confound him like this?

Sufiya let out a sigh that Omar interpreted as incredulity. Her glaring eyes were not quite what he had hoped for. He had hoped more for a lack of certainty, a certain frisson of fear, and a look that asked him to expand and comfort. Instead she just hit the lock on the cash register.

"What do you want?" she asked and then picked up an elephant spike that Omar noticed had a price label dangling from it.

"Well," said Omar. "That is for you to decide."

He tried to smile warmly but somehow only succeeded in angering her further.

"Get out of my way," she said, brandishing the elephant spike, "Go and bother someone else. I have work to do. Go away!"

Omar backed away from her as she swept past him and began picking her way over the boxes of mildewed brass, bails of dusty embroidered cloth, and broken heads of temple gods. He had to act quickly before she went out by the back door. He had to make her understand that she had no right to push him aside like that or talk to him in that manner. He had not wanted to use the weapon of Adam's infidelity but he had come prepared to do so.

"Will Adam ever let you know that he attended a licentious gathering?"

He wished he could have been far more direct but somehow to be so would have undermined his pretensions to being on Police duty. He had to maintain the formalities while hoping that with Sufiya the formality would break down and she would see in him a friend and not a bringer of bad news.

"If you are not careful," said Sufiya with what Omar took to be a weakening tone. "I will report you to your superiors."

"Don't you want to know what gathering I am talking about?" asked Omar.

"Get out!"she yelled. "Get out! I will report you! I will!"

"I just want to get some facts here," he said, feeling perhaps that he had pushed a little too hard. He tried to defuse the situation with a smile and a few steps backward away from her. "There is no need to get alarmed," he said. "This is a routine enquiry."

"I shall report you to Rashid," she said. "He is a very good friend of ours and a party member. He will know who your superiors are."

Rashid? Omar had to think a moment about whom this person was. Rashid? A party member? Who cared about party members anymore? What was this person?

"I'm sorry you feel that way," said Omar, "But I think you must agree that your husband has some explaining to do."

Omar walked over to the front door, a little worried about this Rashid character. The name rang a bell but he had no direct dealings with him.

"You don't get my meaning," said Omar, not sure what he meant, "What I'm trying to say here is that I have some kind of drug taking orgy that I'm accused of letting happen and, accusations of prostitution . . . You see what my position is? You see what has been happening here? And I should now begin doing something but I am not sure what it is other than gathering information to see...I mean, they are gypsies and some people round here would shoot them just for that, but we are enlightened people now. But even so..."

Omar was fishing for ideas and coming up with very little. It had all been very clear to him when he first heard about the goings on in the desert. What a golden opportunity to traduce Adam and provide a shoulder for Sufiya to cry on. Somehow things were not going the way he hoped.

Sufiya stared at Omar with her mouth open and he thought she looked beautiful. Then the frozen moment disintegrated and Sufiya began waving her hands and shouting incomprehensible insults.

Omar quickly stepped out of the shop and trembled at the irrationality of the woman.

"Love," he sang sadly to himself as he stood before the shop confused as to what he should do next. "Oh Careless Love . . ." He did not know any more of the words but never truer words had been spoken. "Oh foolish love," he whispered. Perhaps now that he had told Sufiya of the treachery of her husband, she would in time, come to see Omar as a protector and not a threat.

"Singing to yourself?" said Adam.

Omar turned and found Adam standing before him with a shovel in his hand. Omar flinched.

"What a morning," said Adam. "Digging out my father's belongings. Hardly worth the effort really. But there you go, we have to do these things."

"Pardon?" said Omar.

"A sand dune. Well it's been creeping up for years but suddenly the wall gives way and it rolls forward into the house. He is lucky he wasn't inside at the time."

Omar took a deep breath and nodded saying, "Yes, yes, yes. Lucky."

The words echoed around Omar's head and he kept nodding.

"You don't look too well," said Adam, "Don't tell me you were over the dunes the other night?"

Omar shook his head.

"You'd be the only one who wasn't. I tell you this town is rotten. You should do something about those gypsies. They are a disgrace and I bet they are the bandits that we have been hearing of. You should do something about them. I heard they were passing out drugs and alcohol. There is many a hangover today. But not me. I feel good. I have a clear conscience. But I would not be in certain other people's shoes. Are you sure you are feeling all right?"

Omar raised his hand and gave a wave. "No, no, I'm fine," he said and headed rapidly towards his car thinking how inhuman Adam was, how oblivious to the sufferings of others!

***

"You will have to get him clean," said Rashid as he leant back in his swivel chair.

45

Adam, sitting opposite, nodded.

"And he must not spit in front of the guests," said Rashid.

Adam nodded again and thought how embarrassing it was to be sitting there, knowing that it was Sufiya who had rung up Rashid, demanding work for Saleem. Why Rashid had agreed, Adam could only guess, and what he guessed, he did not really like.

"Nor smoke," continued Rashid.

"That's going to be harder," said Adam. "But it is not a completely irredeemable fault, surely?"

Adam awaited a reply but his mind was barely in focus. All he kept thinking about was how close he was to losing everything. If he had gone with Amina then somehow Omar would have known and had conclusive proof and that would have been that. As it was, his life was going to go on much as it was before. Not that it was that bad. He was making progress, but he felt much the same and, if there was anything certain in his life, he did not want to feel much the same.

"We'll put him in a uniform," said Rashid. "That'd make him at least look better. You will make sure he always wears it?"

"Oh yes," said Adam thinking that it was probably best if he just agreed with everything Rashid and Sufiya had concocted between them.

"And can you make him brush his teeth?" added Rashid.

"I doubt it," said Adam, making a mental note to buy himself a toothbrush.

"Oh well," said Rashid. "I don't suppose it's that important."

Adam smiled inanely. A deal had been struck. Not only was Rashid going to give his father a job, he was going to let Adam set up a little stall in the hotel. The price of employing his father was an extortionate rent and the ignominy of knowing that it had all been sorted out by Sufiya without any input from himself. Still, maybe, as Castrol would say, this would open the doors upon a new lifestyle.

Rashid swivelled around, opened the door of his fridge and in English asked, "Then what'll it be?"

A row of bottles glinted in the glare of the light. Adam peered in.

"Ice and a slice?" asked Rashid.

This was a turn up, thought Adam, who felt scruffy in comparison to Rashid and could not imagine that his business dealings would lead to socialising with the man.

Rashid shovelled a handful of crushed ice from the ice bucket into a glass.

"So are you ready for the great opening yet?" asked Rashid.

As Rashid poured copious amounts of gin, Adam looked at the bookshelf above the air-conditioner. A book on advanced level economics caught his eye. He stood up, pulled out the book and flicked through its pages hoping that the image of himself, book in hand, thoughtful, would impress upon Rashid that he was not dealing with a peasant.

"Is this what us businessmen are doing?" asked Adam examining a particularly complicated looking chart, wondering if this somehow explained the curious nature of his inadvertent success.

Rashid handed Adam his drink and then glanced at the book. He shook his head.

"This is theory," said Rashid. "It is written by men in universities who study business but do not do it."

Adam felt the book being rested from his hand and watched as Rashid carefully placed it back on the shelf.

"The party has done away with all that stuff," added Rashid.

Adam took a sip of his gin and stirred the ice with his finger.

"I hope my father doesn't cause you too much trouble," said Adam. "I do appreciate what you're doing for me."

Rashid smiled the bureaucrat's smile that told Adam a favour demands one in return. But what sort of favour would a man like Rashid want? Perhaps he wanted the same favours that Omar apparently wanted with his wife? Adam scanned the bookshelf for other books in the hope of finding clues to this riddle. On the top shelf was a biography of Lenin. He had heard all about him in school and somehow this Russian had managed to liberate Adam's country, but then somehow become a very shadowy figure.

"Is he a great man, in your opinion?" asked Adam, assuming he was still alive somewhere.

It was a simple question but Rashid started to nervously fidget with a pencil from his desk before replying. Maybe, thought Adam, Rashid knew Lenin and was a bit frightened of him.

"He was a man of the moment," he said. "A simple man. Don't you think that for all the complicatedness of life, all the filling in forms, sitting on committees, planning the mobilisation of disparate economic forces, life is essentially simple?"

Adam was inclined to think it was all too complicated so opted for the formula: "You're born, you die, but I don't think it's very simple."

Rashid laughed out loud. Somehow Adam could not equate the wearing of such expensive suits with the tendency to laugh readily. Rashid is an enigma, he said to himself, but Lenin frightens him.

"You are priceless," said Rashid, "You talk straight from the heart and have no worries about betraying yourself."

Adam finished his drink and wondered if he had said the wrong thing.

"I don't think I have anything to betray," said Adam, presenting his empty glass for Rashid to refill. "This is the way I am."

"Precisely," said Rashid. "And I envy you. My own background is suspect. My attitudes are not always the most correct. I have to work at being acceptable to the new society. I admit it."

"Surely you are acceptable!" said Adam, warming to the alcohol and the apparent treatment as an equal.

"Very good," said Rashid. "You are learning this game very quickly. Flattery can get you a long way. But let me tell you this. Let us make a bargain. We tell each other the truth. We don't mince words. We watch each other's backs. I do what I can for you. You do what you can for me. This place is a desert, in more ways than one, and there are very few people who really understand what is required. The capital has many different groups of people far more powerful than us, but if we stick together, if we keep our eyes and ears open, we will be able to ally ourselves with the right factions, and maybe become rich and powerful enough to be able to tell them to get lost whenever we feel like it."

Adam held his glass up in the air. "Here's to always being truthful with each other," he said, wondering what lies were being told him.

"You don't understand what I'm saying do you?" said Rashid.

Adam shook his head.

"I've been hearing things. Things are happening in the capital. Maybe none of us will survive."

Rashid solemnly held his glass up then drained it.

"One day I will do you a great favour," said Rashid. "And if you do not repay it, you will gain a great enemy. I'm a survivor. There will always be Rashid. No matter where they send him, no matter how low they think they can throw him, Rashid always comes back, stronger and wiser."

Adam gulped his drink then suddenly Rashid's tone changed.

"Your father's duties are light but responsible: he is to keep awake and walk the perimeter fence every hour. There is a book in which he is to fill in the time of his journey and any event that occurs."

Adam nodded and agreed that he would explain everything to the old man. He was sure he would be able to cope. Not an educated man, but not a fool either. Even he could keep watch.

"And remember," finished Rashid. "I can do you the favours. But there will come a time when you can do me the favours. I will call on those favours and the bigger ones I do for you, the bigger will be those you have to do for me. That's how it works. That's how we get into things deeper and deeper. Do you have that sort of ambition Adam?"

"I - I," stuttered Adam, "I do."

Rashid nodded sagely and Adam felt he had made some unholy pact with the devil.

"A good answer Adam. The truth. Always tell me the truth. It will get you further than you bargained for. My regards to Sufiya. Close the door firmly when you leave."

In one movement Adam's glass was removed from his hand, and he found the door being shut tight behind him. Hm, thought Adam, I think we must be getting on together.

***

Adam sat in his truck listening intently to the cab radio where the perky female presenter extolled the virtues of a film about a lady bandit and her lascivious ways.

"I have already made my plans to go and see that," Adam told the radio. Then he gave the plastic doll hanging from his mirror, a flick to set the bells inside it jangling. He was parked outside his father's collapsing compound while Sufiya checked that Saleem had everything that was necessary. As far as Adam was concerned, Saleem merely needed the clothes he stood up in because nothing else was of value, but Sufiya knew better and insisted on making sure there was nothing valuable left behind.

As Sufiya hurled the last piece of luggage onto the truck, Saleem finished a cigarette, then with a deep sigh, joined Adam in the cab.

"We will now go to the cinema at the Hotel," announced Adam as Saleem settled into his seat. "And we will eat and see a movie and you will like it."

Saleem gave a grunt of disapproval. "How many years did I live with your mother there?" he said, not pausing for a reply, "Thirty years? Yes. Thirty. And now they are gone. Like she is."

Sufiya climbed into the cab beside Saleem and switched the radio off. The movie of the week's notorious theme song had just begun. It was full of all sorts of panting and sighing.

"Such a thing," she said, "Should be listened to only by adults alone together in private. And probably not even then."

"See," groaned Saleem. "Even she does not want to go to the cinema."

"No," said Sufiya. "That is not the case. I just don't want to listen to that music. And after coming all this way to pick you up, I most certainly do not want to cook for you two, then make up your bed. And I most certainly don't want to have you miserable and moping about tonight. So we are having a treat."

"That's right," said Adam, "We are after all a family with new prospects, widening horizons, and more to the point, money in our pockets."

"We've already been to the cinema. Don't you remember?" said Saleem. "When you were children, everyone would gather behind the village. They projected the films onto a big screen perched on the back of a lorry."

"Oh yes," said Sufiya, fondly, "I remember. Everyone would get so excited. We'd be told by our teachers that the films were coming and we would spend what seemed like months waiting. Every night we would go and sit on the road and look out for the lorries. And when they finally came ..."

"The films were always about feeding yourself properly and cleaning your bum after going to the toilet! Not what I'd call worth the price of a ticket," said Saleem.

"I was meaning to talk to you about that," said Adam as he glanced into his mirror to check that the heap of junk that passed for Saleem's worldly goods was safely stowed at the back. He wondered if there was anything he could get a decent price for. Tourists would buy almost anything, but he was not sure even they would stoop to buying his father's dirty sheets. He ground the gears and jerkily pulled away from the house. As the truck bumped and rolled over the dusty road towards town, Gypsy children ran out of the crumbling compounds, their dust-caked faces and big brown eyes watching.

"I should not leave," said Saleem. "I cannot leave."

"Too late," said Adam. "You've left."

"Take me back!"

"Don't be stupid," said Sufiya.

"And remember," said Adam, as if it needed saying when it had already been explained to Saleem umpteen dozen times, almost as if meant to cheer him up, "This is just going to be a temporary arrangement until we can get you set up with accommodation at the Hotel."

"I do not want to be a night-watchman," murmured Saleem. "I am quite content with my lot."

"From now on," said Adam. "You will have to be discontented."

He hammered the horn and revved the engine to pick up speed enough to overtake the chugging town bus.

"In the real world," said Adam, warming to his theme, "No-one is contented. Unless they are dead."

"I'm an old man," Saleem replied. "I soon will be dead."

"Then what are you worried about?" said Adam, pointing out the positive side, "It is not so much that you have failed to take care of the property the state handed to you, but that in the end all flesh fails, all lives dwindle away to irrelevance, and there is no point in being miserable about it. Much better to grab the money when you can, get a decent room somewhere, with air-conditioning, and of course a decent suit."

"What are you drivelling on about?" commented Saleem, pulling out the tobacco he had loose in his pyjama pocket. He began trying to roll a cigarette as the truck swayed and bounced. As he delicately held up the as yet unrolled cigarette, trying to get his tongue to the paper to make the seal, there was silence. Even the howling engine held its breath until a bump jolted Saleems head and instead of licking the cigarette-paper's edge, he managed to stick his tongue into the tobacco and recoil from the bitter taste only to tip the remaining strands of tobacco onto the floor. What made it all the worse was that Adam and Sufiya laughed at him.

"One day," said Saleem, "You will be like me."

"Oh God, no!" howled Adam in mock terror.

"And your son will mock you."

"If he gets like you then he will deserve to be mocked," said Sufiya, nudging the old man with her elbow.

"That's it!" said Saleem, grabbing the steering wheel and giving it a yank that sent them hurtling off the road over the desert.

Adam wrestled Saleem's hand off the wheel and hit the brakes, bringing the truck to a skidding halt that had both Saleem and Sufiya sliding off their seats and slapping their palms against the windscreen. The engine spluttered to a stop.

"I only hope for your sake, it will start," said Adam through clenched teeth.

Saleem struggled to clamber over Sufiya and get at the door but she slapped him away and shouted at him to sit down and not be an idiot.

"That's right," said Adam, "This is going to be the last but greatest stage of your life."

With his left hand held in the air, fingers crossed, he turned the ignition key and the engine stuttered into life.

"There," he said, "Everything is perfect. Now sit down, shut up. And we promise not to laugh at you."

Adam drove back onto the road and felt pleased at how he had handled himself. There was a certain completeness in the situation, he thought. With his mother dead - a most upsetting period since they only found half of her body, the rest thought to have been eaten by wild animals - there was only his father left of the family.

"Let me explain your duties," said Adam noting that his father had slumped back in his seat and surrendered to a sullen stupor. "Your job will not be too difficult. You will have to walk the perimeter fence of the Hotel checking for lascivious lady bandits, like in the movies. If you are lucky, you might find one. But it will do you no good unless you regularly brush your teeth. So remember that. And then of course you will have to fill in a report book."

That woke Saleem up.

"Report book!" he said.

"You are not completely illiterate so it should be no problem."

"I am completely illiterate!"

"All you need to write is your name."

"I don't know how to write my name."

"I will teach you. And I will teach you to write No Problem! That's all you need to know. Your name and No Problem!"

"And if there is a problem?"

"Then you take a bribe and keep your mouth shut like everybody else! Now, does that sound fair to you? Is that the sort of behaviour you feel within your capability?"

Saleem gave a grunt and seemed to resign himself to his fate.

"Ahaa," said Adam, "The prospect of a little bit on the side makes you less apprehensive."

"Apprehensive?" questioned Saleem, "Don't you ever call your father, *Apprehensive*."

Adam was enjoying this day: Sufiya was giggling, and he had put in an order for a sign for his new "outlet", which he understood was the correct word. And now, they arrived at the gates of the hotel complex, its twinkling lights already lit even though night had yet to fall. What is more it gave him a chance to flash his pass card at the Guard, who nodded and raised the barrier allowing him to take his place in the staff car park. What a privilege, he thought, and then looked up at the big hand painted poster advertising the Lady Bandit film. A large breasted lady wielding a whip was sitting astride a stallion. The stallion wielded something even more dangerous.

"The artist, did he make a mistake?" asked Sufiya.

"I see nothing amiss," said Adam, making a great show of sticking his head out of the truck side window to get a better look.

"That thing there," said Sufiya, "Would surely slow such an animal down. Especially over rough ground."

"Huh," said Saleem, "That is nothing!"

"Well, let us see the film and decide for ourselves," said Adam, taking his cue to park the truck and hurry his passengers out of their seats. "We must hurry to get the tickets. It is a very popular show."

Saleem slowed down and protested that his belongings were on the back of the truck for all to see and steal. But Adam threw a tarpaulin over them and derided the sanity of anyone who might want to steal any of those items.

"Hurry hurry hurry," he said, keeping the momentum going.

As the three of them queued to buy tickets, Adam watched the hotel guests walking straight through to the auditorium.

"They do not have to queue because they were allowed to phone ahead," he whispered knowingly to Sufiya. "One day we too will have a credit card and be able to jump the queue."

Presently though, thought Adam, the best he could hope for was that his father would not spit in the cinema, at least not too loudly.

"Have this on me," said a voice.

Adam turned and saw Rashid approaching, his suit as sharp as a freshly folded new dollar note, and his teeth gleaming white. He put one arm around Sufiya's shoulder and the other about Adam's. Sufiya giggled. Adam had never seen any other man touch her. Nor had he seen any husband allow any other man touch their wives. What he had seen were desperate fistfights leading to drawn knives, smashed bottles, and everlasting enmity. Good suit or no suit, Rashid could be construed as dishonouring Sufiya. Except that she was giggling which meant that Sufiya was doing the dishonouring and required chastisement, in public. However, since Rashid was offering to pay for the cinema tickets and had mentioned there would be favours needing repaying, Adam decided to let Rashid have his way, within limits, and chastise Sufiya in private. The thought of it excited him.

"I should pay," said Adam as Rashid began ushering the whole family towards the auditorium.

"No," said Rashid. "This is my cinema and you are my friend and today my guest. Please. Enjoy yourself. Have a good time."

Rashid left them in the darkness.

"You have slimy friends", said Saleem, taking his seat. "In my day we would have cut his throat."

"Shush!" said Sufiya. "He is a modern man from the city. He means no harm."

"He needs teaching a lesson," said Saleem.

"Shush!" said Adam. "I will buy you a toothbrush."

"A what?" said Saleem.

"Shush!" said Sufiya.

"What was that about a toothbrush? What is that cuckolded husband of yours talking about?"

"If I was ever to run off with anyone," said Sufiya, "You do not think I would return to Adam if I knew I had to put up with you?"

"Shut up, both of you," said Adam. "Enjoy the film!"

"I need a cigarette," said Saleem after watching a few advertisements for cigarettes.

"Then get one!" said Adam. "Here. Here's some money."

"Sssh!" said Sufiya, "It has started."

A stallion reared up as a young girl who was to become the great outlaw beat it into submission. Slavering jaws chomped on a bit and the girl screamed as her father dragged her out of the compound. She was not to torment the horse but to prepare for her wedding. This was a sudden revelation to the twelve-year-old. The marriage was going to be to a fat rich oaf of a landowner, who also was slathering. On the way to the marriage ceremony the girl, hidden beneath a scarlet embroidered headdress, sang a haunting melody full of longing for the day when true love would be victorious over false love. She also hid a pair of scissors in her bra. Adam wondered if this was not carrying things a little too far.

***

"Where would I find such money?" said Saleem to Ali who had just that moment made a suggestion about Saleem and Amina, who, he assured Saleem, "Really liked him."

Ali wobbled his head from side to side. He had been doing that all night during the evening's performance for the tourists. Saleem had sat beside the pool, smoked, and watched as Amina went through her paces. He found it all slightly irritating. She was fine, he thought, but Ali was outrageously hamming it up. All that neck wobbling and eyebrow raising! It was a spectacle he was making of himself and a not too good one at that! After the performance he had joined Saleem for a smoke beneath a palm beside the bar.

"You," continued Ali, "Are now a man of substance and such a man needs a woman."

News travelled fast. Saleem, as father of the up and coming young Adam of "Adam'S Boutique" was a personal friend of the manager and well in with the party higher ups, so the story went. Saleem was thus soon to be a man with a fortune.

"But in the mean time," said Ali, "Perhaps we can extend you a little credit?"

Amina arrived to remind Ali that everyone was waiting for him. She had changed clothes and wore a pair of jeans and a T-shirt she must have bought in the Hotel with some of her earnings.

"What have I told you?" snarled Ali as she beckoned to him to hurry up.

He sighed and turned to Saleem.

"Look what is happening," he said, "She is not taking a blind bit of notice of what I say. She must never appear like that in front of the customers. They will not pay her so much."

Saleem agreed. Amina looked smaller, slighter, younger, and plain dressed as she was. His eyes half closed as smoke curled up from his mouth. The T-shirt, stretched over her young breasts, made her look fragile and childish. So young, he thought to himself, so young. His wife must have been that age when he first met her. He too could not have been much older. Had he too been a child? It seemed impossible that he could have one time been a child. What on earth had happened in the meantime?

"What are you looking at?" said Amina, her wide eyes set above her bony cheeks bored straight into Saleem's.

Ali giggled and put his hand on Amina's bottom to push her ahead of him. Amina wriggled out of his grasp and then turned and scowled at Saleem.

"Look sexy," whispered Ali into her ear, "Give him a smile. Give him a wiggle."

Ali gave Saleem a wink.

"See what I mean?" he said, "You are honoured."

Then they were gone, leaving Saleem desperately trying to suck up the last dregs of smoke from his sodden cigarette stub. Saleem hurled it down and quickly lit himself another. This was ridiculous, he thought to himself, an old man like him ogling such a girl. She could be his granddaughter. But then Saleem listened to the pounding of his heart. Odd, he thought, most odd. He pondered how much money he would be earning as a security guard. It would not be much but was it possible that he could afford to marry again? An old man like himself? No, not marriage, that really would be obscene. But, perhaps something else? Yes, yes, he knew he was capable.

"You stupid old man," said Adam.

Saleem sighed and looked at the ashen face of his son.

"Is the movie over?" asked Saleem, swivelling around on his barstool, spraying sparks of cigarette-ash as he turned. He flicked the stub towards the pool where it sizzled in the water. "I hear the girl castrates the landlord. People have been fainting all over the state, so the waiters tell me."

"Come along will you!" ordered Adam.

"Don't speak to your father like that," said Saleem.

"I was not speaking to you like anything," said Adam.

Adam noticed that Sufiya had caught sight of something in the sky.

"What are you gawking at?" he said.

Sufiya pointed upwards and Adam and Saleem turned to see.

For a moment nothing stirred but then a shooting star streaked across the sky. Sufiya placed her hand on her stomach.

"I think you now have friends in high places," she said, "Probably very high places. And maybe a few low ones too."

"What's she talking about?" demanded Saleem.

Adam and Sufiya did not answer him but infuriatingly looked into each other's eyes and seemed to forget that Saleem existed at all.

CHAPTER THREE

A month after the cinema excursion, Adam was in the hotel reception looking at the list of the hotel's shops that hung on the wall. He blessed his father for getting one thing right. By giving him a name that started with "A", he was at the top of the list. The shop was simply called "Adam'S". Rashid had told him this was a very trendy up-to-date sort of thing to call a shop and the capital S at the end was the height of style.

"Ice and a slice?" enquired Rashid as he came up behind Adam and tapped him on the shoulder.

Adam turned round in surprise.

"Oh yes, yes," said Adam.

"A good day's trade was it?" asked Rashid.

It had not been, but Adam did not mind.

"Early days yet," said Rashid. "Word takes time to get out."

Adam looked like something out of The Arabian Nights in his baggy red trousers, with a silk cummerbund, and an open necked collarless shirt. It was supposedly traditional dress though he had never seen anyone, anywhere, wearing such things except in a painting of a Turkish Janissary he vaguely recalled from a book in his shop. But this was the look, the preferred image of the Hotel for its franchise operators. So when behind the counter, this is what he wore, down to the curly toed slippers that were most uncomfortable. Dressed thus, he walked beside tall Rashid admiring the man's dark expensive Western suit. That was the next stage, he said to himself. When he no longer has to wear all this fancy dress but can wear one of those suits, then he will know that he is a man of substance.

"This day is coming to an end," pronounced Rashid, "And to watch the sunset with a cool drink in one's hand must be as close to heaven as one can ever get in this life."

At a poolside table, Rashid ordered drinks for them both and invited Adam to sit with him. The fountain at the end of the pool bore the name "Poolside Paradise."

"Wherever you go," said Rashid, "In the entire world, this is what they dream of."

Adam nodded.

"And it is all built out of extruded plastic," added Rashid. "For a few who can afford it."

Rashid raised his glass in a toast. Adam took a sip of his gin and tonic, and pretended to understand Rashid who he thought looked very handsome and wondered why the man did not seem to have any women in his life, apart from an inexplicable, and he hoped, innocent, friendship with Sufiya. They sat silently for a moment watching the hazy orange sunset engulf everything above. An airliner slowly scored a line across the sky. Adam began to feel uneasy with the silence and then thought he had better try to equal the profundity of Rashid's thoughts.

"Something up there," said Adam looking skywards, "Pulls me forward. Not God, I don't mean God, but the size, the greatness of it, makes me want to expand into it, to step forward into it."

"Into what?" asked Rashid with a raised eyebrow.

"Well, into whatever it is up there," said Adam, not expecting any sort of question.

"Sort of, Club Class?" enquired Rashid.

"Club what?" asked Adam.

"You don't even know what it means and yet you want it!" laughed Rashid.

Adam rapidly glanced about for a clue to the secret of Rashid's laughter. He saw a Sun Shade emblazoned with the words Club Med. He saw a menu with Club Sandwich. He saw an electric trolley parked by the travel bureau that would take the guests to the Gold Club. A brochure lay discarded amongst a nearby weedy tangle of potted palms containing an article about something called the Mile High Club. The Club Class, he thought, yes! Yes!

"And when you have it, then what?" asked Rashid, a crooked smile on his face.

"Then I'll have what you have," said Adam, thinking this was what Rashid wanted him to say. This was flattering to the man and what was the harm in flattering him?

"You would not want what I have," said Rashid.

59

The sun suddenly disappeared and all plunged into darkness until one by one the myriad of tiny lights hung from the tropical trees, rattling with cicadas, speckled with mosquitoes, began to eerily light the pool side. The waiters busily hurried to light the blobs of candles on each of the tables.

"The tourists come out with the moon," whispered Rashid.

On cue, the rest of the tables began to fill up with the pink-faced, crazy-shirted hotel guests murmuring with self-satisfaction.

"And then we seduce them," added Rashid.

A drum beat tapped quietly in the background. Adam turned on hearing it and saw Amina slowly walk to the edge of the pool hissing like a snake, a flaming torch in each hand. The bats began to circle over her head catching the moths about the flames.

Rashid grinned at Adam and then raised his big hands and clapped slowly and loudly until the audience caught on and began wildly applauding. Amina ignored them, her eyes turned ecstatically upwards, as she began to twirl with the torches in hand. Other musicians entered one by one to join the drummer, all dressed in white with red sashes around their waists. The straggly white beard of Ali appeared yellow in the light. Amina's purple skirts spread out about her as she swirled. Her toughened feet stomped upon the concrete floor like jackhammers.

"You don't get this Club Class," mysteriously whispered Rashid into Adam's ear. "This is what we've always had. And now they will pay good money for it. Who is wealthy now? Huh?"

Adam did not understand Rashid's meaning but he nodded as if the deep significance of Rashid's commentary were second nature to him, glad that he did not need a reply because Amina was standing before him rolling the muscles of her stomach and hissing through her black teeth. The whites of her eyes shone out from the surrounding darkness. She hissed and sighed, until Adam reached into his pocket and pulled out a large denomination note. He stuck it onto the sweat of her forehead. With a grin she departed to the next table. Adam felt good for setting the precedent and looked to Rashid for approval, which was given with a slight raising of the palm of his hand from the table. Now all the tourists knew what was required. Adam had given her a good night. She would be grateful to him one day, thought Adam. He had favoured her, and she would one day favour him... Then he thought how he had to get out of this place, at least until she had gone because he would not be able to control himself and that was a certainty. A man like him was irresistible to such creatures and he could only stand so much temptation without succumbing to it. Already he nearly had done so, so it was a genuine danger. Perhaps now was a good time to go into the capital to open that bank account.

"Everything's changing," said Rashid. "Everything is changing and we are the ones who are changing it. We are the new force out here. The army, the police, the party, will have to reckon with us one day. They gain their legitimacy only by allowing us to flourish."

Us? thought Adam. Rashid and him, us? He had never considered there to be anything Us about Rashid. The man was a party member after all. But the more Adam thought about it, the better. Us, yes, he liked that. Us. Even if what they shared was Sufiya, then it was a price worth paying. That is, it would be if he and Amina could get together as well. And then a few more, all at the same time, a harem like his Grandfather. Us. Well, if there was going be an Us, there was one thing Adam was certain that he needed:

"How much does a suit like the one you're wearing cost?" asked Adam.

After a moment's thought, Rashid replied saying, "It's very expensive, Adam. Not at all approved of by certain people. But if I am the manager, I must at least have as good a suit as the customers."

"Then I must have a suit as well."

"Why? It can serve no purpose for you."

"I have plans," said Adam. "I must go to the capital and open a bank account. Whilst I am there, I want to see if there are other hotels who would like to trade with me. And I cannot turn up there dressed like this."

Rashid shook his head and Adam felt a pang of misery overcome him. He knew Rashid was all pose, all show, but even so, to consider Adam unworthy was an insult.

"Why do you look like that?" asked Adam. "I can do the same there and get more money!"

Rashid shook his head again, saying "It is not so simple."

"They are looking for someone as chic as me," said Adam.

"Who knows who they are looking for," said Rashid. "Just sit it out and watch is what I recommend."

"Well that is not my style," said Adam. "I must have a suit, and you must introduce me to people."

"Do you really think that wise?" said Rashid.

"It is a good idea," said Adam.

Rashid got to his feet and placed one hand on Adam's shoulder.

"Have another drink on the house," he said. "I have some work still to do. And as for the suit, I'll see what I can do."

Adam watched Rashid return to the foyer, snap an authoritative finger at a waiter, to make sure Adam would get another drink, and then Amina joined him. Adam craned his neck to get a better look at what was going on. Rashid was bending down to listen to Amina whispering in his ear with her cupped hand. She was giggling, casting sly glances here and there. Rashid put his arm round her shoulder and lead her into his office, where the door shut and nothing more was to be seen.

Adam was not sure he had seen all that. He was also uncertain as to whether he had insulted the man, or been insulted by him. And he felt betrayed for even so much as pitying Rashid's unmarried, isolated state out here in the middle of the desert. Nonetheless, he accepted the man's drinks and several brandies later, Adam stood up, uncertainly, and through a warm haze of incomprehension caught sight of the faces of various tourists. They all appeared to be watching him. Maybe they thought he was part of the floorshow. Adam decided to disappoint them and stagger through the air-conditioned foyer towards the exit. There was a moment when he almost went over to Rashid's still firmly shut door and banged on it but no, he maintained his dignity. Whatever was Rashid's business, was just that, his business and nobody else's.

Finding his truck, Adam found no greater pleasure than that of pissing up against the offside wheel and staring up at the infinite emptiness of a desert sky, a shimmering moon, a passing satellite blinking steadily as slowly it crossed. If ever God revived, tonight would be a night for him to take a good deep breath, thought Adam, an Aladdin among the jewels. What did he care about Amina any way? She was only a fantasy and Sufiya was real, and if Amina and Rashid were together there was even less likelihood of there having been Sufiya and Rashid. Not that he ever really believed that.

The rattling sputum of a familiar throat woke him from his reverie and he turned to see Saleem in his security guard's uniform. The buttons were done up incorrectly, the lapels were weak and curled over, and already there was a stain down the front, but his father at work, be-uniformed, amused him.

Adam ducked down and hid to watch the spectacle. The sharply peaked cap and thick leather belt hung with a set of keys and a dangerous looking stick, gave Saleem an uncharacteristic menace, but even so, there was no mistaking that shambling walk, that unshaven chin, the unkempt hair. If Saleem had looked any different, Adam would have felt all the worse. Just as he had wanted to change the man, he now hoped he would never change. The thing he hated when he was a boy, he now found all too human and frail and pitiable. The man's attempt at a swagger as he went on about his duties, made Adam smile.

He sobered a little at the thought of the sad reduction of his father to that of an employee instead of the keeper of the desert, but that was progress, he thought. But he suspected that what went through his father's mind, as he plodded along the perimeter fence, was at least a dull resentment.

Things, then, were settled. Adam was expanding his retail empire and his father was guarding the tourists that made it all possible. This was to be their future and that was not so bad. Nothing much might happen in the desert but now at least Adam could be someone of some stature, at least within the limits of No 3 New Town.

Adam climbed into his truck, inadvertently hitting his head on the door arch, and turned the ignition to begin his bumpy way back home. As he drove deeper into the darkness away from the pink glow of the Hotel Complex, he turned to his radio for companionship and sang loudly along with it.

"Cruel Cruel Cruel Little Lady!" he sang. "When will you hand back my heart?"

Then he remembered when he last heard that song. The wicked landlord in the movie had sung it to his new bride just before the infamous castration scene. He should not have been singing about his heart, thought Adam.

When he returned home his head felt thick with smoke and drink, and Sufiya gave him no sympathy.

"It was a business drink," he explained, "That is all it was. When Rashid asks me to have a drink, what can I do? He is an important man."

Even so, Sufiya refused him aspirin, or even to get him a glass of water.

"This will not happen every night," he assured her. "But this was a special night. You cannot blame me for the state I am in. And look, I hit my face on the door as I climbed into my truck. I am in pain!"

"It is no more than you deserve. I hope it really hurts," she said.

Going through to the bedroom, Adam pretended to be less pained and took great care not to slur his words.

"I have made a decision tonight," he told her.

"Oh yes," she said, "And is it to spend all our money on drink and trying to live up to your new friend's wealth?"

"No!" he said, waving her suggestion away. "No! I am going to go to the capital and do some business."

"You are just being stupid and drunk," she said.

"I do not understand," said Adam as he watched Sufiya wriggling into her pyjama bottoms. "You yourself told me to go to the city and open up a bank account. You even suggested I send my father."

"Then you should still send him," she said, and in the gloom of the yellow light, she examined her face in the mirror.

"But I need to go if I am to expand the business," said Adam.

Adam swung his feet back to the floor and stood to admire himself in Sufiya's half-length mirror with its mottled silver backing.

"I will get Rashid to give me one of his old suits so that I can make a good impression."

"He is bigger than you!"

"It can be made to fit," explained Adam, pumping his muscles and standing sideways trying to imagine how he would look.

"If you want a suit," she said, pushing him out of her way and heading for the bed, "Then you should buy yourself one and not go asking for any favours."

"What do you mean by that? Rashid is a good friend!" said Adam.

Adam watched Sufiya carefully as she pulled the sheets over her. Adam was dripping from the heat of his alcohol content and Sufiya seemed to be wearing more clothes than she ever used to.

"Why are you dressed like that?" asked Adam. He went over to the bed and stripped back the covers. Sufiya turned away from him.

"Is it because you want me to take your clothes off?" said Adam, slipping onto the mattress beside her. He began to run his hand up the side of her thigh.

"I am late," she said.

"Ah," said Adam. For a moment he did not know whether to think this was a good thing or a bad thing.

"Does that mean you are going to have a baby?"

"It is a possibility," muttered Sufiya.

For a few minutes, Adam tried to gather his thoughts on the matter. He had wanted this, he kept telling himself, and Sufiya had, more or less, also wanted it. So why was he not jumping up and down with excitement? Adam stood up and struck a pose of self-importance.

"Then this makes it all the more important that I go to the city and get my business done! I have a responsibility not only to myself now, but to the future as well. My son will be proud of me, he announced. Or my daughter! I don't care which, but they will be proud! And so will you. No matter what you say. I will go. I have to have a good business. That is the way of the future."

He placed his hand upon her stomach.

"Can you actually feel anything?"

"I don't know what I feel," she said, "Other than that I am supposed to feel happy, and all I feel is sad because my husband is a hopeless drunkard and dreamer."

"Me?" said Adam, surprised to hear this.

"Just like his father," she added, rubbing the insult in even deeper.

"Him? He is hopeless, but not a drunkard, whereas I may be drunk, but..."

Adam burst out laughing. And Sufiya burst out crying.

"I'm so happy," she said.

***

Adam walked about the hotel complex feeling his new suit made him at least six inches taller. Rashid had kept his word. Did a man ever have such a friend? And Rashid had been most encouraging, more or less, with only a few reservations, about Adam's plans to go and open a bank account and have a look around to see what kind of business opportunities there were for the likes of him. Yes, Rashid was Adam's best friend.

"Ice and a slice," practised Adam over and over, sounding more and more what he considered to be top grade. "Ice and a slice, please, thank-you."

English was becoming the most important business tool, said Adam to himself. He had read that in the newspaper and sent off for the accompanying tape cassette. He would play it in the truck when he drove to the capital. Everything was turning out just as he had always dreamed - that is, was dreaming now. He had a goal. And a baby on the way - just confirmed by the doctor. Adam looked forward to seeing his father's face when he showed him his suit and told him he was going to become a grandfather.

"Ice and a slice. You're going to be a grandfather, you old bastard! How does the whistle and fluting suiting look to you old chap?"

Such wit would be wasted on his father but Adam was going to give it to him anyway.

Adam walked out of the front gate and turned left to follow the perimeter fence around to where he knew Saleem hid and skived and avoided filling in that report book. All he had to write was 'No Problem' but for some reason Saleem refused to learn even to do that much. If there was something wrong, he told Adam that he would shout. After all, what was the point in writing it in a book that no-one ever read? Adam contemplated telling his father off for being so slovenly in carrying out his duties, but all the other guards had the same old skiving habits, so why should his father behave any differently?

Adam entered the hotel's garden - called The Oasis in the hotel brochure. He approached the vegetation that he suspected hid his shirking father, then stopped and listened. The cicadas became silent. He approached closer and saw Saleem leaning against the perimeter wall with a cigarette dangling from his mouth. Before him, purred Amina. Adam drew back a moment. He saw Saleem pulling a few dollars from his pocket.

"What are you going to do for them?" Saleem kept saying to her. "What are you going to do for me?"

"Nothing," she said, snatching the cigarette from his mouth. "Just give us a cigarette before I have to go on."

"Is this the way you'd treat me when we're married?"

"Marry you?"

Amina cocked her head to one side in one of her dance moves and crossed her eyes.

"You do that once too often and you'll be stuck that way," said Saleem.

"What would an old man like you do for me?" she said, her hands moving into the darkness about his crotch. "What would I find down here," she whispered to him.

This was just too much for Adam and he burst upon them, waving his hands at her.

"Go away! Go away!" he shouted.

"Why should I?" she said and then she slowly walked about giving him sly glances. "I'll be seeing you later," she hissed, "I'll be seeing you both sooner or later."

"What does she mean by that?" said Adam, astonished that she should have even spoken to him. "That girl is -"

"Crazy. Thinks she's a camel," said Saleem.

"And you let her - do whatever it is that she was doing? She's..."

"What do you look like?" said Saleem. "What is that thing you are wearing? You look like some cheap gangster from a movie!"

"It is not me that we should be talking about!" said Adam. "It's you and that girl."

"I wasn't doing anything you weren't trying to do not so long ago," said Saleem.

"I was not trying to do anything with her."

"You practically had your trousers round your ankles and your little dick dribbling."

Adam turned to walk away. This was not the time to make his announcement. It would somehow defile it. This was typical of his father. There was always something to spoil a moment.

"I cannot even give up smoking," shouted his father, running up behind Adam. "Even though there are signs everywhere saying Do Not Smoke! I still do it. It is my nature. And young girls, they are what is in men's nature. And so now I have some money, why

67

not? Why shouldn't I? You said I should maybe take another wife? So why not that girl? She'd have me."

"She'd have anyone," muttered Adam, "Who paid."

"I paid for your mother! So what's the difference?"

Adam walked faster. This was not something he wanted to hear.

"If you did not want me to be tempted by the wickedness of the world," said Saleem, "Then you should have left me alone."

"To be tempted is one thing, but to succumb another."

"I am a man!" said Saleem, pleading, "What else can I do?"

"Men think of the consequences of their actions." said Adam, turning round, "Men think of their loved ones. Men think of their wives, and their mothers. And they think of their reputation. Men hesitate. Men make a mark upon the world. They do not shame themselves."

"I only gave her a cigarette!" shouted Saleem, "That is hardly a matter for shame!"

"It is what it would have led to that is the matter of shame!"

"You're a sanctimonious fool," declared Saleem, "In a stupid suit."

Saleem turned and slunk away leaving Adam fumbling for words to express his emotions. But he could find none, and returned to the hotel booth where he worked beneath his own name. He worked there for the rest of the day and it was not a good day's business. He found it hard to turn on the old charm. Something about the customers' attitude towards him in the suit made it harder for him to be the chirpy rascal of a Desert Arts salesman. The suit seemed to make American matrons suspicious of him. But he was sure things would be different when he got into the Capital. There they would see him differently. There, to be considered a yokel from the sticks was not good. The suit was a good idea, he kept telling himself, even when someone called out "Waiter!" as he walked by the bar to pick up his truck for the journey home. And at home, he found Sufiya exhausted.

"First one coach load, then another," she said. "I almost closed up and said I could not take any more. Then I thought, what would you say? Keep taking the money until you drop? Is that what you would say?"

Adam said nothing but stood posed, watching her in the gloomy light of the kitchen. He wanted her to say something about

68

his suit. But she seemed too exhausted, slumped in her seat by the kitchen table, to even look in his direction.

"If you want to eat, you will have to cook for the both of us."

"You will have to tell me what I am supposed to do," said Adam. "But I will cook. If that is what you want."

Adam sighed, took off his suit jacket and went through to the bedroom to find his usual clothes.

"Is that the suit?" said Sufiya at last as she followed him. "You look like a waiter, or is it that gangster in the movie? You know, the brother whose younger brother became the policeman..."

"I do not look like a gangster and I do not look like a waiter. You are just showing your ignorance of what is fashionable."

Adam carefully hung the jacket on a coat hanger and brushed it free of hairs and dust. It was a little shiny in places and the button holes were a bit frayed but Rashid had sold it to him, for a reasonable sum, and one of the hotel staff had cut it down to size for him - which made the trousers a bit wide about the ankles and a little low about the crutch but he had been assured by one of the women in the clothes' shop that the baggy look was very fashionable.

To hell with his family, he thought. They knew nothing and he would show them up for their ignorance. Then he took off his trousers and took great care to make sure they hung straight on the hanger, then hooked the lot over a peg on the back of the bedroom door. It was his space suit, he thought, just the thing to let him breath when he walked on the moon. He pulled on his old clothes, walked through to the kitchen and began to search out the ingredients for the evening's meal.

"What do you think you're doing?" said Sufiya watching him ransacking the cupboards.

Adam thought it was patently obvious what he was doing, especially since she had told him to do it. By the time Adam had recovered his composure, he found Sufiya had taken charge of the kitchen and reduced Adam to merely watching the black iron frying pan and giving it the occasional stir.

"You are all alike," she said. "And that Omar is just the same. He has been watching me again."

"Then Omar is a man of great distinction and good taste," said Adam bitterly. "Perhaps we were brothers in a previous life. I'll go and ask Castrol what he thinks. Maybe he can light some incense

69

and say some mumbo jumbo and find out if we were pigs of the same litter."

"Well I am sure that suit would fit Omar," she said throwing in another handful of bean curd into the mix.

"And soon we all of us will be the same size, so I am just jumping the gun by a matter of weeks. Foresight is definitely my strong point. Whereas yours momentarily escapes me."

There, thought Adam, the suit was working its magic on him and he was getting stronger. Only these small minded petty people with their provincial attitudes could do nothing but mock and try to hold him back. Well he was not having any more of that! From now on, he was going to be a dynamo of action.

***

As far as Saleem could see, the next two days were uneventful. He watched Adam go to work and come home and the words "dynamo" and "action" never crossed his mind. But then he was refusing to speak to him. But then, they never really saw each other long enough to refuse to have very long conversations, which was most likely just as well. Finally though, Saleem woke up one morning and found Adam was packed and ready to leave for the capital. He wore his suit and gibbered excitedly about feeling sharp, prepared and dynamo like. No-one, apparently, had ever gone to the capital looking so sharp, so well prepared and so dynamo like. He even had a briefcase containing his proposals all neatly typed out with only the barest minimum of spelling mistakes and missed words. Truly he was to be the No 3 New Town's first businessman.

"Ask him what all the other shopkeepers and carpet makers and Hoteliers and Restauranteurs are, if not businessmen?" grumbled Saleem to Sufiya, who ignored him and busied herself picking up all the things she thought Adam might need, such as sharp pencils, a stack of unused paper, and a packed lunch.

"My great friend, Rashid," said Adam, explaining himself to Sufiya as she re-knotted his tie and tucked his shirt tail in, "Has given me sound advice: presentation is 90 per cent of the solution. As a salesman, I understand that idea completely."

So now is the moment of truth, thought Saleem as he lounged in the doorway, cigarette in hand, unshaven and scruffy and unconvinced. Adam turned to him and said, "No mischief!"

Saleem did not know whether to punch his son or ignore him. He decided on ignoring him and puffed away on his cigarette pretending not to have heard the words.

"Ask your husband when he's going to come back," said Saleem to Sufiya. "Ask him, because I've seen people like him. They go to the city and then come back maybe once, twice, then stay a little longer there and find themselves another woman, a city woman, and leave their village women behind. Especially when their village women are pregnant."

"Ignore him," said Adam, loading his cases into the cab of his truck. "I'll be back when I'll be back. It shouldn't take long at all."

Sufiya stood back from the truck and waved as Adam started it up, ground the gears and set off clunking down the road.

"He'd do better with a new truck than that stupid suit," Saleem.

"It makes him feel better," explained Sufiya. "I don't know why but that is just the way he is and maybe he is right."

"Well," said Saleem, "I don't know who he takes after. Certainly not me."

He lit up another cigarette with his nicotine stained fingers.

"No," said Suffiya returning to the shop.

Saleem gave another look towards the horizon where Adam's truck still belched out its pollution, then, with a sigh, took a long drag on his cigarette, so long that he nearly smoked the whole of it in one go. It was bad for him. He could feel his lungs rebelling. But he was convinced that his smoking was the fault of having money. Before he had always craved a smoke but had never been able to indulge - well, not as much, or at least, with as good quality. That is, those really bad for you. That is, those you did not roll yourself. But what else was he to do with his money? What would he be saving it for? And so why should he not indulge in his only pleasure?

Saleem smoked and spat and watched the dust settle, only to be disturbed again by Omar driving up in his police car and sitting for a moment wrestling the door with his stomach wedged beneath the steering wheel. Finally he managed to rock himself free and get out, fix his peaked cap more or less into position, and almost

71

manage to do up the buttons on his uniform, except that one was missing and the other promptly unloosened itself. Saleem screwed up his eyes and followed every movement as if Omar was the devil incarnate, the very force of nature that was bringing the desert into the villages, drying up the wells, frightening the camels, the children, the women, not to mention plagues of tourists. And more than likely darkening the very sun at the same time as it was getting hotter! But other than that, Saleem felt he had nothing really against the man.

"I see you are working at the hotel," said Omar, offering cigarettes. Saleem accepted one and stuck it behind his ear for later.

"Isn't everyone?" he said, with a puff of smoke, "We're all fetching and carrying for the tourists now."

"Since most people's aim is to get out of this camel shit town, it is hard to see what the attraction is for these people," said Omar. "But then I guess if you have lots of money, you want to go everywhere and this is certainly somewhere."

Saleem gave a stupid grin as he pondered the philosophical sophistication of Omar's remark.

"I hear Adam's gone into the capital," added Omar, looking uninterested in an answer, "Be away long will he?"

Omar must have been watching to see if Adam had gone yet, thought Saleem. What business of his was it?

"When will Adam be back?" asked Omar with a touch more aggression.

"When his business is done."

"Your daughter-in-law in, is she?"

Saleem pretended to be a bit hard of hearing or stupid, or both, and merely shrugged and puffed at his cigarette.

"Is it true about your daughter-in-law and Rashid? Is that why Adam's run off?" asked Omar.

"Not as far I know," drawled Saleem. "Is that why you're hanging around here?"

"Gypsy trouble," said Omar with a yawn, "Usual things: soliciting, begging, littering, thieving, drugs. I'm warning people. In fact I told Rashid, your boss, he should control them since he employs them. Either that, or get rid of them. Outsiders, huh! The likes of Rashid come here with their fancy ways..."

"How long you been living here now?" asked Saleem.

"Too long," said Omar. "And even if I'd been here twenty years, you people would still treat me much the same."

Saleem nodded in agreement.

"You are the police," he said, as if that explained everything.

Omar gave a grunt and pushed passed Saleem.

"You stay here a moment," said Omar, opening the door of the shop, "I've some private business."

"What sort of private business?"

"It wouldn't be private if I told you," said Omar, "You just stay there and wait until I tell you that you can enter again."

Omar straightened his uniform then, taking deep breaths, entered the shop. Saleem quickly crouched down by the door trying to overhear what was happening.

"My husband will be back soon," Saleem heard Sufiya say.

"He's gone to the Capital, so I heard," said Omar.

"Don't you ever take a hint?" said Sufiya. "Adam will be back soon, so you can go away."

Good on you, thought Saleem.

"I merely want to talk to you a moment," said Omar. "It's about your mother-in-law's death."

Saleem strained to hear more clearly.

"What about her?"

"Well," said Omar, "I have been thinking and I just want to make sure there is no connection."

Saleem's mouth dropped open. What was all this?

"You did not investigate Jamilla's death," said Sufiya. "So what are you saying now? Are you saying you should have done more to find the truck driver that ran her down?"

"No," said Omar, "I just want you to answer a few questions for me, will you? Please?"

Saleem inched the door open slightly and saw Omar begin to admire some of the brass candlesticks on display. "Are these things locally made?" he asked holding one of them up to examine the bottom.

"Everything is local produce," said Sufiya pointing at the sign on the wall.

Omar nodded and carefully replaced the candlestick on the shelf.

"Remember," said Omar, "I asked you about a party in the desert. Some sort of gathering that other wives complained to me about?"

"And this has got something to do with my mother-in-law?" asked Sufiya.

"Who knows," said Omar. "The dancers were in the desert doing who knows what. And Jamilla was killed on the road nearby not too many months before. Since nothing much else has happened in this godforsaken place, I was just wondering why the sudden flurry of activity?"

In the gloom of the shop, Saleem could make out Omar picking up a ring from one of the shelves.

"Tell me about these?" he said. "Does anyone else sell these?"

"No," said Sufiya. "They were copied from an old ring worn by Adam's mother herself."

Omar nodded and seemed to be looking around for something else.

"What do you really want?" asked Sufiya.

"How long is Adam going to be out of Town?"

"Sergeant Sayeed," said Sufiya. "Are you serving any useful purpose here?"

Saleem muttered to himself that he could see no useful purpose on the planet for the likes of Omar.

"No," said Omar, seemingly agreeing with Saleem's thought, "Not yet. I was just..."

"Just what?"

"We are a long time dead," said Omar, "And there are not many opportunities for happiness, or to help those we admire... "

Saleem craned to get a better look at what was happening.

"You know how much I admire you and I know it is a difficult thing to ask of you, but could you be in the least flattered by my attentions, which are not malicious, or evil, or dishonourable. Because they are natural. I would just like to have some hope here, and perhaps, with Adam not here, we might meet once, just once, just to see, just to..."

"And what has this got to do with Jamilla, and all that cock and bull stuff?"

Saleem began to shudder with indignation at the thought that his son was being made such a fool of, even if he was a sanctimonious prig and a fool anyway.

"It has made me think all the harder about this, and made me realise that I should try to explain myself to you... And, and, I fear that you might be in some sort of danger from those who are preying on women in the region. You see my reasoning here? Do you understand the connections that I am seeing? Because they make me fearful for all here, not just you, but you, I fear for the most... A man like Rashid, for instance. He is a friend of yours, but I don't like him. And I don't like him talking the way he did to me. About you. Saying those things, to me, about you, was not his business. Was... Why would he say these things for you? Ask yourself this? Ask yourself what a man like that would want in return as a favour from you? That is how these people work. They are city people and there is not anything for nothing with them. You are putting your head in his noose. And I am ashamed for having driven you there. But haven't you any feelings for me, who is so discrete, and so caring..."

Enough was enough. Saleem got to his feet and barged through the door, frightening Omar so much that he jumped and entangled himself in the dangling wind chimes.

"It gets hot out there without the air conditioning," said Saleem glaring at Sufiya who blushed before his gaze.

"That's right," said Omar, coughing and nodding to Saleem, and to Sufiya and then to Saleem again, "I shall be talking to you later."

Then in three strides he was gone. Saleem peered out of the window and watched Omar return to his car. Then he cast a quick look over the state of Sufiya's clothing. Nothing amiss, thought Saleem, no dishevelment, no signs of co-operation in this outrage. He wished she had protested though. If only she had screamed or something. He would have to keep a very close eye on her. His son had made a very good choice for a wife but sometimes an attractive wife could be more trouble than they were worth.

"That Omar is a menace," said Sufiya pulling a face as though she had stepped in something disgusting. "I have warned Adam about him but he does not seem to take any action."

"It is up to you to take action?" said Saleem.

"And what can I do?" said Sufiya, "Omar is a police officer. I have complained to Rashid but he says nothing. So who else can I complain to? And what is it I complain about? Omar has not touched me, he has merely told me he would like to."

Sufiya shuddered at the thought and then proceeded to busy herself putting back in place anything that Omar might have touched.

Saleem watched her for a moment and then wondered what was the best thing to do and what would stop Sufiya running to Rashid for protection. It was there that he saw lay the biggest danger. Though no-one ever saw Sufiya talking to Rashid, nor did they ever see them together and yet, people talked about them.

"You haven't seen your father lately," said Saleem. "Have you told him he is going to be a grandfather?"

"You know then," said Sufiya.

"I may be old but I am not deaf. And I am not stupid. So why don't you go and tell him while you can still travel comfortably?"

"They say it is not safe in the mountains at the moment. And with my brother being arrested, I don't know whether it is a good idea."

"Of course it is. We can see if there is something to be done for your brother and tell your father of your good news."

"And who will look after the shop?"

"It isn't that busy at the moment. The tourists are having a holiday from being tourists. Even the hotel is half-empty. So now it is maybe a good time to go and see him. And maybe with you gone, Omar will find some other girl to annoy. Wasn't it only the other year he was chasing after the postmaster's daughter?"

"But she is so ugly!"

"Well he probably thought she was most available. And when she was not interested he thought he might as well go for the best because his chances were much the same there."

Sufiya nodded in agreement and seemed to catch sight of her reflection in the window.

"And I haven't been out of town for years," continued Saleem, "Last time I went on a journey was with Jamilla about six years ago to see her sister. She spent all the time telling me how useless I was. Much like your husband."

"He doesn't say that," said Sufiya.

"Oh no? Well everyone has been saying it for years and maybe they are right. But you people never had to live through what I lived through. I saw my Grandfather hanged."

"No you didn't. Your father saw that."

"Well, someone saw it. But I did see my Grandfather buried."

"Along with his mistress."

"One of his wives. Alive at that."

"Yes yes. We've heard the story."

"Yes well. And we didn't see a chicken for twenty years. That sort of thing soon leaves you thinking that only the most useful trees are chopped down. But now things are different. And I'm still fit. And I don't fall asleep like other old men. I'm..."

Saleem searched for the word that would describe his state to his daughter-in-law. He wanted to tell her that he was getting enormous erections whenever he saw young girls. And for that matter had been getting them every time he heard so much as bedspring creak coming from Sufiya's bedroom, but telling her such a thing was too indelicate.

"Well," said Saleem, "I'm having a second spring and feel like going somewhere while the weather is good."

Saleem liked what he heard himself say. He would deal with Sufiya's problem and then deal with his own. Yes, suddenly he had a plan for his life.

CHAPTER FOUR

A bulldozer roared into action, shovelled the desert up and pushed it back. A jackhammer started its steady thudding search for water, a thudding that rumbled the ground beneath Saleem's feet. He had gone to find Amina. He had business with her, negotiations to conduct, understandings to be formed. After escorting Sufiya to her father's house, Saleem planned to return and, without the embarrassment of relatives watching, pursue his liaison with the little whore, as he fondly imagined Amina to be. A fait accompli, he reasoned, was the way to introduce Amina as his wife. That she was younger than his son would make a scandal, but it was not such a bad scandal for a man to have. And had not his son told him to find a new wife? Thus before leaving he just wanted to make sure that his dream stood a chance.

When Saleem looked about Amina's compound, there were no signs of life. Rubbish blew up into dusty spirals and a door creaked but there was no-one there. Saleem looked into the main building. Some straw mattresses lay ransacked and scattered about the room. A black streak of soot showed where a fire had once cooked.

Saleem felt very alone and out of habit hurried towards the only place where he really felt at home. He found that his house had not been engulfed by the dunes. On the contrary, outside it there was an expensive four-wheel drive truck and a collection of workmen in yellow plastic hats were shoring up the walls with scaffolding and cleaning the frieze.

"This is my house," shouted Saleem at the workmen, "Who gave you permission?"

The workmen showed nothing but bewilderment at his question. Like little dark monkeys up a ladder, thought Saleem. He walked over to the gate and looked in to see a yellow baseball cap upon the pale head of a European. The government must be letting anyone work here now, thought Saleem.

78

"It is not very flattering to you white devils!" said Saleem pointing at the long nosed pictures on the frieze.

"I hope the area never loses its local colour," said the European in Saleem's language. Saleem tried not to betray any element of surprise. Having Europeans working there was bad enough, but allowing them to speak the language as well? It was like handing them a stick to beat you.

"What are you doing here?" said Saleem, seeing in this person perhaps the reason for the gypsy's disappearance.

"Eastern Adventures," said the European, "We're renovating all these buildings. It is going to be a cultural heritage site."

He handed Saleem a card bearing the name of the company.

"What's that?" asked Saleem becoming all the more confused.

The man explained how the village had been sold to a development company that was going to restore the buildings to their original state and turn the place into an authentic desert village. People from the city would be able to come and stay for the weekends. There would be horse riding, swimming and cultural events.

"But there's no water!" said Saleem.

"Not now," said the European, "But there will be."

"And it is my house," added Saleem.

"The land was sold by the state to the developers and, because of the lack of water, there were no tenants."

"Tenants? I never paid rent. It was my house. I always lived here."

"There was nobody living here when we arrived. And half the place had fallen down so I don't think anyone would have wanted to live here."

"I did!"

"If you have legal titles I suggest to take it up with the authorities."

Saleem could feel the logic of his position slipping away. He lived there, but he did not now. He owned the place, but only the state owned property - until now. He turned and looked upon the ruined streets of the village, the noise of the jackhammer thudding its way towards some theoretical water table. There was nothing left of his life, nothing left of Jamilla, and no Amina. Tomorrow he would take Sufiya to see her father and protect his miserable uncaring son's interests. Maybe he should steal Suffiya from him?

Adam did not deserve her, but to do such a thing would not be honourable - as if *honour* was something Saleem could afford.

***

After the morning shift at the hotel, Saleem returned to the shop and packed the few things he felt he needed: a new pair of pyjamas, a pair of slippers, a bar of soap. Then he thought better of the bar of soap. There was no place to wash on the train and he was sure that at their destination, soap existed.

"The way Adam talks to me," said Saleem, explaining to Sufiya his luggage requirements, "Some might think I never used the stuff or gave it a second thought, but they would be wrong. It is merely that I did not waste water in the desert, not that water is a problem anymore. The Europeans, it seems, can make it appear anywhere they like."

Sufiya just nodded and went about shuttering up the windows, covering the stock and hiding the money she was not taking with her. Saleem could not tell whether she was listening or not.

"The revolution has failed," he pronounced, "And now it will all be like it was before, except this time it will not be real, it will all be pretend. We will all play at being natives and the Europeans will all play at being colonialists and what will it mean?"

"I have never heard you say anything on this subject before," she said, "Why do you say it now?"

"I have many thoughts," said Saleem, "It's time people heard them."

Then Castrol arrived to take them to the rail pickup. This was one of the many little services that Castrol provided for a small fee.

"Saleem!" Castrol said on seeing Saleem struggling with the luggage. "What are you doing?"

"I am going with my pregnant daughter-in-law. How is she to travel in that condition without assistance?"

"Pregnant," said Castrol. "Congratulations. Omar won't like it."

"And what has it got to do with him?" said Sufiya, bristling with indignation at the mention of the name.

"And Rashid won't like you running off like this. Isn't Saleem supposed to be guarding his customers from thieves like us?"

Saleem heaved the luggage into the back of the truck, wheezing from the exertion.

"Rashid has more important things to think about than me," said Saleem pushing Sufiya up the step into the cab of the truck.

"Stop pushing!" said Sufiya.

"Rashid," said Castrol, "He did Adam a big favour taking you on."

"And I did him a big favour working for him," said Saleem, "And besides, this is my paid holiday. Official. I saw the Personnel Officer and he said I had a paid holiday and so I am taking it in advance and they can pay me later when I am supposed to have it, but I shall work then instead. That's fair isn't it?"

"A paid holiday?" said Castrol, frowning.

"That is right," said Saleem. "Just like all the tourists have. And now I too am a tourist. I arranged it properly. So why you should think Rashid is concerned about these things, I do not know. And I know even less why *you* should think anything about these matters!"

"I'm just letting you know what others might think."

"What you think others think and what they think are two different matters."

Saleem felt most aggrieved that he should be interrogated by a mere mechanic and sat himself squashed up against the door with Sufiya plumply squeezed between him and the gear stick. He noticed that Castrol's grease-laden face showed that he was still struggling with the concept of paid holiday.

"A paid holiday is my entitlement," said Saleem proudly. "As an employee I have several days paid holiday to enable me to travel and see things. It is not only Westerners now who can do these things. We can all do them. It's the law. Stupid or not."

Castrol engaged the gears and smoothly pulled away from the shop.

"Well when you used to come to my garage you would have said it was stupid. You would have argued with everybody. Told them they were not working hard enough and probably informed the police about them as well."

"That was a long time ago," said Saleem, "And I most certainly would not have called the police even then."

"And well, what is the point of going to all these places for holidays?" added Castrol. "I can see them on the television. And if people are not shooting at each other, they are unhappy about something or other. I can stay home for all that."

"That is neither here nor there," said Saleem. "It is an entitlement and that is that. My right. That is what the man said."

"Your right?" said Castrol, "Everyone has rights now. Too many people if you ask me."

"Who is asking you?" said Saleem, "Did you hear me ask you for permission? Aren't we paying you for this privilege? I don't hear you complaining about that?"

For the rest of the journey they travelled in silence. The dead dog squashed out six feet across the road evinced no comment. The low flying jet sending up eddies of dust, caused little more than a few blinks of the eye. As Castrol put Saleem and Sufiya down at the pick up point, he stared down the length of the railway track.

"What are you looking at?" said Saleem. "Are you wishing you were going somewhere?"

The rail stretched off towards the horizon. Either side of it was nothing, barely even scrub. Castrol shook his head.

"There's nothing out there for me," he said, "Everything is here."

Suddenly he revved up his engine, and gave a honk of his horn as a farewell shot.

"Oh," said Sufiya, rushing back to the cab. "I nearly forgot. Please post this letter will you?"

She handed Castrol a scruffy envelope.

"It has not got a stamp on it," said Castrol.

"I don't know what the fee is. But if you find out," said Sufiya with a smile, "I will pay you it double when I return. Now that is fair, isn't it?"

Castrol took the letter, put it into the oily pocket of his overalls, and drove off. When his dust had settled, Sufiya returned and stood with Saleem staring down the railway line. A fly buzzed about her head. She swatted at it and it decided to buzz about Saleem's head.

"What was in the letter," asked Saleem.

"Nothing," she said.

"If it is nothing then why did you write it in the first place?"

"Just to let Adam know where we are. That is all."

Saleem wondered whether the letter was to Omar or Rashid. She could be making an arrangement with either of them. She seemed so quiet. She had some sort of a treacherous plan, he was sure. Women were like that. Even Jamilla had not been entirely trustworthy. He had always had to keep an eye on her. Women did that, they left you, they betrayed you, they made their promises, they tempted you, and they died!

Saleem saw the train coming. People were hanging off the side of it, hanging off the roof, and as the train slowed down, hooting its steam whistle, they were leaping off and tumbling over in the dust to be the first to rush off to a piece of bush for their toilet.

The train clanged to a standstill and hissed a sigh of relief. A hundred or so men, some businessmen, some farmers, some soldiers in scruffy uniforms, began to wander up and down the track looking for old friends, stretching legs, looking to see if there was anything to purchase.

Sufiya and Saleem gathered up their bags and went to the first carriage. A stern young woman in a uniform that, shockingly, showed her knees, blocked their way.

"Tickets," she said and held her hand out.

"I believe we can purchase them here?" said Sufiya.

The woman sucked on her teeth and then called back into the carriage. Out came a man, his uniform equally smart though the dye from the collar seemed to have stained the back of his neck blue.

"How many tickets do you want," asked the man with a sly smile.

Saleem watched him looking Sufiya up and down. There were obviously ways to obtain free tickets. Sufiya announced that she required two.

"Two?" said the man with a laugh. "You want two? They are very rare."

There followed a negotiation, which bewildered Saleem. He kept thinking that he should intervene here, being the man, but Sufiya was making lightning calculations about the mark up these two officials were making. In the end Sufiya snatched out of the man's hand a couple of grubby tickets and paid thirty foreign exchange certificates which made her hiss as she climbed up the steps.

"If you see me later," said the Ticket Officer, "I might be able to find some special offers."

"What was that all about?" asked Saleem as they inched down the crowded, urine and smoke smelling corridor to the compartment with the same number as their tickets.

"They think they are the lords of the line," muttered Sufiya.

Saleem surveyed the six other men crammed into the compartment. It looked, so he imagined, like a brothel's waiting room. There were six bunks available and Saleem and Sufiya made eight people.

"I hope," announced Sufiya, "That you all have the correct tickets? Otherwise, I shall have to call the Inspector."

No-one moved but Sufiya barged in, pulled down the top bunk and threw her bag onto it. No-one protested.

"I am going to the end of the line," she announced.

The other passengers nodded. The air was stifling and stank of garlic. Saleem began to feel hungry.

"I have paid for two bunks, guaranteed!" announced Sufiya.

The train lurched, sending Saleem sprawling over three of the passengers.

"Sorry," he said, dragging himself back up.

"I am now going to examine the facilities on this train," said Sufiya, "And when I return I shall return to my bunk. Is that understood?"

Sufiya, put her hands on her hips and glared around the compartment making eye contact with everyone there. Then she nodded her approval and left the carriage.

Saleem grinned sheepishly at the men, who still did not move from their seats.

"She is a strong willed woman," explained Saleem.

"Then you shall have to keep her under control," piped up a voice.

Everyone in the compartment muttered and groaned about how women were impossible, and how nothing short of a good beating was the only way to treat them. Saleem excused himself and went looking for Sufiya.

As he pushed passed standing passengers, he found the carriage windows too dirty to see through. It set him wondering what the train might be passing. He pulled down one of the windows. Through the swirling smoke from the stack of the engine, he could see the desert interrupted only by a flash of telegraph pole. A vapour trail lazily unwound against the blue sky. Then he heard the roar of a jet fighter plane coming low over them. With a flash of flame from its engines, it rose up into the sky. He admired the technology. Amazing, he thought, so much power, so much . . .

And then his attention was caught by Omar's car belching fumes as it raced along the dust track beside the train. Was it Omar's car? Small and squat, the rusty door frames, the dirty windows: it could not be anyone else's. Why was it rushing along at such a reckless pace? Saleem watched as slowly Omar inched past the carriage. Was he going to stop the train? Then the train hit a downward gradient and began to speed up, slowly pulling past Omar, whose car bounced over a hump and veered across the road for a moment before regaining control. Saleem tried to stretch his neck out of the window to catch a better view, but the gap at the top of the window was too narrow.

Saleem wondered if Sufiya would leap from a moving train into Omar's arms? She had tricked him into taking the train and thus left her with a chance of escaping with Omar. No, it was too absurd.

Saleem found Sufiya in the restaurant car packed with dollar payers. Each table groaned with cheap champagne and a fat old cook merrily ran between them with plates full of prime steak and deep-fried chipped potato. Saleem licked his lips at the smell and joined Sufiya at her table.

"I can not afford the steak," she said, "I do not have dollars. Although I could have purchased some. But I refused to. It is not right that we should have to do this. It is not right that I should have to deal with such people."

"Don't get upset," said Saleem, hoping he could perhaps persuade her to pay dollar prices. "I am looking after you."

"Is that what you are doing?"

Sufiya stood up to make her way back along the corridor. Saleem sighed and followed. He was hungry and was sure that Sufiya could persuade someone to give them food, somehow.

"Mind," he said, "If you perhaps paid for one meal between the two of us..."

Sufiya pushed passed men who seemed to step back into her path. They were first class travellers, gold watched and Western clothed, like cigarette advertisements. But even so, their hair was greasy, their faces flecked with the smut of the steam engine, and a hint of the desert in their squinting eyes.

The rhythm of the train altered as it approached a station.

"There'll be food to buy at the station," said Sufiya confidently.

Saleem pulled a corridor window down letting in a blast of cool sooty air. He and Sufiya stared out and in the distance saw an orange glow raising itself up over the desert. The train slowed down. Outside a few stone buildings slowly passed. Then the train clunked to a satisfied standstill, its whistle giving a slow hoot. Sufiya made for the carriage intersection. Saleem followed on.

Clambering down the iron steps of the carriage, Saleem found that the station was not much of a station. A couple of rail lines, no platforms, but a breezeblock waiting room connected to a shed. Before the waiting room a couple of old ladies sold various kinds of food from baskets and aluminium hot pots sitting at their feet. Sufiya went over and examined the food: eggs boiled in tea, some potatoes, a few sausages. She purchased eggs and potatoes. A crowd had by now gathered and the old women were doing a brisk trade. Saleem kept watch as Sufiya took her goods and stood aside. He was not sure what he was watching for, but looking into the waiting room he saw a couple of drunks lying on their sides in the middle of the dirty floor. Their shoes were worn through and tied on with string. Their heads miraculously stuck straight out from their shoulders, without touching the floor. Maybe they were dead. A few bottles of spirits lying beside them indicated they were at least dead drunk.

There was a scream.

"Sufiya!" snapped a voice.

Saleem recognized the voice through the hubbub of the station crowds. Where had it come from?

"What are you doing here?" demanded Sufiya.

Saleem began to push his way towards her. The red of her veil flitted in and out of the black of the food sellers'. He could see Omar and he could see Sufiya and he could hear their conversation but he never seemed to get any closer to them. Somehow he had to stop them talking. Somehow, if they continued to talk, then all would be lost. His son would be forever his enemy. His grandchild would never know him...

"Get off me," shouted Sufiya.

"Saleem!" shouted Omar as Saleem burst through the crowd and confronted him.

At that point Saleem froze a half-second. What was he to do now he was there, now he had stopped them talking? What could he do? He could not tackle Omar and Omar was incomprehensibly yelling at him.

Saleem backed away. He could not hit the man, he was too strong, and he was a policeman. Saleem considered all the possibilities of what he should do as Sufiya and Omar now again shouted at each other. She was not co-operating and all heads seemed to have turned to look at Omar struggling with Sufiya. Saleem saw a couple of the characters that were crowding out their compartment and grabbed their arms.

"There he is!" he yelled. "He is the man she has been trying to run away with!"

Other men followed Saleem and soon Omar and Sufiya were surrounded.

"You should be ashamed of yourself," said one of the men, giving Omar a prod.

"And you a police officer," said another.

"Never trust the police," said another.

"Think they can do what they like," said another.

Omar shuddered as a fist punched into his shoulder knocking him backwards. Someone tripped him from behind and he sprawled backwards. A scream rang out and Omar disappeared from Saleem's sight, hidden by the backs of heads crowding in on him.

Saleem found Sufiya, who was so confused by the situation she at first tried to run from Saleem and then, on seeing soldiers running along the platform, returned to Saleem and ran with him back to the train. A whistle pierced the air and people ran for the train, clambering up the iron steps as the train began to slowly inch forward. Those with arms laden with loaves and hot potatoes threw their booty into the arms of people hanging from the windows and then athletically leapt and clung to the sides of the train.

"Sufiya!" yelled out a voice.

The train began to pick up speed as it pulled out of the station. Sufiya squatted in the corridor breathlessly eating the potatoes she managed to purchase. Saleem squatted beside her and slowly and stiffly peeled a boiled egg and pushed it into his mouth. He chewed, opening and shutting his mouth, as if he wanted to say something but then the train's monotonous drone with it iron

87

wheels groaning and straining at their burden, disrupted his thoughts.

"That was exciting," giggled Sufiya.

***

"Where d'you want to go?" asked the skinny barelegged cyclo Man as he cheerfully leapt up out of the passenger seat of his cyclo. "Nice suit," he added.

Unknowing that Sufiya was riding the train to her father's, Adam emerged from Madam Dai's Business Hotel and stood on the steps striking a pose before the grandly ornate doors. He felt most efficient. He had spent the previous day resting from his journey, lying in his room watching TV, but now he had to face the city and there it was spread out before him in all its steamy clattering glory. The muddy river could be made out at the end of the street where a rusty tanker was moored. Just across the road was the clutter of blue and white striped plastic awnings that hid the start of the market street cluttered with bicycles and baskets and chickens, while this side of the road began a long potholed boulevard lined with dusty trees dangling with electric cable. And everywhere were people: mostly five per moped that dangerously swayed and wove their way through the traffic obeying no laws of traffic other than the biggest always has the right of way.

"You can hire me for the entire day," said the cyclo Man flashing his yellowing teeth.

"I don't want to hire you," said Adam. "You are too expensive!"

Adam walked on down the street and hesitated as he tried to cross the road in the face of the oncoming traffic. The cyclo Man peddled up beside him.

"If not satisfied, you don't have to pay," he said with a buck-toothed grin. "You'd be crazy not to take this offer!"

It was an extraordinary offer and Adam had to admire the gall of it. So making a great show of reluctance, Adam climbed into the passenger seat and sat back trying to feel like a great man - a great man in a suit.

"Take me to..." Adam paused a moment and then said with great authority, "The Bank."

"Ah," said the cyclo Man, "So you are going to the bank. Any particular bank?"

"Which one do you recommend?" said Adam rather puzzled by the question. He had never considered the possibility of a choice in the matter.

"Well," said the cyclo Man ringing his bell merrily at a truck hurtling towards him on the wrong side of the road. "They are all as bad as each other."

"In what way?"

"They charge you money for putting your money in and they charge you money for taking it out and then pay you interest that in no way covers their fees."

"But I get a credit card don't I?" asked Adam, a little concerned about this sudden influx of disturbing information.

"Oh yes," said the cyclo driver. "And they charge you money for that as well."

"Then," said Adam, "Why is it that rich people have bank accounts and poor people do not?"

"Maybe," said the cyclo Man, "That's how the rich become poor."

Round the mildewed fountains barely trickling with slimy water, by the cream coloured baroque facade of what was now the town hall instead of the Emperor's Palace, the cyclo-Man peddled. In and out of the hordes, ringing his bell, shouting abuse, he peddled. Then he peddled Adam up a street lined with trestle tables groaning with black and silver lacquer-ware, each with a squat black clad grandmother on a stool beside a red clay pot for the day's takings, towards the all glass walled Army Bank. Breathlessly he stopped and let Adam leap out and shakily push his way through the glass doors.

"I will wait for you!" yelled cyclo Man, sweat dripping from the end of his nose. "You are going to be my special customer. I have a feeling."

"Hmm," muttered Adam, his nerves still jangling, "I also have a feeling."

As Adam marched across the marble floor, a security guard with a large shotgun stood by the counter sipping at a cup of coffee, eyeing him. Adam tried to ignore this. "I am wearing a suit," he said to himself, "And there is no reason to expect to be thrown out." He went up to the counter. Feigning confidence, he held up his cash box and rapped on the glass partition with his knuckles. No-one came to his assistance. Then he noticed the closed sign on that window and looked around to see if anyone had noticed him. No, they all seemed preoccupied with their own business.

At one counter a backpacking Westerner in shorts and T-shirt was arguing loudly with the teller. Adam went over to him.

"Excuse me," said Adam in his best English. "Can I help you?"

The backpacker turned round and glared at Adam.

"Come again?" said the backpacker, his face red with sunburn.

"You seem to be having a problem?"

The backpacker looked at Adam and then shook his head.

"Say that slowly will you?"

Adam repeated himself. The backpacker remained puzzled.

"Yousim beaving problem?" paraphrased the backpacker, then suddenly a light went on in his eyes. "Oh Oh, I get it! Yeh, you can say that again. But don't try. No, but it's just she doesn't understand me. I'm trying to change this local toilet paper back into dollars."

Adam nodded on hearing all this, then turned to the bank teller and explained how this gentleman had been given money used for toilet paper and was trying to change it for dollars. She explained that this establishment, being an Army Bank, dealt only in dollars and did not accept toilet paper.

"They do not deal in toilet paper," Adam informed the backpacker.

The young man looked at Adam and then back at the Bank Teller. He shook his head and walked away leaving Adam to get on with his own business.

"Tourists!" said the Teller, tutting and turning back to the ledger she was slowly writing numbers in.

"Tourists!" said Adam, adding a few tuts of his own, "They always seem to have diarrhoea."

The Teller looked up from her ledger and, with a sigh, put her pen down. Adam beamed the friendliest smile he could imagine and then said he wished to open an account with the cash that he was carrying. He held up his cash box and tapped it as if that would somehow show how much it was worth. Much to his great pleasure the process proved plain sailing. He did not even have to fill in the form himself. The Teller filled it in, he signed it, and then he asked for a Credit Card. She told him that he would have to put in an application with proof of his annual income.

"No problem. A reference from my friend the Hotel Manager will soon deal with that," said Adam with a smile.

As Adam walked out of the bank, he felt at least six inches taller. At the front door Adam even dropped a few coins into a legless beggar's scrawny hand. The hand appeared from nowhere and then disappeared from Adam's vision and mind. He not only pretended to be a big man, he was a big man. It was official. He had the suit. He had the bank account. He had a credit card on the way. There was no more need for him to feel ill at ease in the city. The city belonged to him. This was the sort of place where a man like himself should be.

"Hallo Hallo!" cried the cyclo Man, waving his skinny brown arm above his head.

Adam held up his hand, snapped his fingers and the cyclo Man, his shirt flapping exposing his ribs, peddled his machine across the oncoming traffic.

"Where next?" asked the cyclo Man, looking barely capable of pedalling his own weight let alone that of Adam's.

From his pocket, Adam produced his notes of introduction and checked the address.

"Let me see," he said, "Let me see now. I have so many important meetings to make..."

Behind him the backpacker wrestled with an endlessly unfolding map. Adam, on seeing this, could not help but wish to be of further assistance. He glanced at the cyclo-Man and explained, "I find this happening all the time. These people are always in need of help from me. It is always the case when one has linguistic skills."

Adam went over to the backpacker and said he did not know the place that well but he would try to help him. However, before he could help, the cyclo Man had already grabbed the map and was pouring over it muttering how inaccurate it was.

"All these places are much too near to each other," declared the cyclo-Man. "You need me to show you how to get there. Very cheap."

"But I am hiring you!" said Adam.

"But he pays tourist rates," explained the cyclo Man. "Do you want to pay double? If you do, I will throw in a visit to my Grandmother to sample our true customs."

"Pay double?" enquired Adam, feeling at a loss as to what he should do. Should he pay double and be robbed? No, that was beneath his dignity.

The backpacker, whose red burnt face beamed with a happy innocent smile, found himself being ushered into the cyclo.

"He is of course trying to cheat you," said Adam bitterly.

"That's all right," said the backpacker. "He gets a little bit of extra money and I feel morally superior. It's probably a fair trade."

As Adam watched his cyclo disappear into the traffic, he thought how being a big man in town was obviously not enough, one had to be a Westerner as well. This was perhaps what some of the politicians he had seen on the hotel TV meant by "Counter-Revolutionary Tendencies." He would vote for those guys, if there was a vote, and people would be forced to do business with people they could not cheat, people like him and not foreigners like the backpacker.

***

When Omar began to recover his wits about him, he was being dragged backwards by two soldiers holding each of his arms. A crowd of onlookers melted away back onto the departing train.

"Sufiya!" he yelled.

He seemed to call it out for a long time and could hear himself calling it as if far far away. His mind operated quite independently of the situation and quite lucidly, during the scuffle, recalled that he had, after only eight months in No 3 New Town, begun a similar vigil at the altar of the post office keeper's daughter. She was thirteen then and Omar had found her attractive though few others did. That had been eight years ago. She had four children now, all strangely ugly, and, so Omar now realised, all taking after their mother. He hoped that when he awoke from his current obsession he would not find Sufiya so ugly, and God-forbid that it should be eight years in the desert of desperation uglier than the Post Office Keeper's daughter.

Omar regained his attachment to the here and now when he hit the floor with a thud and discovered that he was lying in the dust and dried mud of the stationmaster's hut. Looming above him were the two soldiers with crumpled unbuttoned uniforms and automatic rifles on their shoulders. Their sixteen-year-old faces had fifty-year-old eyes.

"I'm a policeman!" he yelled at them.

One of them knelt down beside him and examined Omar's torn bloodstained shirt. Then he flipped the ripped epaulette on Omar's shoulder.

"ID?" he said.

Omar tried to sit up but his back gave him a twinge. Then he saw the bloody mess of his right hand and wondered how it had got in that condition.

"I was trying to arrest a suspect," he said as he sat up to nurse his hand. "Look in my back pocket." Then he thought better of letting them get hold of his wallet. "No," he said, "I'll get it." Grimacing, he pulled out his ID, handed it over and tapped the side of his holster.

"I wouldn't be wearing this if I wasn't police," he said.

"Touch that again," said one of the youngsters, his kalashnikov aimed at Omar's brain, "And you're scrambled eggs."

His partner examined the ID and gestured for Omar to stand up.

Slowly Omar got to his feet and watched the soldier making a telephone call. Omar found it all the more painful as the soldier slowly and hesitatingly picked his way round the telephone numbers, first getting them wrong and having to start again, and then getting another wrong number.

"Do you need glasses or something?" he snapped.

The soldier gave him a myopic glare.

"I don't suppose you really have to hit anything with those guns," said Omar, "So long as you just pull the trigger and make a lot of noise."

"You'll be making a lot of noise if I pull this trigger," said the other youth, a grin spreading across his face like an axe wound.

Eventually someone answered the telephone. The soldier whispered into it, holding his hand up to his mouth and casting glances towards an increasingly impatient Omar.

"Oh for crying out loud!" said Omar, "They're getting away. While you're holding me here, they are getting away! Can't you understand that?"

93

"Can you understand you are in a restricted zone?" said the soldier, getting through on the phone to Colonel Khan's office, the area army commander.

"Restricted zone!" said Omar, "Every bloody where's a restricted zone to someone! But not to me! I am chasing after a dangerous criminal. Do you understand?"

Colonel Khan's office did have a record of a local police sergeant called Omar Sayid and did have the authority to give him free passage through restricted zones, but they had not done so.

"I didn't have time to request a pass," declared Omar, "I didn't know this was a war zone anyway!"

Omar began pacing up and down in exasperation as the soldier explained how Omar was to be escorted out of the area and to report to Omar's boss, Police Lieutenant Chan.

"Something about irregularities," said the soldier with glee.

**

Adam walked towards his first real business meeting, swearing that he would take great delight in finding that cyclo driver on some other occasion, taking him for a long exhausting pedal and then leaving him to wait for payment. "I'll be back in a minute," he rehearsed in his mind and then gleefully saw himself running out the back door of some establishment and catching a public bus home. Yes, thought Adam, that would teach him a lesson. Unfortunately he knew that there were so few places in the city that a man like himself could afford to go, that any cyclo Man worth his salt would find him within an hour.

"Hallo! Hallo!" heard Adam. He stepped back from the kerb to avoid some unseen danger. But it was just some girl shouting, so he tried to ignore it. The cry got louder and more insistent. "Hallo! Hallo! Mr! Remember me!" Adam did not know any females that would be in the city and could not think of any that he should remember from anywhere. Adam looked around and saw a slight figure in the back of a cyclo frantically waving. "Hallo! Hallo!" she said. Her dark hair and complexion did not ring any bells. She looked like a million other girls he had seen whizzing about the capital on the backs of motorcycles.

"Share my cyclo," said the girl.

94

Adam squinted and tried to make out who she was or what she might want of him, though he had a shrewd idea of what a strange girl in town might want with a big man in a suit. She was attractive in a childlike manner, looking even more childlike because she was wearing a pair of white shorts, but he did not know her at all and decided that she was merely pretending to know him. It was a ruse to make it easier for him to allow himself to be picked up. Well, the ruse would be on her! Even though he needed a cyclo, under no circumstances would a prostitute pick him up. Then he noticed the elegant manner in which the fingers of her hand bent back.

Amina grinned and showed her blackened teeth. How Adam had managed not to notice those, he could not imagine. But she was so different. Without the clothes, without the music, the desert, without the hiss of snakes and insects, she was someone else. She had a cheery smiling face, for a start.

"I am doing three nights at one of the big hotels," she declared, "It is very good money. Much better than I could earn in that fly blown back of beyond place. Are you going anywhere?"

Adam flinched as a wild herd of bicycles suddenly lurched out of a side street. "I must go to The Majesty Hotel. I must..."

Amina gave a cheeky grin and squashed to one side to let Adam join her. Adam was bewildered by this girl. Her manner, her poise, her confidence, had come from nowhere. Either that or all that Fruit of The Desert stuff had been just an act. Instead of being a slave girl trained from birth to please men, she was the product of one of the wooden shacks sprawling among the rubbish heaps and river tributaries at the edge of the city.

"Rashid said you would be in town," she added, as he sat squeezed in beside her.

"He did, did he?"

"I have ditched Ali and his friends," she said as the cyclo lurched around the fountains, "My manager says I can do better on my own and take a bigger share of the takings."

"Manager?" said Adam.

"Rashid," she said proudly, "He got me this job. Paid old Ali his blood money - what a phoney *he* is! - and here I am now with a real contract. It is all written down. And I am learning to read it. I think one should read these things very carefully, don't you?"

"Oh yes," said Adam, "Very carefully. If you can."

"Well maybe you can look at it for me, not that I do not trust my manager. But I do not think one can trust anyone at any time. Is that a wise thing to think?"

"Most likely," said Adam, not quite sure how he should take this.

"Can you believe I was with those clowns for five years?" she said rolling her eyes in disgust at the thought. "But they lost the Government grant they used to give to folk troupes and after that it was just drifting here and there with no real idea of career development. The state used to do all that for you anyway. But now, I think I'm going to benefit from the new scheme of things, don't you?"

Adam kept nodding as she spoke, "Uh huh," he kept saying, trying to keep up with this flow of unexpected ideas.

"This is the place," she announced.

"Oh yeh," said Adam, beginning to get out of the cyclo before it had even stopped.

"I've a roll of film to develop," announced Amina, "So if you don't mind, I'll come in with you. The hotel receptions here get them developed."

"A roll of film?" asked Adam.

"Oh yes," she said, "I bought a camera and I've been going about the sights. I am educating myself."

The two of them pushed through the revolving doors and hit the air-conditioned air which sent a shudder through Adam's body. Amina, though, did not shudder.

"What a dump," she said, looking around at the gleaming marble floors and huge icicles of chandeliers. "This is so phoney."

"No," said Adam. "It is genuine. It is a hotel."

"It sure is that," said Amina with a laugh.

"Then why did you say it was not?"

"Because I am the real thing and I know when things are trying so hard to be real when they are not. They are phoney. They will have a floor show where they sing our songs with a disco beat. I can tell. Maybe I will show them how it is done."

Amina skipped off towards the cash desk, giving a little turn and a tiny wave, before getting down to her business. The moon maiden, thought Adam, where is the moon girl? The cold made him shudder again. These city places were unhealthy in the way they froze you as soon as you walked in off the streets. He wrapped his suit around him, did up an extra button, then went to the information desk and showed the clerk his letter of introduction. The clerk phoned through to Mrs Tang and asked if Adam would take a seat. Gladly Adam sat in one of the red armchairs in the coffee lounge. He snapped his fingers for a waitress and ordered a pot of tea. Amina then joined Adam at his table.

"I hate these places," she said. "They are the same wherever you go. They are totally at odds with the local culture."

"Where have you heard all this?" asked Adam.

"People I meet, tourists, they all say the same. They do. We should listen to them. Because this is what they say."

When Mrs Tang, a smart Keff woman in a black skirt and jacket, and lots of gold about her wrists and neck, appeared, Adam stood up and self-consciously shook her hand.

"And this is my friend Amina," he said. "She is an authentic dance artiste."

Amina did not stand, she merely lounged limply in her armchair and held her hand in front of her mouth as she grinned. Adam noticed that the T-shirt showed her nipples, and the tight shorts showed everything else. He became even more nervous.

"I've come here to speak to you about a business proposition," continued Adam, trying to bring his mind back to the business in hand. Then he went on about how he had discovered the secret of selling to tourists and how they searched for the truly authentic. He turned to Amina for her to confirm this.

"Authentic? Yeh, why not?" said Amina.

"This illustrates my point," said Adam, who went on to say how all the products that he sold had a story attached to them.

"But we already have a souvenir shop," said Mrs Tang. "And each item has a written description attached. If you can do it cheaper, then we would be interested."

"You're talking about selling souvenirs?" butted in Amina.

Adam held his hand up and shook his head. "Please please," he said, "Let me finish here first, then we can talk over old times."

Adam turned his back on Amina and tried to explain to Mrs Tang how Amina was his Uncle's daughter and they had not seen each other for a long time, not since she had been for dancing lessons with the old gypsy dancer that lived the life of a recluse at a desert oasis far away. Somehow he could not quite get into his stride because the expression of Mrs Tang's face was one of impatience and not interest. If he had been telling an American such a thing they would have believed every single word and bought something.

"It's all shit," said Amina, "Every shop sells the same thing. And in the end no-one makes money."

Mrs Tang seemed at a loss for words. Adam was also at a loss for words. He wished Amina had also been at a loss for words. Suddenly with a few polite words, Mrs Tang informed them that there was a phone call waiting, and if Adam left his card then she would be in touch at some later date. Then she shook his hand and walked away leaving Adam feeling six inches shorter.

"What a bitch," he heard Amina say as they hit the revolving doors and headed for their awaiting cyclo. "But never mind. We'll go to my place and you can forget all about business."

Amina waved her hand before Adam's face and with her long fingers beckoned him to sit beside her.

"You should get yourself a decent suit if you want to do business in the capital," she said, "You should wear something like Rashid wears. Now there's a snappy dresser. I mean, look at you. You look like a hick from the sticks in that get up. You should at least have got one that fits."

"That is where you are wrong," said Adam indignantly, "This is very fashionable. You should keep abreast of the times."

Amina pulled a face.

"If you say so," said Amina, "But you look like a gangster."

Adam could have left her right that moment. He had the will power to do so. He was not under her spell. This was not the desert with its dark night and marijuana cigarettes. And she was not the girl he dreamt of. Besides, he was not here for that sort of thing. This was a business trip. There was the future to consider, a future where there were bigger and better things for him to be doing than cavorting with some T-shirt girl. How he wished that he were with Sufiya right that moment. But instead, he was with Amina and she had him sitting beside her in a cyclo that seemed hell bent on killing them both. He should get out, he kept telling himself. But he did not. Instead, he bumped through the muddy narrow streets of China Town as scrawny chickens ran for cover, and muddy bare arsed children stood bemused and simplemindedly scratching their heads as the cyclo bounced and crashed its way passed them.

"Nearly there," said Amina, as she waved at a group of girls sitting on milk crates outside one of the dilapidated low slate roofed buildings. The girls waved, jeered, and stuck their chests out for Adam.

"That is not a nice place," said Amina, "But they are my friends."

Adam glanced over his shoulders at the not so nice place. It looked little different from anywhere else around him. The cyclo now ran through a graveyard of monstrous mausoleums, all leaning to one side, subsiding and crumbling. Thunder cracked the skies wide open and tremendous flashes of lightning bounced from cloud to cloud. The cyclo driver hoisted an umbrella and with one hand holding it, and the other on the handle bars, brought the ride to a halt outside of what Amina declared was a nice place because it had drainage.

Amina leapt out up to her ankles in the mud and chivvied Adam along. His suit was drenched through, and the rain blinded him. He handed the cycloman a bank note and the man was gone without so much as a mention of giving change.

"The hotel found me this place," said Amina pulling at Adam's sleeve and they ran through the front door of her house. "I share it with others in the show. They are all very nice."

Inside the low ceilinged building Adam found a sparsely furnished room with white washed walls, a TV set in one corner and a few cushions scattered about a low Japanese style table.

Amina pointed to a poster on the wall. In bold characters it announced an Hotel's Floor Show, featuring Amina. There was a small blurred photograph of her in costume, posing with a huge ring through her nose.

"See," she said, "I am famous. You are going to make love to a famous dancer."

So that was what he was going to do, thought Adam, as he looked at the emaciated child before him with her T-shirt soaked to her skin and her thin legs poking from her shorts.

"This is the bedroom," she said, "We have not long before the others return home. Then I will make you some tea. City prices mind. You understand that?"

Adam felt compelled to nod and follow wherever Amina led. In the bedroom, which smelt of cleaning powder, Amina unceremoniously pulled off her T-shirt revealing her small breasts.

She was more like a boy than a girl, thought Adam. Perhaps she was a boy? This gave Adam a shudder of alarm that he suspected transmitted itself to Amina as passion. But when she pulled off her shorts, he was assured that she was definitely a girl. Even so, alarm was still the ruling emotion as she began drying herself with a towel.

"You get ready now," she said, "Put your things over there. They are quite safe."

Adam again did as he was told. The rain beat down on the roof and the thunder crashed. Flies idiotically floated around his body as he stripped. They began to bite him and as he slapped them, huge wields rose up on his skin. Amina though, was giggling and dancing before him, leading him by the hand towards the bed.

"Hisss," she said.

Adam slapped at another mosquito bite.

"Oooh," she squirmed as she pulled Adam on top of her.

Adam banged his head against the wall and then ricked his neck. Finally he settled into a reasonably comfortable position as she whispered, "Fuck me!"

Perhaps it was the words, because it could not have been the sights or any other aspect of the ambience, but Adam managed to gain an erection and then the proceedings followed on mechanically with Adam trying to keep his mind on the job. Amina squirmed and squealed and hissed, which helped him to concentrate but just as he was reaching some point of no return, his mind flashed up an image of Sufiya craning her neck and looking on disapprovingly. He almost lost it for a moment until he brought to mind the slippery moon girls draped in flowing rippling liquid gravityless gowns. Then just when he was about to reach a satisfactory conclusion, the whole imagery exploded as the Lady Banditress, galloped up on a slavering horse, scissors in hand. Amina's panting brought him to consciousness again and he opened his eyes to find her checking between her legs.

"Are you finished?" she asked.

Adam nodded his head. He always found it difficult to speak after these events, and even more difficult after such non-events.

"You didn't make a sound!" she said, "So I was not sure."

"Finished," said Adam with a strangulated voice.

Amina sighed and swooned to one side.

"You are so gentle," she said, "You are my favourite. Thirty dollars but for you twenty-five. Twenty for the second time. So we shall meet again? Huh?"

Adam sat up on the side of the bed and listened as the rain continued. He whacked another mosquito, splattering its blood, which had once been Adam's blood, over the welts on his arm.

"Don't you get bitten here?" he asked.

"They don't seem to like me," said Amina.

Adam pulled his underpants on. This was not how it was supposed to be.

"Do you know how to find your way home?" asked Amina.

Adam nodded and rapidly pulled the rest of his wet clothes back on. This was definitely not how it was supposed to be.

"There is a card on the table. You should take it. It has my address, and contact number. You can call me at the hotel. I am there most nights."

Adam hurriedly walked through to the main room and saw a collection of business cards spread out on the top of the Japanese table. He did not pick one up but left and splashed through the rain in search of a cyclo. However, because of the rain, all cyclos were upturned with their drivers huddled beneath them playing cards. He thought this served him right. A man of his undoubted stupidity, treachery, and impotence, deserved to walk.

CHAPTER FIVE

Omar had a very unsatisfactory time. He had the misfortune of being driven through the night-time desert by a couple of psychotic country boy soldiers who had insisted on shooting from the army truck windows at everything that moved and many things that did not. When they were not shooting they were giggling inanely. They could not believe their luck in getting the job of delivering Omar to Police HQ. And knowing how the bureaucracy worked, they looked forward to a very long stay in the capital. They told Omar several times that they intended to fit themselves out with the latest fashions. They had six months of pay and had had no opportunity to spend any of it, therefore now was the time. When Omar was pushed out of the lorry in the pouring rain, instead of feeling nerves as he stood before Police HQ, he felt more relief.

Omar found his way to Chan's office and sat in the scruffy reception room awaiting his meeting. The only air conditioning came from a fan that slowly circled in the centre of the ceiling. Omar could smell burning from somewhere and then noticed that all electricity came into the place via the one socket. Six plugs of various sizes stacked up on an array of adapters to run not only the fan, the fridge, a photocopier, and an electric typewriter but also the computer. A little Keff secretary, looking as if she was dressed for a discotec in her tight lycra dress, sat behind her desk putting newspaper cuttings into various files then stacking them on various overloaded shelves behind her head.

"Soon you will put it all onto the computer disk?" asked Omar.

The Secretary looked wistfully at the computer.

"One day we will get a copy of the computer manual."

An intercom buzzed and finally Omar was allowed into his immediate boss's office. Lieutenant Chan was several years younger than Omar and in a much smarter military green uniform.

He looked thin and intense as he sat bolt upright in his swivel chair, his hands folded before him on the desk.

"Don't bother sitting," said the Lieutenant, "I know all the excuses. Just put them down on paper and we'll file them away. Essentially you are getting out of touch with developments in the capital, so listen up. Nothing must be seen to discourage foreign investment. And with the open door policy we have to be wary of our image in the press. The danger areas are as follows: any dealings with foreign nationals, any dealings with Ethnic Minorities considered to have cultures under threat - though why they should concern themselves with that now, one can only guess at - and any dealings with endangered animal species . . . You haven't got any pandas in the desert have you?"

"No, sir," said Omar.

"Good," said the Lieutenant who then thought a moment. "Oh, and pollution and dissidents . . . You haven't got any dissidents in the desert have you?"

"None that I know of, sir," said Omar.

"Good. Unless you're one. You're not a dissident, are you?"

"No, sir," said Omar.

"Good. How long have you been out there?"

"Eight years, sir," said Omar.

"Aah," said the Lieutenant, "And you are wondering if you will ever get a job in the city?"

"It has been crossing my mind, sir."

"Yes," said the Lieutenant with a deep sigh as he leaned back in his chair and put his hands behind his head, "But frankly, it's not what it's cracked up to be. I think with all the changes out there you'll probably be better off. They're thinking of building a casino complex you know?"

"No, I didn't know sir," said Omar, shifting on his feet and feeling uncomfortable in the heat.

"Yes it is going to be Fun City up there all right. Fun City! Stick it out for a couple of years more and you will be the one with the plum job. We'll all envy you. You'll have some real crime then. Get some drugs runners and international gangsters of all kinds. Be great fun. Much better fun than playing politics in the city."

Although Omar resented the fact that this young Keff wielded so much power over him, he could not help liking him.

"Of course you know you have a black mark against you now?" said the Lieutenant, returning to a more businesslike pose at his desk, "Just don't get caught with your hands in someone's till or dick in someone's wife. Understand? We have a quota of corrupt policemen that we are supposed to lock away. Most likely forever. Not a pleasant prospect. Oh and er, by the way, I should tell that uncle of yours to pack his bags and run for the border."

"Uncle?"

"Barbur Sayeed is your uncle, is he not? And is he not the man who pulled strings to get you your sergeant's stripes even though you failed the examination?"

"I did not fail! There were extenuating circumstances and my good character was taken into account..."

"Well. Your Uncle's good character is under scrutiny right this moment."

"Uncle Barbur's? What's he done, sir?"

"I don't know, but I heard his name bandied about. If he is guilty, he should run for it."

"And if he isn't?"

"Then it could be really bad for him because he'll only stay and try to prove his innocence. Which as you know, when we think you're guilty, denial is only taken as proof of guilt. If I was him, I should run for it and save us all a lot of bother . . ."

"He and my father haven't spoken for years. And I think Uncle Barbur has forgotten all about me."

"Well that's a bit of luck for you isn't it? Denounce the bastard while the going's good and you'll get your name down for a new car allowance."

"I always had my suspicions about Uncle Barbur."

"You've done the right thing Sergeant. Just fill in the forms when you've time. Now, er, this woman... Has she given you any cause for taking such an interest in her?"

Omar was still taking in all this information. Things had not quite gone the way he expected them to go.

"Er," said Omar, gathering his wits, "It was in pursuit of the suspect that caused me to be picked up by the military in a so-called restricted zone."

"Oh, fuck their restricted zones," said Chan, "Military men are all cretins. Just let me hear about this suspect. What is she suspected of?"

"Helping in procuring girls. There has been a lot of trouble in the region. Gypsies you know. And erm, the mother-in-law of Sufiya, that's the woman in question..."

"The mother-in-law?"

"No. No. She's the wife. The mother-in-law was run down by a truck and with the bandits in the region, who we all suspect were the gypsies before they started working at the hotel..."

Lieutenant Chan held up his hand for Omar to stop.

"You're talking a load of crap Omar. It's the sort of bullshit the donkey boys of the desert tell you when they want to sell you a quick fuck with their sister. So don't go on with it because you'll only make me angry. Let me remind you that the reason you are in the position you are in is because of that incident that took place not long after the exam results came through. Remember? The girl, the rape accusations..."

"That was a lie! Is that in my report? How's that got into my report?"

"Everything gets into the report. Lie or not, you were bothering her with your constant unwanted attention and now I find you up to your old tricks again. Choose your women better, Omar. Lose some weight. Pull yourself together."

"Yes sir."

"Why should you risk your entire career on her?"

"I didn't know I was risking my entire career on her," said Omar. "After eight years in No 3 New Town, I didn't know I still had a career."

Chan swung his chair around and stared out of the window.

"Just don't do anything stupid," said Chan, "You stick it out where you are. And sooner or later things will change for you. Oh, and er, remember there are party people banished to your region and sending reports in to try to demonstrate their loyalty."

"Tell me who sir," said Omar, "Give me a name and I will sort it out."

Chan opened up a file he had on his desk and scanned down the page. He laughed to himself and nodded as he read. Then slapped the file shut.

"Leave this Sufiya alone. And this Rashid, well, is he a personal friend of this Adam?"

"It has been said, though I wouldn't think it was too close."

"Maybe Rashid and the woman then, huh? Have you thought of that connection?"

Omar had not really thought that to be any problem. If anything the rumours simply meant Sufiya was fair game.

"Just make sure you are, erm, reasonable friends with this Rashid. Not too close, not too distant. Just enough."

"I'm not sure I know what you mean sir."

"No. It's a difficult balance to strike. But if you get it wrong you're a dead man. That should be enough of an incentive for you to work it out yourself. Now bugger off and er, this Adam character... Husbands don't forget and forgive. If he is going to stir up trouble for you, deal with it now. Money usually does the trick. And if money fails, well, I'll leave that to your imagination. But don't make things worse for yourself. Be a little subtle about it. Be friendly to him. Say it was all a misunderstanding. Maybe he'll accept all that Donkey Boy Bullshit you were trying to pass off on me. Now go on, piss off."

Omar saluted, clicked his heels and marched out of the door. He needed a drink and he needed to think things through. Perhaps it was very fortuitous to be in town right that moment. From his inside pocket, he pulled out the letter Castrol had given him and read it again. It was not exactly very clear what Sufiya was talking about but if she could play games with Adam, then so could Omar. Sufiya, thought Omar, is a woman who likes to torment her men. He had thought that right from the start when he first noticed her casually sitting in that dark shop window of hers, her sari loosely hanging off her shoulder and, he was sure, one of her breasts quietly exposed. She must have known he was watching her.

***

Adam returned to the hotel feeling wet, weary, a little nervy; his day of shocks had left his nerves jangling like bicycle bells. Every so often a hot flush overcame him as he imagined Sufiya somehow knowing at a glance what had happened to him. Still, it was over. There was no reason to think she could find out anything. Even so, he showered very thoroughly. There were all sorts of diseases he could now have and scouring his body with scalding hot water was one way of trying to get rid of them. No matter what he did though, he still itched and was that a swelling? And that pimple, was that a sign of something worse? And was there not a hint of some horrible discharge lurking about the tip of his penis? Worse thoughts came to mind. Some diseases took years to show. The worst diseases took years to show! Ten, fifteen years from now, things would start turning blue and falling off, no matter how scolding hot the shower, or how much he scrubbed. He would not mind half as much if he had enjoyed himself, but he had not. If he could have beaten himself up for being so stupid then he would have done so. Instead, he went downstairs to have dinner.

In the dining room he found there were no spare tables, at least none for a single person and as Adam wandered the cramped ill-ventilated room feeling stupid and out of place, he was suddenly confronted by the morning's backpacker: all gangling hand-shaking, back patting, elbow squeezing good will and rangy sunburnt, skin peeling, innocence. The blonde haired, blue eyed, freckle faced kid from Tacoma, announced his name, "Herman", his rank, "Taking a siesta from this semester," and his number, "If you ever get to Tacoma, look us up." Adam fixed himself a smile that took some difficulty maintaining as Herman dragged him over to his table where Adam found himself sitting with some more young Americans seeking, as they told him, an authentic experience. Since by now Adam had decided the day a complete disaster, he thought he might as well go for broke and really punish himself by spending the rest of evening with them. He deserved it. If he could not beat himself up, then enduring Herman and his friends' inane prattle would have to suffice.

After an uneventful meal of broken English conversation consisting of attempts at explaining the entire philosophy and geographical make up of each other's hometowns, Adam and the boys retreated to the bar. Adam's father seemed mild in comparison to the belching and beer swilling exhibited by these creatures. Once again Adam found himself in a tortured conversation, this time about beer and its medicinal purposes. There was a very long and heated discussion on why Locals could neither hold their beer, nor brew anything tasting better than gnats' piss. Adam tried to convince himself that not only was he cleansing himself in suffering; he was also going to improve his English. Unfortunately the English these people spoke might as well have been Serbo-Croat for all the vocabulary he managed to recognise. He found the hoots of laughter that greeted him every time he ordered another ice and a slice most disconcerting.

"The Native inhabitant of these regions, so I hear," said one, a youth of darkish complexion and drooping heavy smokers' eyelids, "Is among the nicest people that money can buy."

There were hoots of laughter at that.

"But they ain't got no clue!" he continued, intermittently swigging on his bottle, "Have you got a clue, Adam?"

"A clue?" said Adam, stretching his neck forward in the hope that this act will somehow make the conversation understandable, "No, I haven't got a clue. Do I need one?"

"There you are, just as the man says!"

More hoots of laughter.

"When they say 'Yes,' they can mean yes, maybe, no. When they say 'right away,' they can mean any time between this year and never. And there's that blank expression that comes over them when you ask them a question about anything. They look as if to say, that's just stuff, it's always there, so what? They ain't got no curiosity about shit. Have you got any curiosity Adam?"

"I am very curious!" declared Adam who was greeted by more howls. "But most certainly not about shit!"

"That's right," said Herman slapping him on the back with a big pink blotchy hand that Adam immediately resented.

There was something deeply dull about these foreigners, thought Adam. Their concerns were alien, their obsession with vast amounts of beer incomprehensible, and their means of support a complete mystery. How could such people, not a suit among them, be so rich, be so powerful, be such demons in the eyes of the rest of the world, and yet, be everywhere, even in Daoistan which had kept them out for so long, even in Daoistan that fought them for so long, so heroically, and... Adam tried to think of the heroic history of his country but could not come up with any specifics. He was sure though, that it happened otherwise the place would be full of them and they would be running all the businesses... Which seemed to be what was happening anyway. Them and the Japanese that is, who he had not actually met, but had overheard some of the city folk griping about them buying up all the property. So even they were plundering his land. An image of a land laid waste by plunderers filled his mind. The country would be turned into nothing but a desert. There would be nothing but old ruins if these foreigners had their way, old ruins that tourists loved so much...

"Why do you like ruins so much?" asked Adam, barely coherent. "You come and look at old rocks. Maybe you want it all to be old rocks and ruins. That is what I think you like to see! Rocks. Ruins. Old junk. Antiques. Authentic bits of old wood. And, and, and you want to throw your small change at cute little black children. And, and, and take photos of ignorant peasants who know nothing..."

This was greeted with even more incomprehensible laughter. Adam would have continued his attack, but found himself looking up into the dark glasses of someone presenting him with a letter. The fat stomach seemed familiar, and the whole manner of the person, but something was missing. Adam took the letter and blearily attempted to focus on the address. It said: "To Adam Sariputra, Business Man, Visiting sundry hotels to do business. Please Forward to wherever he is likely to be."

"It is from my wife," said Adam, ripping open the letter. "She is a very ingenious woman."

"Three cheers for Adam's wife!" shouted Herman and immediately roused a few cheers from the others.

Adam ignored them and began to read: "Dear Husband, since you have been away there have been terrible things happening. There have been accusations of a most unfounded nature. There is not a single word of truth in any of this. So I write as we flee in case you hear otherwise. And I must tell you of what happened when Omar Sayid thought he could take advantage of the threat he imposed for the desert incident we do not speak about but I trust you as it did not happen. And I too am not doing as he will say if you arrive and find me not there. Yet what proof otherwise than my word, a poor woman, in the hope that it will get to you before you are alarmed as you might be to find all gone. If I had been a man then it would have been another matter. So rest assured I am not defiled and our child is untouched but not for want of trying of some people. We are all innocent except those that are not. I hope you are feeling well and business has not been unsuccessful, your ever loving wife, Sufiya. P.S. Nearly forgot to say the point of this. Am going to my father's, if I am not already there when you get it. It would be better not to be here when Omar is there. This will be much better. So there is nothing left to worry about."

Adam did not know what to make of it. Something terrible had happened or perhaps it had not happened yet. Then he recognised the person who had handed him the letter. The lack of uniform had thrown him.

"Adam," said Omar, dragging a chair over to sit with him at the beer bottle strewn table. "I was coming looking for you so Castrol gave me your wife's letter to read."

"Castrol?" said Adam.

Omar nodded.

"To read?"

"I meant deliver. But, I could not help but notice that the envelope was open and the paper falling out. She is a scatter-brained woman. Why didn't she post it like anyone normal? But then you know your wife. Always something, eh? Never know what to make of her. All sorts of strange things going on in that woman's head. Mmm? So how's things going then?"

Adam shouted out for a couple of beers.

"I've over spent my budget," said Adam. "And I miss my wife. Is that the sort of thing an international businessman does? Is it? We're supposed to be hard-nosed, profit oriented, and all I keep thinking about now is heading back home to see how my wife and the baby are coming along."

Adam made a despairing gesture in the very thick and humid air.

"Let's not play games here," whispered Omar to Adam. "You are not the sort of person who does not understand these things. You are a man of passion. I know. And that motivates everything you do. It is the secret you have."

Omar pushed Adam's gin and tonic aside and lowered his head across the table to get as close to Adam's face as possible.

"When the dancer threatened to tell your wife," whispered Omar, "What went through your mind? That you would lose your business? Lose your best worker? So you thought, just pay her off. Just give her enough money to send her on her way, and that would solve everything? That cross your mind did it?"

Adam's drink sodden brain throbbed to the sound of Omar's strange words. The sight of one of his drinking companion's T-shirt bearing the cryptic message, "No Pens, No Dollars, No Hash Hish," hovered at the edge of Adam's left eye. He began to wonder

110

if he was hallucinating because of the workings of some terrible venereal virus.

"Then you thought you'd deal with me," continued Omar. "Pull a few strings. Get friends to tell a few lies..."

"Deal with you about what?" said Adam, rather puzzled.

"Deal with me as in put in the knife and twist it."

"What knife? What twist?"

Omar stood up and gave Adam a hard, calculated stare that made Adam shudder. Then he dragged Adam from his chair, and butted him in the face, sending him sprawling across the top of the table spraying beer, gin, and broken glass in all directions.

"You may pay off all the gypsies in the world and send them on their way just to hide your betrayal of your wife, but you do not get your friends to send in slanderous reports to my boss, who does not believe any of them any way!"

Omar then turned, and left, muttering, "Well that was subtle wasn't it?"

"What you need," said Herman as he helped Adam to his feet, "Is another drink."

CHAPTER SIX

With his wife's letter tucked in his shirt pocket, his nose swollen up like a purple onion, and slivers of glass still falling out of his hair, Adam quickly packed his things. He had a hangover from the night before but he felt coldly analytical about the whole situation. His trip to the big city had been a disaster, but there were things he had learnt, for instance: never trust a Westerner in a T-shirt bearing inscrutable slogans; never look away from a policeman; and don't attempt to have sex with fifteen year old girls, because it is never quite what it is cracked up to be. These things he had learnt and now Adam's wife was in need of him; his wife and future child! And although he felt a twinge of guilt about the incident with Amina, he was glad he got it out of his system. As he strapped up the lid of his suitcase, the simplicity of thrusting a penis into any woman, struck him as a peculiarly misunderstood phenomena. In simplicity was truth. And the truth was that, when it came down to it, he might as well have been fucking his wife. How to work the heat up was another matter, but yes, spending all that money, failing to do any business, and being accused of whatever it was Omar was accusing him of - murder? It might as well have been murder. Either that or having a good-looking wife. The man was insane. Whatever it was, it was worth the lesson and thus a worthwhile experience. It was - It was like a cold shower, irritating but refreshing. It made Adam long for home.

Adam went to the check out desk with every intention of paying but there was nobody there. He banged the desk bell several times with the flat of his hand and still nobody came to take his money. Instead he could hear sirens wailing outside. His first thought was that Omar, this time in official capacity, was returning to take him away and finish the job he started last night but that was mere paranoia. But if nobody was going to take his money he thought he would leave anyway. If the Hotel really wanted him to

112

pay his bill they could send it to his address. After all, this was not a time to be hanging around awaiting petty officials to sort out the procedures. He had a wife to look after and that was far more important.

When Adam walked out of Madam Dai's Business Hotel onto the streets, the sirens stopped and the whole city seemed strangely quiet. He walked towards the lorry park where he hoped his truck was still to be found. Normally within ten seconds of hitting the pavement a cyclo Man would be giving chase and crying out, "Where you want to go?" But there was nobody. Then rain began falling in large rubbery blobs that exploded on the pavement becoming instant mud. As usual, a naked, eyeless, limbless beggar lay in the gutter, his money tin on his chest and as the rain created clean streaks on his filth encrusted body, he sang:

"When the Robber Mistress calls, she is the one who has all the balls . . ."

And the more it rained, the more spirited the rendition and the more bewildering, no doubt, the lack of coins pleasingly clanking into the tin. Business for everyone was not good, thought Adam, pleased that he had gone into a different line than the beggar, even if right that moment his own seemed more precarious. Adam, then, with his suit soaked and hair bedraggled, his face a question mark, cut as pathetic a sight as he felt.

When he reached the lorry park, he looked through the muddy rain at the surrounding grey dilapidated buildings, trying to avoid staring too directly at the rows of soldiers with guns at the ready and bayonets drawn that filled the spaces between the trucks. He casually glanced about to see where his truck was and found half a dozen soldiers crouched down in the back and a couple more in the cab waiting to join the convoy that was being put together by the exit into the main road. The look on the soldiers' faces told Adam that this was not a good time to be arguing over a small matter of whether or not he had given permission for them to ride his truck.

Adam promptly turned around and headed back towards the Hotel where he hoped someone might be able to tell him what was happening. A hand tapped him on his back and he felt that maybe he should stop, but then maybe he should just run and hope that whoever it was could not shoot straight.

"Wait!" said Amina.

Adam recognised the voice.

113

"Rashid told me to come and find you. You've got transport haven't you?"

"No," said Adam slowly, highly suspicious of what Amina wanted.

"They're closing the hotels and throwing us all out and there is a lot of trouble and I phoned Rashid and he said to go with you until things are better and you will give me a lift back to him and he will sort these things out for us, OK?"

Amina then grabbed Adam's arm.

"Where's your truck?"

Adam pushed her away.

"The army have got it. So we're stuck here."

Amina looked disturbed as she tried to think what to do.

"What's happened?" asked Adam.

Amina shook her head.

"All I know is that people like me are being rounded up and I don't think that it is a good idea for me to stay here for the time being. Come on, come with me..."

Amina began pulling at Adam's suit sleeve and he reluctantly followed after her, his suitcase becoming heavier and heavier as they hurried. He certainly wanted to leave the city, so if she knew a way out, then why should he not follow her?

She took him to the main road which was eerily silent except for a few shop keepers standing uncertainly in their shop doorways peering one way and then another as if waiting for the arrival of someone very important.

Adam could feel that he should not be on the street. There might have been some sort of curfew called. But then they arrived at a small side street booth full of flowers and telephones. A large pock faced man pondered what to do with the flowers and the wedding car complete with ribbons that was parked beside him.

"What is happening?" asked Adam.

"Don't you know?" said the pock faced man, playing with a bunch of keys in his hand and trying to listen to a small radio through an ear-piece.

"I haven't seen any news," said Adam. "I didn't think to look."

The pock faced man sucked on his teeth then explained, "Something called the Army Council made an announcement about reorganising the constitution and well, as you can see... No-one is working today. Except me. And I'm going home in a minute."

The man gestured at the empty streets where only a few dogs ventured out of the shadows to cross the road.

"Isn't there anybody travelling today? Are the trains working?" asked Amina.

The man shrugged and then slapped the top of his car.

"When I drove this here there were a few people on the roads and nobody said we could not go about our business. In fact, they said that we should carry about business as usual. I haven't heard of any shooting. I haven't heard any disturbance. But by the looks I'd say not many people are taking chances, not even to get married."

Then Amina entered into negotiations with the man. This was a car hire booth and he had a car to hire, a Mercedes at that, and well, if nobody would be using it today, so maybe as a favour, Amina could hire it for a discount.

"If you can give me proof of who you are and when you will bring it back," said the man, "Then you might as well have it."

"No problem," said Amina, flashing her credit card.

"You've got a credit card!" exclaimed Adam, watching closely the procedure.

The man took her card and examined it, then dialled the credit card company, punched in the numbers on the telephone and the automatic credit confirmation gave him the yes answer and so there was indeed no problem at all.

"These are wonderful things," she said, "You must get one. I am sure Rashid will give you a reference."

This was very depressing, thought Adam, whose nose began to throb all the harder. And very unfair.

"Get in the car!" chivvied Amina, thrusting the car keys into Adam's hand. She took his bag and walked round to the boot. "Hurry up!" she yelled.

"Your girlfriend is in a big hurry," said the pock faced man locking up his booth and handing Adam a spare bunch of flowers. "They won't keep," he explained.

Adam unlocked the car door, climbed in and turned on the engine. Amina leapt in beside him.

"Right!" she said. "Let's go."

Adam contemplated the automatic gear stick a moment and then tentatively slipped it into start. He had heard of these sorts of gears before. He just had to remember there was no clutch and so not to hit the brakes whenever he felt like changing gear. The car inched forward and then, gaining confidence Adam juddered along the empty road. He decided to head for the western highway, which he felt, being the newest of the roads, was probably the better for heading up far north to his father-in-law's home.

Ten minutes later they discovered themselves moving slowly beside long lines of military vehicles and a soldier waving them down.

"Drive on!" demanded Amina, clutching his arm. He pushed her away and calmly stopped the car, wound down the window and smiled a big friendly purple nosed smile.

"What's the problem?" he enquired.

The soldier poked his head in through the wound down window and flinched at the blast of cold air from the air conditioner. The face of the soldier was that of a sixteen-year-old and his hair stank of coconut oil.

Adam, still smiling, said, "I am taking my wife to see my parents. We got married yesterday. What's all the trouble? We got up and the place is empty? What's going on?"

The soldier gave no discernible expression but pulled his head back and walked around the wedding car kicking the tyres and inspecting the lights and festive ribbons. Then he returned to the window and stuck his head in again. Amina smiled nervously, as he looked about the interior then slapped the roof of the car and waved them through.

"If it had been a policeman," said Adam, "I bet I would have had to pay some money."

"You were brilliant," said Amina, much relaxed, and searching about her pockets. She pulled out a tube of fruit pastilles. "Lucky I found you. I knew you would drive me out of that place."

Adam took the proffered sweet and slowly chewed it as he made good time along the near empty road. He gunned the engine and honked the horn as they raced through chicken hut villages, lush jungle and over rattling iron surfaced military bridges. Above, a jet fighter rushed across the sky.

"Is this the right way?" she said.

"Yes," said Adam, though he was not being very honest with her. Nor did he really know if he was going the right way himself, in as much as on the one hand he wanted to get back to No. 3 New

116

Town and put to rest this thing with Omar, but on the other he wanted to avoid doing anything rash. He was sure there was some mistake, some slight that Omar had taken very wrongly and that Sufiya was to blame and yet not to blame. Sufiya could behave in ways that men could misconstrue. He himself could wonder about her relationship with Rashid even though there was nothing between them. There could not be anything between them, because there was no opportunity. Even if they had the opportunity, then he was sure nothing would happen. Still, he thought it better to go to his wife and have her explain everything to him before he went off at half cock. To settle a score with a man was one thing, but to do it without understanding what the real problem was, was to create even more problems for himself.

As Amina lolled sleepily beside him, the steamy heat gave way to mountain air and rocky winding roads. Driving down from the mountains after a detour for more petrol, he drove across a railway track and took the road through a housing development scheme consisting of ramshackle breezeblock blockhouses standing amidst seas of rubble. More military hardware was lined up beside the railway passing through the centre of this wasteland.

"It might be a good idea if you take the train back to No. 3," said Adam indicating that now was a good opportunity for her to get out.

Amina awoke from her doze. They had been travelling all day and the last thing she considered was taking a train journey as well.

"I don't think it's a good idea for you to come to my father-in-laws home," explained Adam rather shamefaced. "You understand?"

Amina did not at first understand. She thought she was getting closer to No. 3 New Town and somehow she had missed when Adam had taken this huge detour. Even after Adam had explained what he was doing she refused to understand his reasoning.

"I have to go there first," he pleaded.

"Then you take the train," said Amina. "This is my car! I'm sure I can get someone to drive me."

Adam looked out of the dirt-streaked window and watched drunken soldiers lazily sitting on their haunches in small groups. They swigged from bottles of The Spirit of Daoistan and hurled the empties into the air to spectacularly shatter upon the gun barrel of a broken down tank. Bravely, Adam opened the car door, stiffly climbed out, stretched and looked over the heads of the soldiers. The sun was setting and against a wall along one of the railway sidings a couple of young men stood with their heads bowed down and their hands tied behind their backs. Another group of soldiers stood about six feet away from them. The officer in charge raised his pistol and then the other soldiers raggedly shot at the men until they fell down. The officer walked over and shot them again.

"What is this?" asked Adam casually of one of the soldiers sharing a bottle.

"Drug dealers," said the soldier with a dismissive wave of his hand.

Adam climbed back inside the car.

"I thought you were leaving me?" said Amina rather hurt.

"It would not be good for either of us," said Adam.

Adam pushed the automatic gear stick into start and continued to drive past the half-finished housing blocks. How insane, he thought, to be taking this prostitute to see his wife. Has he not punished himself enough? He should kick her out now. He should, but he could not. And soon he had driven away from the railway and was driving along the winding dirt roads with farmers' fields on either side. Then the fields gave way to muddy ponds, and telegraph poles and finally low mud brick houses with grey slate roofs. Adam drove the car into the village square still preparing in his mind a list of excuses for Amina's presence, a tone of voice, an attitude to take, and never settled on what he considered to be quite the right one.

As soon as he pulled up the hand brake, Adam leapt out of the car and became suddenly conscious of how he must smell but put that aside as irrational, since he had showered the previous day. He flexed his shoulders and tried to rid his bearing of any hint of the failure he suffered in the city. He was here because his wife, he told himself, had called for him and it was his duty to run to her rescue. For the moment he forgot about Amina and saw Sufiya standing in the doorway of her father's house. His eyes were drawn to her stomach. No sign of the baby yet, he thought.

"What have you been doing?" said Sufiya examining Adam's swollen nose.

Adam almost hugged her but then noticed that Amina had climbed out of the car and was sitting on the bonnet awaiting an introduction. Almost on cue the sun disappeared and darkness

118

descended. Adam heard a match strike and someone spit. He turned again, this time to see Saleem sauntering over to him.

"So you got here," said Saleem puffing his cigarette into life.

With his face lit by the glow of his cigarette, Saleem continued:

"There was no need to rush though. We've everything under control."

Adam wondered what exactly was the everything that Saleem had under control. The strange look of his father rang alarm bells in his mind. Why was the old man so straight backed and sprightly, for instance? What tonic had he been taking to make him look so young and fit? Something had happened, thought Adam.

Saleem looked at Amina who wiped her nose on the back of her hand. He went very quiet and just stared.

"Yes, yes, yes," said Adam, running over to Amina and taking her by the arm over to see Sufiya and Saleem. "She was in the city. Believe me, she rescued me. They impounded the truck. And she had a credit card... Her... Yes, a credit card. And things were happening so she thought it safer not to be in the capital, though it looks worse here. What is happening?"

"You should not have brought her," said Saleem.

"She brought me!" snapped Adam. "It was necessary. And, and I thought you would like to see her. I thought, I shall show my father that I understand him. And, am happy with whatever decisions he makes."

Amina raised her eyebrows and then giggled at Saleem.

"She is not necessary," said Saleem flashing a look that Adam thought looked almost as if it was full of hatred. Why the man should suddenly hate her, he could not imagine?

Feeling a chill in the air, Adam rushed to get both their bags from the car and push her past his father and his wife with as little unpleasantness as possible.

"This is my wife," he announced to Amina, as he led Amina into the dark house where he whispered, "And don't you forget it."

Within the candle-lit gloom Sufiya's father sat looking old, dark and sinister. His face lit up in recognition of Adam.

"It's Adam," announced Sufiya.

The old man stiffened with formality, his old suit laden with dust, his cap pulled deep over his forehead, and glassily looked Amina over.

"No, father," said Sufiya, "That's Adam and this is someone else."

"This is Amina, a friend. She is a friend of Rashid's," said Adam, handing his wife his suitcase and then pushing Amina forward perhaps half hoping that his father-in-law would take a fancy to her. "I'm sure you have a lot in common."

Much to Adam's annoyance, Amina giggled when he said that. It was almost as if she thought him ridiculous.

Sufiya held tightly onto the case, and with her other hand grabbed Amina by the elbow and took her away. Saleem beckoned to Adam to join him at the table. Adam was not sure what was best to be done: either run after Amina and Sufiya, and keep an ear on what might be said, or try to act calm as if nothing had happened. He opted for calm, though he felt anything but.

"They are shooting people," whispered Saleem. "But do not tell Sufiya this, because her brother is in danger."

Sufiya's father groaned as he moved to sit beside them.

"He is upset," said Saleem, "He is an old man now and cannot deal with this the way he would have done."

Saleem patted the old man's arm, sending up clouds of dust.

"There was a time when he would have taken his rifle to them," said Saleem.

Sufiya's father suddenly looked fierce and Adam could feel himself regressing to sixteen years old when he first met the old man. Saleem continued:

"And as for that whore you've brought into his house, he would also have shot you for it. But I'm not here to complain about your behaviour. There are more important things. I've been talking to some of the young men that have not been arrested yet. We have a plan to get her brother out. We will bribe the soldiers."

"What with, father?"

"Well, we could use that whore you brought, but I'm not going to talk about her. What we were thinking of was bringing a shipment of drugs across the border," said Saleem. "That's all the soldiers want. Drugs. Drink. It's easy. And we'll have her brother out free."

Sufiya's father gave a grunt that Adam took to be a grunt of approval and then Sufiya returned to the living room and a hush fell on them.

"Well," said Adam standing, "I could do with a wash and change of clothes."

He took Sufiya's hand and she led him off to the privacy of her room where at last, Adam could touch her. They were in the room of her childhood. Even the bed was that of her childhood and they would have to share it that night. About them Sufiya's childhood dolls dustily looked down from a shelf upon which was one English book, "Toad of Toad Hall." Adam sat on the corner of the bed and groaned as he lay back and listened to both his bones and the bedsprings creaking.

"It has been awful without you," he said.

"So you find yourself a girlfriend," said Sufiya. "And you lost the truck," she added. "And what else?"

"Forgive me," he said feebly, beginning to think he was in some feverish nightmare. He would wake up eventually, he told himself.

"So explain this insult to me?" she said.

"I overestimated myself," he tried to explain. "I could not make them understand what I was about. They did not laugh at me but they did not treat me with any respect."

"And that is why you find this girl and think you can march in here without explanation?"

"I'm explaining now."

"And you have spent everything? What on? Explain. I'm listening."

"Business is a very expensive affair. I could have spent more. I did not even have enough. That's one of the reasons why they had no confidence in me. If I was already rich, I could have got richer, but since I am not . . . It was as if they spoke another language."

"And which one of them did this scratching and bruising? It was that girl no doubt giving you what you always want me to give you. And this is where it leads you."

"It was Omar."

"He did this to you?"

Sufiya slumped onto the corner of the bed and let Adam place his hand on her stomach. There would be a future, he thought. He felt it coming, but it was not quite the future he had in mind when he first had the idea of Adam's Franchise.

"But there are more important things than Omar," he said. "Our trust. Our love. And I now know that we are strong, and that

121

apart, we are nothing! But nothing will break us apart again. Nothing will destroy our trust for each other. We will always be true, won't we? There will never be any lies between us?"

Sufiya glared at him then seemed to be about to strike him. He held up his hand in protest.

"Let me sleep!" he said, "Let me sleep! I'm saying nothing that makes sense. I'm tired! I'm..."

Adam closed his eyes and feigned sleep, hoping that Sufiya would take him at his word. He found himself dreaming of everything rushing at him: lights and then trucks and then guns were firing and then there was Amina with her writhing snaky belly, hissing at him, her eyes popping from her skull. And amidst flame and smoke stood Saleem, hacking away at Adam with a chopper. Jamilla, his mother also loomed up from beneath the earth destroying all the grave stones, reducing them to powder, her hands winding in the wind like flowers blowing one way then another. She asked him why he had not found her? He tossed her a coin and she turned into a snake that Saleem hacked into pieces. The pieces then became a prostitute with red and black underwear flashing like so many neon lights. A limbless beggar laughed and sang as he lay in the road with truck after truck running over him. All the hands of the limbless, all the hands amputated by mad Saleem, all the limbs entwined in passion, in mangled remains, writhed in the air before Adam. Then cocks began to crow and in the distance guns rumbled and aircraft screeched low overhead...

***

As Omar climbed out of the army truck, he caught a glimpse of himself in the wing mirror. "You have a very highly developed sense of self-preservation," he said to his image and felt rather pleased with himself.

"What?" said the truck's pink lycra clad driver.

"I was just congratulating myself on coming back," said Omar.

"What to? To the arsehole of the universe?" said the driver's equally pink clad companion, much disappointed that they had only managed two nights in the city and a visit to a sports shop. They had hoped on hitting the high fashion shops of the hotels but they had been side tracked by the vision of a hunting rifle and some very interesting pictures of young girls in leotards.

"Right now," said Omar surveying the dusty old No 3 New Town, brimming with affection for it, "I can think of no better place to be in."

"Suit yourself," said the driver, wrenching the truck into gear. With a honk of the horn the truck was on its way and Omar was left standing feeling crumpled and grubby in a uniform he had not been able to change since he chased Saleem off into the hills, not that he would have changed if he could, but somehow not having the opportunity had made it feel grubby whereas if he had had the opportunity he would not have noticed.

Omar unlocked the front door of his office, which also doubled as his apartment. He found nothing much had changed. There was the usual layer of dust over everything and a few more flies lying dead on top of his files, but as far as he could see, bandits had not come into town and no-one had missed him. He was about to stretch out in the hammock slung in the corner of the office for periods of great thought and a few beers, when the telephone rang. A secretary on the other end told him that he would be receiving a letter this week informing him of his change of rank to lieutenant and that he should either come to the capital or send the measurements in for his new uniform.

"Do I get a raise as well?" asked Omar, wondering if this was some joke. Apparently he got a raise as well and a car allowance. After congratulating him, the secretary put the phone down leaving Omar stunned. Now he knew there was a god.

After changing his uniform and freshening up, Omar walked across the street to Castrol's garage for some serious bragging.

"Where's that car catalogue of yours," demanded Omar on entrance.

"Omar!" said Castrol, "Where've you been?"

"Get us some tea and give me that glossy one with the exciting foreign cars that promise to flood our markets any time now," said Omar, "And I will tell you of the extraordinary mood of the capital. Things have been going on there that are either very good for us or very bad, I'm not sure which, but in the meantime I get a new car out of it."

"All hell has been let loose here," said Castrol as he began to fill his kettle with water.

"Yeh, I can see," said Omar, glancing out to the empty street. A sleepy dog lay gathering flies in the centre of the road and in the

123

distance he could hear the singular thud thud thud of a lone pile-driver.

"It's quiet today because people are frightened," explained Castrol. "There have been bandit raids on the road. I'm surprised you managed not to see the army out there. There's been road blocks and shootings and all sorts of happenings. The news has been full of it."

"Full of what?" asked Omar.

"A busload of tourists was machine-gunned and robbed," continued Castrol, "One had his feet hacked off and was then forced to run over broken glass. A major incident so I'm led to believe."

"And who has led you to believe this?" asked Omar, impatiently watching Castrol pour the boiled water into the teapot.

"Everyone knows," said Castrol, "And I myself saw the marks of the bandits. One of my trucks was shot up. There are holes all over it. A very expensive repair job that means. In fact I'm rather angry. This will kill business. The hotel will soon lose its guests. So everyone wants something done to sort out all these troublemakers. A posse of some sort."

"A what?" spluttered Omar, "Have you been watching too many episodes of what is it? What is it you get on that TV of yours? Banana?"

"Bonanza," said Castrol, "It is a very old cowboy series. Much loved by the baby boomer generation. A large number of the cast are already dead."

"They weren't shot by these bandits were they?" asked Omar.

"Of course not!" said Castrol.

"Then why should you take it so personally!" said Omar, shaking his head, "Now fix me that tea!"

Castrol began to pour the tea out.

"What else is new?" asked Omar, thinking that he might as well have all the inanity.

"Rashid," continued Castrol, "Is involved in some new development up by the old village."

"Is that so?"

"And markings have been laid out for a new road," added Castrol.

"In short," said Omar, "I would have to have been away thirty years for anything new to have happened."

"Oh no," said Castrol, "Adam has not returned and his shops remain firmly shut."

"And that's it?" said Omar.

"I think so," said Castrol.

"And the military takeover in the Capital escaped your notice?"

Castrol gave a bit of thought to that announcement.

"I'm not sure I understand."

"The bandits and the shooting and the army and all those sort of disturbances," said Omar, "Didn't indicate to you some political upheaval?"

"Not here."

"No," said Omar with a deep sigh, "Probably not."

As Castrol pondered and puzzled, his tea halfway to his mouth, Omar picked up the car catalogue and flashed a glossy picture of the desirable vehicle at Castrol.

"Do you think this will suit my image?" said Omar holding up a picture of a sensible solid four-wheel drive. Castrol still looked puzzled. "I have been promoted," explained Omar. "I have broken through the system. Someone who is now up there has taken a shine to me and the result is a decent car allowance."

Castrol became suddenly excited. "You've solved some great crime?" he said, "Is that why they're so pleased with you?" Castrol opened up a can of lager. "It should be champagne," he said putting the tin down on top of an oily workbench. "But what crime could it be? The only crime I thought might be committed around here was one that you were considering committing, that is, the rape, pillage and otherwise of the sumptuous Sufiya."

"I restrained myself," said Omar, carefully choosing his words, "And that, apparently is why I am now king of the shit pile. It is all to do with the new balance of power you see."

"So then if you have the power, you should use it!" said Castrol, "I have work to do and although it is not glamorous like yours, it is necessary. Only I can't do it with those bloody bandits shooting up passing trade."

"There are no bandits," said Omar, "Those were merely rumours spread by ignorant people who could not tell which side of the bread the butter was."

"A rumour?" said Castrol, his brow deeply knotted, "Why would they spread such a rumour?"

"People have been bandit barmy ever since they saw that film."

"I blame the gypsies," said Castrol, "They move on and suddenly a bus is robbed."

"There was no bus. There was no robbery. Otherwise I would have been told. I, you see, know everything because I am told everything. Or at least I will be."

Omar finished off the tea, stood up and yawned.

"I shall go and write my report."

Seeing how Castrol looked impressed, Omar thought that his visit had not been wasted.

"So the revolution is over?" said Castrol. "The party is overthrown?"

"I wouldn't put it quite like that," said Omar, "But well, things aren't going to be the same anymore and someone is going to benefit from it and so far it looks like me!"

Omar watched as Castrol bent down and rummaged in the cupboard beneath where he kept the kettle. When he stood up again, Castrol was holding what looked like a Schoolroom globe except that it was black and painted on it was a big blue eye.

"It was my father's," explained Castrol as he gave it a spin. "It's the great universal see all, know all, that watches all our actions and decides whether we will be saved or not."

"Saved for what?"

"I'll have to read the instruction booklet. But it made my father an important man in his time. This was a long time before you came. But he was an important man."

"I thought he was a raving mad man?"

"That was during the revolution, now people will think differently. You'll see."

Omar was not sure he would see. But he patted Castrol on his back and thanked him for the tea then set off back to his office. What a pleasant sort of person Omar thought himself to be. He tolerated all sorts, befriended the weak, the stupid, the crazed and maintained a quiet dignity as he oversaw and protected the poor demented flock that was given into his responsibility. And soon, he thought, he would get some respect from the bastards or else.

In his office, sitting before his rattling old Remington typewriter, he began to fill out official forms. He wanted to have in writing some kind of story that justified all his actions and fulfilled

126

what he felt to be the nudge and the wink that had been given him. Everyone must be implicated, he thought. There must be some incriminating evidence about everyone so that the authorities can keep control - even though he was not quite sure which authorities were in control at the moment. This report was going to tell a terrifying story of a young girl's ordeal. She had been sold into slavery at a young age, used for all sorts of depraved acts, and then when finally seizing a chance to escape she was raped by a lascivious old man and his son. No, he thought. Rape was nothing. Murder was the only thing. And so murder it was. He was particularly pleased with his description of a Ritual Murder. Then with a flourish on the keys he concluded that he could not tolerate such behaviour in his region and vowed that he would hunt down all those involved, especially those high ups involved in the cover up. After a little more thought he decided on not saying that there had been a cover up or that high ups had been involved. He X-ed that out and left it that he would hunt down all those involved. He attached this to his request for a clarification of his powers of investigation, in particular, whether he could search property while the suspects were not in residence.

On sober deliberation, Omar retyped his report. He reduced the purple to officialese but still held to the description of the murder as "Ritual" and the victim as "Poor and Downtrodden" but emerging from her slavery on the crest of the new government reforms. He paused over the word 'government'. Then thought he should leave it there, for whoever was in power, was indeed the government and he supported them wholeheartedly, especially since they had put their faith in him. He needed a body though. That was the great flaw in this scheme. Sooner or later, however, he reasoned that one would turn up in the desert, as they always did. Maybe the other half of Saleem's wife Jamilla would turn up. There must be bits of it somewhere out there. If there were, it would be enough.

The phone rang and Rashid's pleasant, friendly voice congratulated Omar on his promotion.

"See what a bit of goodwill from a friend can do for a man, eh?" said Rashid.

Omar was so surprised to get the call that he could think of very little to say.

"So you come and have dinner with me," said Rashid, "And we'll discuss things further."

Omar panicked. What did this mean? How did Rashid know so much? What did he mean by friend? Which friend? He had no friends.

"I, I, I," stuttered Omar, "Shall have to check my diary."

Omar stalled and then searched through his desk drawers for the diary he had for the past eight years. He found the yellowing object and brought it near to the telephone receiver. Then he flicked through the blank pages and hummed and hahhed, until he reluctantly came to the conclusion that he could squeeze Rashid in. Then he put the telephone down, sweat dripping from his forehead.

The next day he distracted himself by chatting to whoever he came upon, telling them where he had been, what he had been doing, and of course his promotion. They in turn greeted him with a fixed mask-like expression. He persisted in talking, though, telling the story of what he now assumed to be his own adventures, and they became increasingly lurid in the telling. Apparently, he had been in the Capital to pledge allegiance to the new order and report who in No 3 Newtown was essentially sound and who was not. It had been his special revolutionary remit.

"This country," confided Omar to everyone, "Is going places and I have it on good authority that this particular region is the place to be for the time being. This is where the bulk of the new investments is coming. And I am here to make sure that law and order prevail and thus encourage the investors and money people to trust us."

After that the mask-like expressions of the shopkeepers and tradesmen softened. They all expressed their concern about the recent banditry and Omar agreed it was a terrible thing that something should be done about but there was only one of him. Soon, however, he reassured them, he would be able to recruit some assistants. The town was to have a proper police force. And he was to be at its head. His local experience had at last paid off.

By the time he arrived at the hotel, Omar had worked himself up into a frenzy of self-promotion, and nervous anticipation. The town at last accepted him, so he thought, and distrusted them all intensely. And as Rashid greeted him in the Hotel foyer, Rashid struck him as a complete mystery. A little conscious of the smell of

128

his own sweat, Omar tried to relax as this expensively dressed man accompanied him to a dining table.

"I hope you don't mind my telling you," said Rashid, clicking his fingers at a waiter to bring on the prearranged best. "But I did mention how you had eschewed the use of pull and influence to move out of the region."

"Whom did you tell that to?" asked Omar, a little flustered by the bevy of waiters cleaning glasses and trying to lay napkins across his lap.

"Friends of mine," said Rashid mysteriously, "Of course they said, why ever not? Is the guy a fool? Ha ha!"

Omar wondered if he was supposed to smile.

"No," continued Rashid, "I told them you loved it here. That you were a genuine son of the soil."

"Is that so," said Omar, checking to see which spoon Rashid used on his soup.

By the time Omar had finished the meal, drank a bottle of wine, and endured Rashid's fawning, he began to suspect that his promotion was something to do with someone's dislike of Rashid. Someone in authority thought it would be amusing to give Omar enough power to keep Rashid in check. It really was all a question of a balance of power. That was definitely the game, thought Omar. As more money came into the area, Rashid would gain more and more power unless someone opposed him and only the police or the army could do that. That seemed a pretty reasonable assumption to make, thought Omar as he began to sample Rashid's prime brandy and feel a lot more relaxed about the whole situation. It was not such a mystery after all.

"In these times of uncertainty," said Rashid, offering a toast, "It pays to have friends."

"And you are of course my friend?" asked Omar.

"Of course!" said Rashid.

Bizarre, thought Omar, truly bizarre, considering it was most likely Rashid who had reported him to his superiors for chasing after Sufiya.

"And what is Adam to you?" asked Omar.

"He is another friend," said Rashid, "Why do you ask?"

"And what about my Uncle?" asked Omar.

"What about your Uncle?" asked Rashid, apparently puzzled by the question.

What do you know about my Uncle?" asked Omar.

"What should I know about your Uncle?" Rashid gave what Omar took to be an ironic smile. "Friends," continued Rashid, "Do each other favours. And each favour requires a bigger in return. That is the manner in which everyone gets involved up to their necks and cannot turn back. In this way great acts are performed. Great achievements are managed. Timidity is overcome. Power is gained. Do you understand me?"

Omar listened to Rashid talking and was glad he had only one friend. And the last thing Omar would do for him, was a favour.

"This is a small community," said Rashid, "But it is made up of people who are going to be this country's future. The army, the party, the petty shopkeepers and peasants, all legitimise their power by allowing the likes of us to make money and to maintain civil stability. Big Business and The Law go hand in hand . . ."

Rashid continued in this vein and Omar pretended to listen attentively, allowing his brandy soaked eyes to glaze over in the light of Rashid's gleaming charming white teeth, and the sunlight from the gardens that shone onto Rashid's shiny suit.

"In what sense is The Law going to be hand in hand with Big Business?" asked Omar, hoping he was about to receive a fat bribe, or at least the offer of one. He began to practice turning it down and taking the moral high ground. But that would depend on how much it was.

"You are the law," explained Rashid. "You can do anything you like."

"And what is it that I like?" asked Omar.

"How can I," said Rashid, "Tell you? It is you who is the law here. You alone make the decisions."

Omar tried to think of exactly what information Rashid could have about him. Could there be a dossier containing a photo of himself lying comatose in his hammock watching the flies land on his smelly feet? Could there be pictures of him, several cans of beer in the stomach and another on the way, falling out of his car and lying in the road singing some lascivious love song? Could there be such a dossier? He never imagined Lieutenant Chan had such a report, even though he imagined him having a pretty damning one, but it would not have these dull everyday sorts of mishaps recorded. Rashid though, he could be the one with all that sort of stuff.

Rashid looked up towards a waiter waiting beside the bar. Suddenly the man picked up a portable telephone and brought it over to Rashid.

"It's for you sir," said the waiter, handing Rashid the phone. Rashid excused himself from Omar for a moment then put his hand over the mouthpiece and turned back to him.

"Colonel Khan," explained Rashid.

Omar nodded back and thought about Colonel Khan. It made sense that that man was a friend or associate of Rashid. The two were of an age, maybe old school pals. And Rashid as a reputed party member would have a direct connection with the military. Then Rashid with a sigh switched the phone off and said that he had suddenly got things to do. So if Omar would excuse him, he would leave him to finish off the brandy and get back to work.

Omar raised his glass to friendship and then found himself sitting on his own wondering if Colonel Khan really had called a mere hotelier and given him some important things to do. He could not believe it but then he could not be sure. Oh well, it was a mystery that sooner or later he would fathom.

As he drove his wavy road back home, running through his head the duties that had been thrust upon him, without any comprehension as to what those duties were, Omar decided that what he really wanted was to lord it about a bit in a new car and a flashy uniform and so long as people respected that desire, he would not send in too damming a report on them.

***

Everything moved fast for Omar. A pathetic letter arrived from his Uncle Babur. How his uncle smuggled it out of the prison he did not know. What Uncle Babur expected him to do for him, he also did not know. Besides, what ever had Babur done for him? But just to show that he was not totally heartless, Omar would get a cousin of his to make enquiries about his Aunt.

That was a politic decision, thought Omar, befitting of a man of his new found status. But he grew a little worried when confronted by Colonel Khan's troop of slack jawed soldiers sitting astride towering groaning rolling eyed camels.

It was first thing in the morning when the soldiers arrived. He

131

had not expected them but they had brought a spare camel for Omar to ride.

The Sergeant of the troop, gave his charge a prod bringing it to his knees. He slid off the saddle and presented Omar with his compliments from Colonel Khan. Then handed him an envelope.

The orders were written in military style and roughly translated into no matter what happened it was all Omar's fault and if anyone was injured then the Colonel himself would personally castrate whoever was at fault, i.e. Omar.

"What are your orders?" asked the Sergeant.

Omar hesitated. He had never had to give orders to anyone before.

"I suppose I want you to find the gypsies that Colonel Khan says I must apprehend, and bring them back here."

This seemed to be part of the price that he would have to pay for his future career.

"You will have to direct us to them, sir. We don't want to deal with just any gypsies, do we?"

"Gypsies!" said Omar, "Gypsies! Well, there were some that passed through not that long ago but I don't know where they are!"

"Not to worry sir. Just get on your camel."

"I'm not prepared for this!"

"I think you have to be sir."

"I'm not in the military. I'm a civilian."

"I don't know anything about that, sir. I just know I have to accompany you on this expedition."

Much against his better judgement Omar found himself aloft on the camel, holding on to the saddle as hard as possible. He had once thought riding a horse was a much more sensible proposition until he rode one and discovered that it had all the charm of being kicked in the seat of the pants. Camels at least merely rolled and teetered from side to side. But the look of a camel and the groan it emitted every time Omar yanked on the spiked ring through its nose, seemed to be building up a deep and terrifying resentment. One day, this beast would bite him to death. Of that much Omar was sure.

Saddled up and blinking in the sunlight, Omar stifled his protests and set off with the troop on its mission. He blamed Rashid for this but could do nothing more than go along with the situation.

As he followed on, he discovered another thing he disliked

132

about riding camels. He had to ride with his arms outstretched. His fellow camel troopers happily sat with their arms resting on the saddle before them, giving a sly dig with a stick when they wanted anything to happen. But Omar could not get the stick to work and unless he was yanking on the nose, his animal always wandered off in the opposite direction to everyone else.

"Surely it is this way?" asked the Sergeant whenever Omar's camel decided to investigate some piece of interesting desert.

"Yes, yes, yes," Omar muttered, yanking frantically at his animal.

After they had picked their way across the grave yard and headed out into the desert, Omar was ready to break down and weep. That morning he had planned on maybe a glass of tea at Castrol, a confirmation of the amount his car allowance would run to, and then cadge another lunch at the hotel. Instead here he was.

"Sergeant," called out Omar, "Couldn't we have used a helicopter to find these people?"

"Not us sir," said the Sergeant, "We're the army not the airforce."

"But you do have helicopters," said Omar as he tried to look at the horizon and stop himself from feeling sick, "I've seen them. Army Helicopters. It's written on the side."

"They're all up north," said the Sergeant, "But don't worry sir because we'd never find them with helicopters. With a helicopter you have to look everywhere, but on the ground you know where people are going, which trails they are following, where they expect to find water. The camels can smell the way. The shit's still warm. And you get a feel for it. Up in the air, desert is just desert."

Omar sighed. There was a sort of logic in operation here and he was a logical man; he prided himself upon it; read scientific publications, or at least articles in magazines he picked up at the hotel - but being on the back of a camel! How ironical that as soon as he got himself a car allowance he ended up on a camel.

The sun was high in the sky now and Omar wearily rolled along the track, sweat dripping off his forehead. He would have fallen asleep if he did not think he would fall off the damned beast. At first he felt thirsty. Then he felt hungry. Then he did not know what he felt. He stared off into the distance and the distance seemed to get no closer. He had only been on the camel for four hours and he already felt half delirious. He should have prepared himself for this, he thought. The Sergeant had assured him that they had all the equipment he needed: food, tents, water, rifles and ammunition. But he was not psychologically prepared for this.

Eight hours went by and the Sergeant called a halt for the day. Omar heard all the camels groaning as they knelt down on the hard sand, his own included. Without warning Omar lurched forward and landed head over heals on his back. He lay there in the sand looking up at the puzzled munching face of his camel, who then proceeded to dribble from its nose. Omar rolled to the side and wiped his face on his sleeve. He sat up and looked around at the laughing soldiers.

The Sergeant helped him to his feet and dusted him, a little too hard for Omar's liking.

"You were asleep!" announced the Sergeant with a laugh. Lucky your camel did not just walk off with you and dump you in the middle of nowhere!"

***

Omar felt sick and stiff. He sat silently with the troopers as they lit a fire and roasted strips of meat on the ends of their bayonets. The conversation ran to and fro, largely concerning the merits of various types of camel. Above, the stars shone and some fell to earth in glittering desert displays. A satellite quickly scooted across the sky and Omar thought how it was even more ridiculous that he was here in the desert with a bunch of bloody savages.

The Sergeant belched, wiped his hands down the front of his trousers and came to sit beside Omar. "Tomorrow we start early and try to reach the oasis before noon. Then we will rest for a couple of hours and head off towards the new highway. The usual way people travel through here is to stop at the Oasis for a couple of days. There are sometimes coach tours there and your people will probably do some begging."

Omar blinked a little at this revelation.

"Coach tours?" he said, "Then I should have taken a bloody coach tour not a camel trek!"

"That is not my concern," said the Sergeant, "But after the oasis I believe we will find that your people have gone off towards the highway because we have been having a lot of trouble with bandits down there. They do a circuit. When we stop them there, they cross back to the other side and begin causing problems on the road into your town."

Omar rolled over and closed his eyes. He could have merely driven to the intersection and taken the new highway across the central plateau. If he had known about this activity along that side he might have avoided all this. But he had not known. In fact, all this was a complete surprise to him. This was information that had never even come his way by the usual vague rumors that drove life out in the desert. This was some new reality, a new policy, a completely new invention!

He groaned along with the camels as he settled his head on his pillow. No-one told him anything, he moaned to himself. The newspapers must have censored all this news. Perhaps this was a godsend, he thought as he drifted off to sleep, keeping him out of the way whilst who knows what else was happening elsewhere. Arrests were probably taking place. Maybe even Rashid was being arrested. He did not care. Serve the bastard right . . .

Barely had the sun risen when Omar was being kicked awake and handed the reins of his camel. Stiff and dirty he climbed onto the beast and as it plodded off on its meandering route, the Sergeant handed Omar a cup of luke warm weak coffee. Omar managed to spill most of it down his front. The Sergeant though, drank his coffee, ate a hearty breakfast of bread, cheese, and slices of salami. Then he brushed his teeth and shaved, all whilst sitting on the camel. Omar watched with amazement as the Sergeant whisked his cut throat razor across his face leaving a blob of shaving cream behind each ear. Omar decided not to tell him he had left the blobs behind. At least this way he would know the man was not perfect. Not only was he not perfect, he was probably stupid. The ability to defecate aboard a camel was not on a par with nuclear physics exactly. Though in the desert, Omar could well believe such men as these thought it was superior.

As the day wore on, Omar counted the animals he saw. They ate the many succulents that grew around him. The place seemed full of deer of some kind. The Sergeant said they were wild horses though they seemed to bear no resemblance to any horse he knew of.

"They are not that good to eat," said the Sergeant, "But if we have to we can survive on them. Anyone can survive out here. There is plenty of water if you really are desperate for a drink. The cactus can be chewed. It tastes like shit, but it is OK. The snakes are good for a stew though. And I have deep fried scorpions. A sort of smoky earthy flavour. Not bad but very fiddly. Have to fry up a lot for a decent meal. There are various disgusting grubs about. All edible."

Nearly everything the Sergeant pointed out as being of great value for survival he added was disgusting. Omar could well believe it.

"If I were lost in a desert," said the Sergeant, "I would be more inclined to eat you. But if you were not available I guess I would eat the wild horses. Drinking the cactus though, yeccch. But if it has to be done, it has to be."

The Oasis came into view. There were no buses in the car park and there was no-one else around. But Omar could hear the noise of the parrots swarming in the trees. As an oasis it was a far cry from paradise but as they descended into the little fertile valley with its muddy strip of river, Omar could feel the slight moistening of the air and a comforting breeze coming through the trees. An underground river emerged at this point and because of the shelter from the hot winds, top soil had been left behind from the time when the whole area was still a forest.

The troop arrived at the river, let the camels drink and then ripped off clothes and lay in the water. Omar, not to be left out, removed his clothes and gingerly stepped into the unpleasant looking water. His feet sank into the silt.

"There's nothing in this shit that will drill a hole in my skin and get into my bloodstream?" asked Omar.

The Sergeant's grin disappeared. He had never thought of the possibility of such a thing.

"What do you mean?" he asked.

"There are things that get into you and make you go blind or worse," said Omar.

The Sergeant barked out an order and all the troopers ran out of the river leaving Omar still soaking.

"How long do these things take to get to your brain?" asked the Sergeant from the river bank.

Omar rose from the water and washed off the mud from his knees.

"Probably about ten seconds," said Omar, wading ashore. "Ten nine eight er er six . . ."

Omar collapsed on the ground.

"No-one is immune!" said Omar in a pathetically weak voice.

He stopped breathing.

After a minute or so, Omar opened one eye to see what the Sergeant was doing. To his disappointment the Sergeant and his men had not all fallen down clutching their heads.

"It's a joke," explained Omar, "I was joking."

Omar stood up and began putting his clothes back on whilst the Sergeant and his men watched, silently.

"That is not a very good joke," announced the Sergeant.

"I think it was rather a good one," said Omar.

But the Sergeant pushed his hand up against Omar's mouth and silenced him.

"What are you . . ."

"Shush!" said the Sergeant.

The troopers rushed to their camels and grabbed their rifles. The Sergeant listened hard. The Parrots rushed into the air and now Omar could hear the noise of a sarangi playing.

The Sergeant and his men hid themselves away from the river and carefully dressed. They did not want to go into battle naked.

Omar held his breath as he saw Ali and his people entering the valley and heading for the river. Omar counted about a dozen of them. It had never crossed his mind before as to why an old man like Ali and a few young male musicians accompanied so many women and children. Now he realised that most of their men had been elsewhere. Maybe they were the bandits robbing the lorries.

Omar turned to the Sergeant and whispered, "All I want is to talk to the old guy and find out what he knows about a murder. As for this banditry thing, well, that is not what I am here for."

"I'm sorry," said the Sergeant, "It is what we're here for."

The Sergeant checked that his men had loaded their weapons. Then nodded to them and they scurried off into the undergrowth. Omar could not follow what was going on.

"Stay here," whispered the Sergeant, thrusting a rifle into Omar's hand then disappearing along with the others.

Beside him the camels began to groan. Omar glared at his and gave it such an eye that the animal quietened immediately.

The women began to set the fires for their cooking and the men washed and joked with each other. Ali was engaged in teaching one of the young boys a tune. A couple of the girls that Omar recognised from the dance troupe, played with their babies. It would not be problematic if Omar stood up and joined them. He could ask a few questions.

Even so he did not dare venture out of his hiding place. This would upset the plans of the soldiers, though what they had in mind was a mystery to him.

***

The first shots rang out and hit the men by the river. They scrambled for their rifles and were hit by more. Some of them managed to get their rifles and begin firing back in all directions.

Omar flung himself hard upon the ground. The next time he looked up there were bodies everywhere. The gun fire continued and the screaming, but it was from further down the river where the women and children had run to. Omar stood up and moved forward so that he could look to where the sounds came from. He could see people running in all directions. Who was who, he was not sure. To see who had been hit first, he ran towards the river and checked a couple of the young men there. One was still alive and groaning. Omar contemplated finishing him off but he had no quarrel with these people. He walked down the river and came across Ali, his eyes wide open looking quite startled and his brains spread out behind him.

By the time Omar had waded across the river to where he last saw the women running, the Sergeant and his men had rounded up the girls and their mothers. They sat huddled together screaming and trying to put their arms around as many of each other as possible. The Sergeant could be heard screaming and shouting orders out. Then he appeared before Omar.

"Are there any still alive up there?" he asked.

"I think one of them is," said Omar.

The Sergeant nodded at his men and two of them took off back up the river.

"How am I going to question any of these people?" asked Omar.

"No problem," said the Sergeant. He pushed his hand into the group of women and dragged one of the girls forward. He pulled her along by her hair. She screamed and wept.

"Ask her," said the Sergeant, throwing her to the ground before Omar.

Omar knelt down before the girl. She looked up into his face.

"What can I ask her?"

"Anything you like," said the Sergeant.

Omar attempted to gather his thoughts about him.

"I have nothing to ask her," said Omar, "And I doubt that she would be able to answer me."

The Sergeant kicked the girl and told her to get back with the others. His men returned and nodded to him.

"Is there anyone else?" he asked the women.

He then counted off all the men he knew of. His own men added a few more numbers and pointed out where they had shot them. Then the Sergeant turned to Omar.

"Have you got everything you wanted?" he said.

"I wanted to talk to the old guy playing the Sarangi," muttered Omar.

"Mmm," said the Sergeant, "Sorry about that. Never mind."

With that he gave a nod to his men who all loaded their rifles and began shooting into the women until they stopped screaming and moving. Omar watched fascinated.

"A bit of a mess that," said the Sergeant. "We wanted to catch the men in the act. I don't know how you're going to explain this."

Omar stood alone watching the Sergeant and his men go about the business of collecting the bodies into one place and sorting out any identifying belongings. Amongst the things they collected together were a few credit cards and wallets belonging to some of the people who had been murdered along the highway.

"That's lucky for you," said the Sergeant. "Makes it a bit easier explaining things."

"You did not have to shoot them all!" Omar suddenly said.

His nerves were on edge and he shook as he spoke.

"They would have escaped otherwise," said the Sergeant, "And we've got to get back home. Imagine what would happen if any of these got news to any of the other groups roaming around the area. We'd be dead meat. Tasty meat mind."

The Sergeant looked at the young girls laid out by the river side.

For a moment Omar thought the man was going to order that they roast one of the bodies but the Sergeant walked over to the bodies and said a prayer. When he finished, the others also said their prayers, then carried on about their business preparing to dispose of the bodies.

"Normally," said the Sergeant, "When anything like this happens we just throw them into the desert somewhere."

"This happens often?" asked Omar beginning to laugh as he remembered how many bodies he had fished out of the desert.

"Oh yes," said the Sergeant, "When they were building the highway there was always some shooting going on."

"Why?" asked Omar.

"These guys," said the Sergeant, "Never quite knew how to treat foreigners. Didn't know whether to rip them off or just kill them and take their wallets."

"I didn't know there were any incidents with tourists," said Omar examining the lined face of the Sergeant. There was a hardness in the face that Omar could not fathom.

"I heard there were lots of problems with tourists," said the Sergeant, "Buses being bombed. Women raped. Throats cut. That sort of thing."

"I haven't heard about any of this," said Omar.

"It's censored," said the Sergeant. "Apparently these people say tourists are destroying our culture."

"They probably are," added Omar, looking up at the sky where ragged vultures now circled.

"What fucking culture?" said the Sergeant, hooting with laughter at the absurdity of all this.

With a whoof of flames, the bodies blazed soaked in their own cooking oil.

Omar and the Sergeant stood back from the heat. Black fumes wafted in their direction stinging their eyes. It was now nighttime and the flames lit up the trees.

"How long will it take?" asked Omar.

The Sergeant looked uncertain. He had never had to deal with such a large scale disposal before.

"We had better stick around until there is nothing left," said the Sergeant.

Omar went away on his own and tried to get some sleep. It was no use protesting about what had happened. He had to get back to his home first. To protest here would mean a bullet in his back. But even to protest back home seemed a futile exercise. Was he not supposed to be in charge of this? He had been set up. Somehow, for some reason, they, whoever they may be, had set him up to take the blame. If there was blame coming in anyone's direction, it was sure to come in his.

That night he barely slept. He dreamt of faces turning towards him, blood exploding from them at all angles, flames licking around them as their flesh peeled from the bones. There was a curious banality in the dreams: skulls, graveyards, blackness, vultures, even water engulfing him. An array of horror movie themes and lurid book covers hurled through the ether into his dreams. By the morning it was hot and sticky and he longed to get back out into the dry heat of the desert, away from the smell of roast meat.

The journey back was largely silent. No-one had any jokes to make, information to impart, or phatic chit chat. A couple of the troopers muttered about the pure bad luck of some people but that was all the comment made on the proceedings. After another day and night they reached the town and said their goodbyes.

"Better than locking these people up," said the Sergeant as his parting shot, "They'd never survive in prison."

Omar watched the troopers lead his camel away. As they rolled up the road back towards the army camp, another day's journey, Omar could feel the ground still rolling beneath him. He had paid his dues. He was as guilty as anyone else. He knew where his loyalties lay.

***

Omar drove to the hotel complex. He felt there was a strange numbness in the air. There was no other way to describe it. Exhaustion, a bit of diarrhoea, aching bones plus a mild buzzing in his head, turned the world into a distant phenomena which he watched from behind cotton wool. He barely noticed the time it took to travel. When he walked into the foyer it was as if he glided above the marble floor. It would not have surprised him to look down and see no reflection of himself at all.

"Omar!" said Rashid, hand outstretched for shaking, and a suit so sharp he could slice a tomato with it.

Rashid took Omar's hand, squeezed his elbow with his other and led him through to the bar. A couple of clicks of his fingers and tea was served.

"We can have something stronger if you wish," said Rashid, "But I understand you've just come back from an expedition into the wilds?"

Omar slumped down into the armchairs, leaned forward

141

and put a slice of lemon into his glass.

"Yes," said Omar, in reply, "I've been into the wilds."

"Yes," said Rashid, "these people they get greedy, start pushing drugs, girls, the usual sort of thing. We can't have anything to do with that here."

Omar sipped at his tea and examined Rashid as he talked. Were there any signs that he knew what happened? He seemed to be talking a lot. There was a nervous edge to his voice. Was he waiting for Omar to say something? Could Omar say something without betraying himself and merely giving Rashid ammunition against him? He could not tell.

"We're part of the new modern state," explained Rashid, "And in periods of rapid change people become uncertain as to who is in charge. Sometimes under those circumstances a demonstration has to be made. In a land with little tradition of law, of nationality even, people obey the rules because they are frightened of those who make the rules. The rules are in development of course, which makes life all the more complicated. You must know all this. If you cannot catch your criminal you beat a confession out of them. You know the confession might be rubbish, but you hope your action deters others. Random terror is the best way of stopping all opposition. No-one can trust anyone. No-one knows from which direction the blow will come. No-one has time to think, or the ability to think straight. They fear you and you have control. Everyone must come to you to find out if what they are doing is acceptable. You are recognised as the arbiter of what is right and what is wrong. But you also are a victim of terror from above. You don't know where it is coming from. And so you too must find someone who torments you directly and make sure that you check with them."

Omar was still not sure that Rashid knew what had happened. Somewhere, he thought, someone must know all the real reasons for everything.

"Our government works in mysterious ways," said Rashid, a gin martini in hand. "Cheers."

***

"So what was it like?" asked Castrol.

Omar had gone to seek distraction at Castrol's place. Somehow he felt he needed Castrol's blessings. He would feel cleaner somehow."

What was what like?" retorted Omar as he sipped at his tea and stared at the satellite TV.

The set was on a toolbox in the courtyard playing to a couple of the local drivers. A quiz show was taking place. A man with a lot of teeth was standing beside a girl in a long cocktail dress and the two of them laughed at each other's jokes.

"What," asked Castrol, "Was going away with our finest on a mission impossible like?"

"It was like having a stick shoved up your arsehole and then stirred around for three days," said Omar.

Castrol laughed.

"That's good," he said, "That's good. What you need is that four-wheeled Range Rover. Have you got the go ahead yet? I can put in an order today. I have a cellular phone. Look . . ."

Castrol scuttled away to his office and then brought out a tiny handset. He had ordered it off an advertisement he saw on TV.

"You have already got a telephone," said Omar as he examined the tiny mechanism.

"Oh yes," said Castrol, "But this one will work anywhere. Wherever I go I can call anyone."

"But you never go anywhere. You are always here," said Omar handing the machine back.

"Maybe now I will go somewhere," said Castrol placing the phone in his pocket.

Omar watched the television for a few minutes. He hoped there would be a news programme on it. What he had seen and been through he felt should count for something in the world. There should be some mention of it. Something so awful should have some impact upon the world but there was no mention anywhere. Nothing had happened.

"So what who did you go after?" asked Castrol, "Those bandits?"

"There are no bandits!" said Omar.

"So who then?"

"I was hoping to find someone to help with my inquiries."

"And did you?"

"No."

143

CHAPTER SEVEN

Saleem was outside hacking the head off a chicken. There were screams and shouts coming from the kitchen. Sufiya was shouting, ostensibly to keep the peace between her father and the black pyjamaed, wizened old aunts that came in most days to keep house for him. But she had been tetchy with every one all day, all except Amina, to whom she was extremely polite. Saleem assumed that she was planning to murder the girl once she had been lulled into a false sense of security, and decided to keep out of the whole business. Whatever there had been between him and Amina was forgotten. He had better things to do. She was just a whore. And his son an idiot.

Saleem held the headless flapping chicken up in the air. The blood flowed onto the ground where he trod it in until there was no more trace. Dropping the chicken and chopper, he pulled out the present his son bought him: a packet of cigarettes. Saleem examined the packet's picture of a camel, and tried to make out the words beneath it: Cigarettes can kill.

"So you're trying to kill your own father?" said Saleem out loud.

Saleem lit a cigarette with a great flourish to show that he did not care what his son's motives were and took a long drag. The smoke curled out from his nostrils and sensuously rolled up his cheeks.

"Aaah," he said, "The food of the gods."

An army truck changing down gear and grumbling through the village gates into the central dirt track interrupted his reverie. At the compound entrance, Saleem watched as half a dozen soldiers leapt from the back of the lorry. Their metal helmets hid their eyes as they took up a defensive position, automatic rifles fixed with bayonets. For a moment they stood still and blank, with faces in shadow. It was as if a grace was being said. Then they broke into a

144

run through the village grabbing anyone under the age of thirty who happened to be standing there.

A low flying jet drowned the uproar, and as suddenly as it had come, trailed away to leave behind silence. The village seemed momentarily empty. Saleem looked into the distance watching the truck full of thin faced young men sullenly held in check by the soldiers, rumble away on the dusty road.

He ventured out of the enclosure as a few defiant whoops began to ring out. Even they soon died as a huddle of old women slowly began walking towards the town. Saleem assumed they must be the boys' mothers.

From out of the shadows much younger boys carrying large rifles emerged and let a few volleys into the air, only to be shouted at by some of the old men now sitting beneath the tree at the village centre. Saleem also shouted at the boys.

"You'll only bring them back," he shouted.

The boys stopped firing and looked rather forlorn. Saleem had seen that look before. He could remember the look on Adam's face. It had been a common expression. Whenever Saleem was forced by the village committee to take up his shovel and clean the highway, or that time when he was forced to make Sufiya abandon her clothes mending business in the light of criticism from the authorities, and... There were a million and one other little things that he could barely recognise as being anything at all; things he could not remember, except for another inexplicable look of disappointment, contempt, or something else. He did not know what it was exactly. Except the look meant Saleem was less than he should have been.

"You want to do something," yelled Saleem, "You come and see me. I know things. You come and see me!"

A couple of the boys jeered and ran off. One though looked back and Saleem felt it meant something. But the village settled into its quiet drone of liquid gas stoves, transistor radios, and howling dogs.

Saleem returned to the compound feeling the dull ache of compliance. Nothing would change, he thought. Those with guns always ruled. He picked up his chopper and cleaned it on the feathers of the chicken. Children though could make a difference, he thought. They had not been beaten. Not yet. And Adam, for all his irritation and arrogance and stupidity, did seem to be rising above some of it.

When Saleem walked into the kitchen he hoped others there would be talking about the intrusion. He hoped there would be anger and a call for action, or a sad resignation. He wanted a reaction that echoed his own in any way.

"There seems to be a lot of activity," said Amina. "Have you been listening to the news lately?"

Amina tucked into a bowl of dahl, mopping it up with chapatis and her black fingers. Her eyes hungrily looked about the room for anything else she might eat. Saleem felt she might eat him if he stepped too close. But in defence he could kill her, he thought, easily. With his chopper. With his bare hands. He could take her body and crush it, molest it, maul and mangle and... He could feel himself working up a sweat.

"They are announcing this and that," she said, "And they are arresting enemies and shooting them. But they do not say who they are or what. And they are creating great confusion. Haven't you been listening to them? Aren't you confused? I'm very surprised you haven't heard anything."

"No," said Sufiya, curtly as she poured hot water from a pot on the stove into a basin. She began to froth up a mug of shaving foam.

"No you are not confused, or no you haven't been listening?"

Saleem thought this an unwise thing to say to Sufiya while she sharpened a cutthroat razor ready to scrape the chin of her father. He was patiently sitting before her swathed in towels stained with week-old blood.

Amina turned towards Saleem and asked if he knew whether the roads were blocked.

"I haven't heard," he said.

"No," said Amina, "No-one here seems to hear or see anything."

"The soldiers were here just a minute ago," said Saleem, waiting for some cry of horror. But none came. Sufiya scraped away at her father's face and Amina grimaced at each ponderous movement of Sufiya's hand.

"You should do it all in one motion," said Amina, "Not lots of little scrapes. You will cut him to pieces."

Sufiya's father let out a groan but Saleem could not tell if it was in agreement or pain. This was one of the reasons Saleem had given up shaving. It was safer just to snip away with a pair of scissors. That way, when old and incapable, one had set the pattern and no-one would think to give one a shave.

"I was thinking," said Amina, "That I should try to go."

"If you think that's a good idea," said Sufiya, "Then, if I was you, I should go right away."

Amina finished her food with a clatter and gave her fingers a quick lick.

"I shall see if that is possible," she said and brushed past Saleem on her way to the yard.

"Owh!" said Sufiya's Father as blood ran down his throat.

Sufiya quickly washed away the soap foam and slapped a piece of chapati over the cut.

"It is nothing," she explained to Saleem as he backed away from her. "He is deaf. He is blind. And he is grateful he can feel anything at all nowadays."

"I'll go and see what that girl is up to," said Saleem, hoping never to have to rely upon a razor to the throat as his only means of human contact. He placed the chicken and chopper on the table and with relief, left the kitchen.

Back outside, Saleem found Amina standing beside the car examining the driver's side.

"Adam will have to drive me back," she said, "The car is under my name and I am paying by the day for it. So it has to go back."

A jet screeched across the sky and made Amina duck. Saleem looked up. There was no danger. This was near the border and the jets had been doing that ever since jets were invented, which must have been several years ago at least.

Amina stood back up, opened the car door and ran her hand over the steering wheel.

"Driving's not that difficult," she said, then sidled up to Saleem. "But could you talk to Adam? He's been avoiding me. And you could persuade him that it would be best to drive me back to the capital where he can pick up his truck."

Saleem wondered what price he should extract from her for persuading Adam. But to hell with her, he thought. It was obvious what she had been up to, though perhaps it was not obvious. After

147

all, why would Adam bring her here if he had slept with her? The boy was a fool if he had. Most likely he was also a fool if he had not. And Saleem felt that he too would be a fool if he did not chance his luck. Whore she was. And perhaps not quite such a mysterious exotic creature as he had thought her to be, but she was alive and it had been a very long time since he had had any contact with a warm body.

Like an inexperienced schoolboy, he grabbed her and planted his lips as close to hers as he could manage. She squirmed, turned her head away from his whiskery chin, pushed him away and wiped her face with her arm. Saleem did not know whether that had been enjoyable or not.

"Have you gone crazy?" she demanded.

"What difference does that make to you?"

"This is not the place for any of that sort of thing."

"It is. I can do what I like. I can take whoever I want for my wife."

Amina's eyes widened and she nervously giggled.

"What is so funny about that? I'm a man of substance! I have a uniform. My son is a big business man. My family is an important one. And I doubt you have a family at all. So why are you laughing?"

Amina stopped giggling and came out from behind the car. Warily she cast a glance towards a group of young men walking through the gates. They were thinly bearded with eyes nervously twitching. Saleem noticed that he and Amina were not alone and took a couple of steps away from her. He did not want to be associated with her. Not if she found him so amusing.

"Welcome boys," said Saleem, gesturing for the gang to sit down and talk for a moment.

***

The first thing that Adam noticed on entering the yard was his father sitting upon his haunches whispering with some youngsters. The next thing was Amina coming towards him. She looked very well, very fresh faced and girlish in her jeans and T-shirt; how he hated the sight of her.

"We should leave," she said.

"We'll talk about that later," he said, "Because it is not that easy."

"Yes it is. You drive me home."

"We'll talk later," he said, walking over to try to listen to what his father was up to.

Amina persisted and held tight to his arm.

"Are you people all so stupid as to not realise that I am not welcome here," she said.

"I was stupid enough to have done you the favour of bringing you here," said Adam, shaking her hand from his arm. He tried to see what his father was up to, hoping that this would be enough to bore Amina and somehow she would just drift away. But Amina refused to drift away and merely pressed up behind him giving him the odd pinch as he tried to ignore her.

Saleem, he saw, was chatting with the boys, offering cigarettes, which Adam considered to be a true first for his father. Perhaps he was learning some degree of civilisation? Adam also noted that one of the boys' shoes was without laces and tied onto his feet by a leather strap around the instep. He must have made that himself, thought Adam as he slapped away Amina's pinching hand.

"Good day," said Adam, wondering if the shoes could be considered an authentic product of the region.

Saleem turned and several of the youngsters stood up.

Adam wondered how many shoes could be made in a week? He would only need a dozen or so of different sizes to test the market. And he would need a new truck of course, to pick up the deliveries. Maybe Amina could help him there. She had a credit card...

"I'm going to take this car and drive it myself!" announced Amina, giving Adam a final punch in the back, which he tried to ignore.

The others stared at her and Saleem made some comment about women's ignorance that made the boys laugh. Amina sneered at them and climbed into the car.

"It cannot be that difficult if you people can do it," said Amina, wrenching the wheel, tugging at the gear stick, and bouncing her feet upon the pedals. "Just give me the key. I'm sure I'll be able to get the hang of it."

How Adam wished she could just drive away but he knew she would not be able to. He feared that next she would tell him that if he did not do as she said she would reveal all to Sufiya.

"Look, what's the rush?" he said, "You have nowhere to go."

"I'm paying for this car by the hour. Unless you want to pay?"

"I'll pay," he said, regretting it but he could think of no other way of calming her down. "Just wait, ok?"

Amina sighed and watched as the young men passed a bottle of the local spirit to each other. Adam also saw this and asked them what was going on. For the moment he hoped everyone would ignore the girl.

"We have guns," said Shoes. "And we have brains. The soldiers are all shit heads. We could walk in there and get everyone out."

Adam tried to listen to the conversation of the boys, though Amina's huge loud yawns and accidental little blips on the horn proved difficult to blot out of his mind. He decided that the boys' talk was alcohol-stoked bravado. Someone had once thrown stones at the soldiers. Someone had once knifed someone else. Another had taken a shot but missed. But, according to Saleem, with his expertise, they could be knocked into a little group of freedom fighters.

"Expertise?" said Adam with a laugh. "What have you been telling them, you old fool?"

"I have been telling them the truth!" snapped Saleem.

"And what truth is this," asked Adam. "I would like to know."

"I know the way the guards think," said Saleem, "I know the ruses they use to make their job easier. I know what they are thinking. I know these things. Because I thought them too."

"They will just shoot you," said Adam.

Shoes announced, "Only those who take what they need with their guns will have any wealth in the future."

Adam turned to face the boys. They all looked dirty and their eyes were glistening, grey, and distracted by the sight of Amina performing a few dance steps around the car. To a silent drumbeat she sidled, stomped, and wove the air with her fingers. Finally she slithered onto the warm car bonnet and lay as if dead.

"And if you haven't got the guns," said Adam, trying to bring their minds back to the point, "What then? You think you cannot get things without guns? There are better weapons."

"Bigger guns," said Shoes, "Maybe better, but there are lots of us and that must count as well."

"That's not what I meant," said Adam, trying to think how he could explain that setting up a manufacturing, transportation and retail operation was most likely going to do the trick.

"Tonight," said Saleem, "we will go to the army camp and watch the comings and goings of the guards at the gates. If there is an opportunity we will attack!"

Adam looked at the shoes on Shoes and thought what a wasted opportunity. They were quite unique in design, almost a "fashion statement." That was a word he had picked up in the big city. He would have to coach these people in the new ways. Glamour, he decided, was subversive. This is what would undermine the oppressor more than anything else. The whole country clamouring to wear these shoes would bring tyranny to its knees.

Adam noticed that now even Shoes was ogling Amina. And maybe that was fine. For Shoes and Amina could be the models of a whole range of ethnic clotheswear. He would have them pose for a catalogue and set up a mail order company. Now that was revolutionary, that was what the country needed, and he would not need to be behind a shop counter for long hours. He merely needed to have the ideas, then put together the package and get an advert on Satellite TV... To hell with the Capital! To hell with hoteliers and other small-minded folk! Mail order was the future!

"What's she doing here?" enquired Shoes.

Amina stirred and rolled over, kicking her heels in the air and resting her chin upon her arms. Adam snapped out of his reverie.

"She's a guest," he explained, and was about to go further and say that she was a model and Shoes could give up his hopeless ambition to be a guerrilla and become a male model alongside of her.

"Since when are gypsies guests?" he asked bitterly. As soon as he pointed his rifle at her, Amina immediately rolled off the car bonnet and ducked down behind the driver's side. Adam was momentarily shocked at this turn of events. So what if she was a gypsy, he thought? Adam, with as much nonchalance as he could muster, pushed the rifle barrel down to point at the ground.

"Ignore him," shouted Adam to Amina. "It's merely a slight misunderstanding."

Shoes slung his rifle over his shoulder.

151

"Perhaps we take her," he said, "And offer her in exchange for our brother."

"I don't think they will want her," said Adam.

"Of course they will," said Shoes. "We hear you're the financial expert, so, how much is she worth? Come on? You're the man who knows. We let her entertain the troops, and that's worth what? Put a sum on this? And the going rate for bribes is what? Come on, you're a business man, you know all this?"

"I tell you what I do know," said Adam, "I know there are far easier ways of getting money for bribes. Those shoes you are wearing, for instance. You get me a thousand pairs and I could sell them at enormous profit to Westerners."

Shoes looked at his shoes and then at Amina yawning and then at his friends who all started to laugh.

"My shoes?" said Shoes.

He lifted his foot, then lifted the other and began to dance around kicking up the dust.

"My shoes! This is his answer. We offer them my shoes and the whole army will crumble before us!"

"One whiff of them, is all it would take," said one of the boys.

This prospect seemed to capture the imagination of them all and they began sniffing the air at each time Shoes kicked up the dust.

"Whaaa!" they kept saying, "Phwoor!"

They began farting and belching. They were going to kill the enemy with flatulence. Blow them away. Massacre them with halitosis. It was going to be the dirtiest campaign known to history!

Adam took this opportunity to grab Amina and rush her towards the door of the house.

"Gypsies!" yelled Shoes, "Poison the wells!"

"It is not the gypsies who have imprisoned my wife's brother," said Adam, uncomfortable at being ridiculed like this. He looked straight at Shoes and made as fierce a face as he could. Amina also poked her tongue out at him.

"You are not to interfere," said Adam. "I will have Sufiya's brother out of jail. If you interfere with this, then you will not know what hit you. Do you understand me?"

Adam noticed that Amina was now making an obscene gesture with her hand. Shoes spat on the floor and turned to Saleem.

"Your son had better be telling the truth," he said. "Otherwise..."

Shoes melodramatically put a bullet into the chamber of his rifle. It made a satisfying click that was followed by the clicks of the guns of the other boys. Then in a slack jawed insolent fashion, they slowly slunk away, dragging the rifles in the dust behind them like so many snake trails in the desert.

Amina squirmed out of Adam's grip and made an even more elaborate obscene gesture with both her arms.

"Little wankers," she yelled after them. But her voice was muffled by Adam's hand slapping itself over her mouth. As she wriggled and cursed, Adam thought how much he hated children en-mass, especially if they were armed with assault weapons. His own children would be different, of that he was sure. As for Saleem, who always seemed more at home with hordes of screaming brats, he was going beyond all the boundaries of idiocy that he had previously managed to stay just this side of. Adam was especially certain of his facts in this matter when he found Saleem clenching his fist and saying with gritted teeth, "Do not shame me. I know how you despise me. Just do not despise me in front of others."

"Nonsense!" said Adam, letting Amina go and pushing Saleem's fist away.

Adam thought he would try to be reasonable. He would be friendly. He would show concern. He would not let the old man think that he considered him to have gone completely insane.

"Tell me all about it," said Adam, recalling a soap opera he had seen playing on Castrol's Satellite TV. Adam, recalling more TV, gave Saleem a hug that at first alarmed Saleem. But miraculously, as far as Adam was concerned, Saleem appeared to calm down, and Adam could have sworn that there was almost a tear in the old man's eye.

"You people!" cursed Amina, trying to stem blood from a cut lip, "Are the stupidest most ignorant people I have ever known!"

"That girl," said Saleem, "Get rid of her."

"I will," said Adam, nodding in full agreement.

"I mean completely," said Saleem, glaring at Amina and drawing his fingers across his throat. "Completely from your mind and heart. Think only of Sufiya."

Adam had a stroke of genius.

"When Sufiya's brother gets out of jail, he will drive her wherever she wants to go."

Adam could well imagine that this would not be a particularly onerous chore for Sufiya's brother.

"And how long will that take?" growled Amina.

Adam let go of his father and threw his hands up.

"Does it matter how long?" said Adam, shaking with irritation, "What is your hurry? What important appointment do you have that cannot wait until my business is finished here?"

"I must get back. I have an audition to go to. State TV is looking for actors and I am on their short list. This is very important."

Adam exchanged a glance with his father. Amina was full of surprises. Where was the moon girl, he thought. This one here is all too much part of this planet.

"If you had such important things to do," he said, "Then why did you run from the city?"

Saleem nodded in agreement with his son and the two of them relished this mutual moment of recognition. They were as one for about the first time in their lives.

"I was told the soldiers were closing down the hotels and places where I work."

"Well, they still will be. So it is still safer to stay here."

Saleem waved his hand before Adam's face.

"No no no," he said, "Not safer. You want her to go. Not stay."

"She'll go when the time is right," said Adam, asserting his authority. It made him think that he was in complete control for a moment.

"Go to your room," he ordered, "and ... and wait until I tell you to come out."

Adam waited for the refusal but Amina merely pouted, sighed, and hesitated for a few moments more. She looked very sexy, thought Adam. He wondered if it would again be legal to have more than one wife. Not that he could afford it, or that Suffiya would allow it. But one day if he became rich...

"I'll wait for you to come and see me then?"

Oh yes, thought Adam. An important man like himself will have lots of these sorts of offers made to him. He will have to get used to it.

154

"No he won't," yelled Saleem after Amina had turned her back on them and started back to her room.

Amina merely seemed to transform herself even more into the temptress. Her walk became sinuous. Her body lithe. She swayed. She silently padded away, around the corner of the house, and nothing was left but her perfume, her footprints...

"Well I thought I handled that well," said Adam.

Saleem gave a grunt.

**

Through the smoky haze that hung over the railway town, Saleem gazed blinking and muttering, "The wrath of the gods."

As for the grey bleak breezeblock apartment that stood amidst the dirt and army green of the tanks and troops, Saleem muttered, "Most obscene."

He could hear the rumbling of trucks in the distance and kept wondering what on earth he was doing here. He listened to the sounds of the market beside the railway: the drunken soldiers, the constant tinkle of broken glass, and the rumbling of the army tanks' diesel engines. It sounded like the collapse of a building.

"Ugh," he shuddered.

He felt a prodding finger in his back and heard some hastily whispered voices. The voices were talking to him and they were not merely hot desert winds blowing. No, he could hear the voice all right. Loud and clear.

"What d'you see?" whispered Shoes.

Saleem did the voice's bidding and peered out of a thicket of bushes.

Strung out beside Saleem, peering through the bushes were the hairless pimply faces of his men. There was another prodding finger in his back. His men were ordering him on. The attack began and Saleem, made a headlong dash for a ditch.

Shoes had chosen the nom de guerre of Ultraman, calling himself after an old Japanese TV program often shown at the Karaoke Store. Its catchword was TRANSFORM! Which appealed to the teenagers who all named their automatic rifles their Transformers.

Ultraman crept up beside Saleem, who was straining to breathe after the group's breathless dash over the ditches and hedges along the edge of town.

"Well?" asked Ultraman with a deep voice. "What is the situation?"

Saleem could see no situation. If the whole bunch of them had walked into the midst of the town, guns in hand, no-one would have challenged them. They looked like everyone else who was wandering about the market. But this was a holy war, so he had to pretend that there were enemies out there.

"Where's the prison?" asked Saleem.

Ultraman tapped Saleem's shoulder and set off pushing his way through the thicket. Super Mario, Nike, Street Fighter, Nintendo and Godzilla followed him. Saleem tried to follow in their wake but the bushes flicked back into his face, the thistles tore at his clothes, and the stones twisted his ankles. Soon he was left behind. How can these people leave their leader behind, he kept thinking.

Saleem sat down for a rest and pulled out his cigarettes. He was about to light up when Ultraman, his face intense and red, his wiry muscles taut about his neck, leapt out of the thicket and glared silently at him. Something about the close-set dark eyes and furrowed brows made Saleem put his cigarettes away and follow on again. Once more Saleem felt his heart pumping faster than ever before. His head ached and the sweat ran from his armpits. He was on hell's treadmill, he thought, running faster and faster until the wheel span so fast it tore his skin to shreds.

The band of freedom fighters slid down an embankment into another murky mosquito filled ditch. Saleem needed a helping hand to climb down, much to the annoyance of the others. Ultraman did not mind standing up to his ankles in foetid water but he muttered deep resentment at Saleem's refusal to come down out of sight of any guards that might glance in their direction. Saleem though, perched half out of the ditch, rested a hand on Ultraman's head.

"I have to keep watch," said Saleem. "Now that we are here."

Before them was the prison area. It looked little different from the town. The breezeblock apartments that acted as a prison, were set in grounds surrounded by barbed wire. The tanks at the gates pointed their guns inwards. Saleem noted this and pointed it out to Ultraman.

"So?" asked Ultraman.

"It means they will not expect us!" declared Saleem.

"We will surprise them and they will run before us!" said Ultraman excitedly knocking the safety catch off his rifle. A flurry of clicks followed as the others did likewise.

Saleem tried to make some more observations.

"There is the peripheral fence," he said, with a sweep of his arm.

The others poked their heads up above the ditch and nodded in agreement.

"And the guards will have various check-in points. They will have to sign a book hanging on the fence and each day these books will be collected for an inspection of the time. This way they know that someone was there at that time."

Ultraman and his friends, nodded again and watched a couple of scruffily uniformed soldiers appear with mobile phones in their hands.

"And," continued Saleem, "I bet there are a few little places where they can skive off, take a quick smoke, have a snooze, consort with women . . ."

"What sort of women?" asked Ultraman. "Will we have to kill them as well?"

"Women!" The word whispered itself around the boys. "Women! Naked! Consorting with the enemy! They will have to be dealt with! Shown what real men can do!"

"Sssh!" said Ultraman.

Saleem tried to see a worthy skiving zone but he was too far away to see anything.

" I can't see from here," he said. "But where they skive is the place to ambush them."

"Aaah," said the boys. "Ambush them!"

Ultraman dragged Saleem down into the ditch and with a grunt told the others to walk along the ditch to where the water disappeared into a pipe.

Saleem did not like the feel of slime and mulch seeping into his shoes. He sensed he would catch something awful. There were worms that could burrow into the soles of one's feet and turn one blind. This was where he could catch those. He had also heard of people catching gonorrhoea falling into stinking ditches. He felt he was sure to catch that as well. And now, as he reached the end of the ditch and had to climb out and run across open ground to some crumbling stonewalls, he felt he was sure to catch a bullet.

Saleem watched as each of the youngsters crawled, slithered and ran across the dusty patch to tumble and roll into the wall weeds two hundred yards away. The pink flowers shivered and a gush of thistledown blew into the air.

"We must all do what is necessary," whispered Ultraman.

Then he prodded Saleem with the barrel of his Transformer.

"Now!" he said, "Go!"

Saleem crawled out of the ditch and stumbled into the dust. He lay there feeling the mud from his shoes draining out onto the floor. He smelt the stench and something somewhere seemed not to be functioning. He could not push himself up to make any sort of dash.

"Run!" grunted Ultraman pulling himself up beside Saleem.

He grabbed Saleem's arm and wrenched Saleem to his feet. Then he hobbled along with Saleem towards the wall opposite. Saleem slumped to the ground and refused to go any further. Ultraman gave him an extra tug but Saleem could not move but looked up and saw that beside the perimeter fence the two soldiers were speaking into their portable phones and nonchalantly clearing their guns for action. Saleem pointed towards them.

"Oh shit," said Ultraman, leaping to his feet.

All the fearless guerrillas leapt out of their hiding places and ran back towards the fields and the sunflowers where they could disappear.

Saleem lay in the dust. He could taste blood in his mouth. He was imploding, he thought. Inside he was empty and his guts, bones, and skin were being sucked inside this emptiness and he would eventually disappear.

"Most unfortunate," he muttered to himself.

"What is it old man?" said one of the soldiers bending down to investigate his find.

Saleem lay in the shadow of the soldiers and waited for them to shoot him.

"Are you hurt?" asked one of them. "Were they trying to rob you?"

Saleem opened his eyes and tried to compose his thoughts.

"They are all hooligans here in the mountains," said one of the soldiers as the two of them pulled Saleem to his feet.

"Where have you come from old man?"

Saleem pointed to the railway track.

"They are always dragging people off the train," said the soldier.

"They find a stranger in the market and then they rob them," said the other. "How much have you lost old man?"

Saleem had nothing in his pocket except his cigarettes, which he pulled out and shakily offered to the soldiers.

"You should report this to the police," said one of the soldiers, declining Saleem's cigarette but offering him one of his own in return.

The other lit it for Saleem.

"The police may not do much but, if everyone reports these crimes, maybe someone in the capital would realise what we are up against here and send more people."

Saleem nodded his head fiercely in agreement.

"Well," said one of the soldiers. "Unless you want to make a complaint you had better go back to the train. It is still waiting there."

"Oh yes yes," said Saleem nodding and bowing to them, backing away and hobbling off towards the railway. "Yes, the train. Still waiting."

The soldiers waved farewell to Saleem and walked back to their posts on the prison fence. Saleem limped towards the milling crowds of the market and turned back along the road towards the village. He was soon out of sight of the soldiers and found that he was not alone on his march. A stone hit him on the back of the head. He listened a moment then began walking again only to find another stone hit him.

Marching behind Saleem were the fierce freedom fighters of the village, each one convinced of their bravery and the betrayal of their chief officer, i.e. Saleem, who sensed their mood very quickly.

"Go away," he muttered as he marched on with the boys marching beside him, spitting at him, hissing at him.

"Do not draw attention to yourselves!" he told them. "Pull yourselves together! Act like men!"

He himself did not know how a man should act, but he thought they would respond to such orders. They did, but only by blowing raspberries at him and running on ahead, calling out obscene names. So much for his military prowess thought Saleem. It had

159

been a stupid thing to do and could have easily gone very much worse than it had. Just one person fearless enough to pull a trigger, could have got them all killed.

Suddenly Saleem wanted to explain to Amina that he would forgive her everything, that he was an old man, but like a child in many ways and liked the company of children and young people, even when they humiliated him. He would be kind to her and look after her. She was after all, an ignorant gypsy as crazy as they came and otherwise destined to die in a brothel. So how could she resist his advances, especially if he was honest about himself with her?

He returned to the darkened village and entered the gate of the enclosure. There was a light in the main building where he suspected Sufiya and Adam to be. He tiptoed past hoping not to set any chickens squawking, and went round the out-house to the hut Amina had been put in. He stood by the door bracing himself to knock and start explaining himself. He was sure she would at first scream but if he played the wounded man, he was sure she would let him in. Before he could begin, he heard voices from within.

"Ten minutes is not long enough!" said a male voice.

"Then stay another ten," said Amina.

"They will notice!" said the voice.

"Then we should go away," said Amina, "We just get in the car and go!"

Saleem heard something stirring and quickly backed away to hide behind the outhouse. The door to Amina's room opened and Adam walked out.

The fool, thought Saleem, as he slid down onto his haunches and rested his back against the cold wooden wall. He pulled out a cigarette and lit it up. The smoke drifted into the dark empty night.

"Most foolish," he muttered. "Most foolish."

CHAPTER EIGHT

"**A**dam!" said Rashid. "Where are you?"

Adam told him how he was with his wife and telephoning from the Karaoke Palace in his father-in-law's village.

"How's business?"

Adam tried to sound enthusiastic, unbowed, vaguely still positive about his trip to the capital, hoping not to betray his infidelities, not while his wife stood beside him. Though that actually added to the excitement. Last night, mm, an idiotic moment but...

"Your timing was very bad," said Rashid, "lots of other things were happening. Lots of things have changed."

Adam told him about Sufiya's brother and tried to blot out a very whorish image his mind could not escape from. Why was she not like that in the city?

"Oh the prisons are overflowing at the moment," said Rashid, failing to dispel the thrill of Adam's secret, "But not to worry, there'll be someone to influence. There always is. Unless there is a judge that can free him legitimately. You'd better find out who the magistrate is. That would be better."

"If he is incorruptible though," said Adam, not believing there was a single incorruptible in the world, "I may get into trouble."

"Adam you are truly an honest man," said Rashid. "But I shall ask around. See what party influence can be used. It means calling in favours though. And I think I need a reward for this, don't you?"

"Such as?" asked Adam, now knowing the best sort of reward for any act of favouritism.

"I should be your partner in business," said Rashid. "I protect you, and take half the profits. I think this is fair, don't you? Considering that half of nothing is nothing."

Adam covered the handset and urgently whispered to Sufiya, "He wants to take half my profits. What shall I do?"

"What is he offering in return?"

"Your brother. Help. Protection. Connections. All the things you want. All the reasons you insist I telephone Rashid. All the things that will make you trust me."

"This is very unfair," said Sufiya.

"What is very unfair? Your friend Rashid or me?"

Sufiya did not answer. Adam took this as acknowledgement that she had been in the wrong treating him the way she did. Adam removed his hand from the mouthpiece.

"I cannot say I like it," said Adam, "But you tell me more good reasons for doing this."

"There have been big changes in state policy and Omar has benefited," said Rashid. "He has a new uniform. A new car. And he doesn't like you does he?"

"No," said Adam. "But so what? You are still someone to reckon with aren't you?"

"Me? Oh you flatter," said Rashid. "I have influence but I am but a small fish."

"But you can stop Omar bothering my wife," said Adam, wondering how many young girls he could employ in a grand scheme to overcome all opposition to his rising in the world. Omar would certainly succumb. Rashid would not. But Amina could be an extra weapon... an extra danger too...

"Well," said Rashid, sounding distant and unconvinced, "Most likely."

"And," whispered Sufiya to Adam, "find my brother work. Get him to do that. Get him to do everything he can."

"My wife's brother is a very useful person," said Adam. "Perhaps there is a job for a young man with his kind of experience."

There was a moment's silence that made Adam think that he had overstepped the line. Hell! Of course he had overstepped the line. From now on, Adam thought, he would always overstep the line. And feel good about it. Guiltless, Adam told himself, is what he felt. And shuddered.

"OK," said Rashid. "I always have room for people of special talents. I assume you are indicating that he is such a person?"

"I think so," said Adam. "He has a talent for trouble I'd say."

Adam relished the word "trouble."

"Well," said Rashid, "I assume he understands whose side he is on?"

Adam gave profuse thanks and quickly put the phone down before Rashid could back out. "Trouble", he said to himself and turned to Sufiya. He gave her a big smile that he thought betrayed nothing. What a skill he had acquired! There was no stopping him now and he explained the situation to Sufiya as they walked back to the house, making great dramatic gestures with his arm. This way he hoped she understood how she was the source of all problems and he was the solution.

"We are losing everything for this brother of yours," he said, "You understand that, don't you?"

"He will be useful to us. Far more useful than that whore of yours."

"She is not my whore!" said Adam rather meekly, and suddenly feeling ridiculous in his strutting and arm waving. He briskly heated up the pace and tried to leave Sufiya behind so that she might not fix those eyes of hers on his. "And you and that Rashid," he shouted back at her, "And that Policeman and whoever, are white as snow! And I am not a mere pimp profiting from your 'friendships'. Or is it suffering? I'm not sure which anymore."

Adam turned and allowed her eyes to bury themselves deep into his. He could feel himself shrivelling away to nothing before her rage. Sufiya hurried towards Adam cursing and flinging her fists in all directions. Adam was stunned to find Sufiya battering him about the head with her knuckles. How many years of pent up frustration did that contain, he thought. How many years had he had that coming? He could not think back to when some behaviour on his part had started to irritate her. But he reasoned that it must have for she could not know his present secret. She could not guess. Except maybe she dug something out of his eyes. But no, she could not! She could. She did. She knew...

But as suddenly as her rage had come, Sufiya ran inside and left Adam frozen on the spot. Amina ran from the house, with a hail of Sufiya's abuse following after her. She shook it from her like a dog, and found Adam.

"We should go now," she demanded. "We should."

"Maybe we should!" barked Adam. But he pushed her aside and went inside the house so that Sufiya could yell at him some more. Maybe he would be able to tell from the tone of her yelling just how much she knew. But what to do if she obviously did know, he did not know. Probably he would accept her hatred and let her drive him in to the ground so that he was no more than the stain on the earth he felt himself to truly be. After that, was too far in the future to contemplate.

***

Saleem took his opportunity. Adam was at the prison dealing with Sufiya's brother. Sufiya was boiling up the cauldron for her father's year long unwashed bedding. The aunts, who had failed to do this for so long, were nowhere to be seen. Taking the chopper from the kitchen, Saleem walked gingerly over to Amina's hut. In the kitchen corner was Sufiya's father's old rifle. It looked a bit rusty but it might have been serviceable. At least for Saleem's purpose, but he was ignorant of guns. A moment's contemplation of the weapon had brought an image of his grandfather to his mind. He could see the man now, with his thick bristly moustache, his baggy pants, his short coat and his rifle casually slung on his shoulder. That was how he himself should be, but when that man was killed, it seemed women, teachers, administrators, officials, and finally his son ruled Saleem. Consequently the only weapon he could wield with any lethality was the chopper he used to hack apart chickens. It would have to do though.

He burst into Amina's room and waved the chopper at her. Amina looked up from a book that she was reading.

"Get up!" shouted Saleem.

Amina stood.

"You have caused enough trouble here," he said and knocked the book from her hand with the chopper.

"Look," said Amina, "I'll do whatever you want!"

Saleem growled again and sidled round her with the chopper pointing towards the door. After a few nudges Amina began to move.

"I'd like to speak to Adam," said Amina. "I really would. I'm sure he could straighten this out."

Saleem prodded Amina towards the compound where the insects were busily drowning out all other sounds.

"Where do you want me to go?" said Amina.

Saleem grunted and gave Amina another prod. Amina began slowly working towards the gate and then through it out onto the dirt track.

"There's nowhere you can run to," said Saleem.

The two of them walked slowly through the village, past the dead jumble of lights that webbed the Karaoke Palace. Saleem gave Amina a particularly fierce prod with the chopper when it looked like she might venture a shout or scream at that moment. Finally they were beyond the barking dogs, braying donkeys, and curious old women, climbing up the mountain path through the forests of the border. Saleem had no idea where he was going, only that anywhere upwards seemed better than downwards. There was poetry in that and that is what he felt was at the heart of his action: poetry. He tried to think of some.

"That girl has got a crazy look," he sang. "She dresses very strangely. Just when you think she wants your love. Another comes in range."

He had a recollection of a podgy effeminate man singing this while dancing around an exceptionally standoffish harlot with an explosive bust-line.

"Most obscene," he chuckled to himself.

"Have you taken some drugs or something?" asked Amina.

Saleem growled and prodded her to walk faster. He would reach his destination when he felt they had walked far enough. Presently, Saleem was enjoying the sense of career development.

Amina's steps became wearier and more dragging. Suddenly she fell over. Saleem almost chopped her except his swipe was half hearted, and missed by a mile. Amina fell into the shadows at his feet but soon Saleem's eyes refocused and there was Amina cowering. She tried to crawl very quickly off the trail into the thick of the forest but Saleem was there ahead of her. Once again Amina went very still.

"If you think I'm moving any further," she said, "You've another think coming."

Saleem looked behind into the forest. They were a long way away from anywhere. Or at least there was enough distance between him and wherever. He would get Amina up and moving again soon enough but in the mean time this called for a smoke. He relaxed as he lit up a cigarette then offered one to Amina. She took it and allowed Saleem to light it. As Amina took a drag she began to shake. He had gotten her into the sort of state he hoped he would.

Saleem dropped the remains of his cigarette onto the floor and extinguished it with a hiss in the mud. Amina's mouth was opening and shutting in front him like some gold fish in a bowl. Blah blah blah blah, it was going. How he hated all this blah blah blah blahing. She was searching about her pockets and then offering him things. He discovered they were her credit cards and her money, but he ignored them and kicked her until she rose to her feet.

"You should never have come here," he told her. "Chasing after my son like that. Causing all that mischief. This is not good. What do you hope to gain by it?"

Her voice in reply echoed meaninglessly about his ears. She was saying something but he could not hear it. He did not want to hear it anyway, but for a moment Saleem wavered. He had no idea what he was going to do to her. He had thought maybe he would frighten her, make her run away and leave them all alone. But then he thought she was too crazy to understand, though he saw no sign of craziness. But she was crazy, which was the way with these girls. It would be a charitable thing to do, to marry her. Even with a little threat of violence. And what woman did not need a little threat of violence to give into a man's demands?

Saleem noticed Amina was running away from him. Maybe he should leave it at that? But he started to chase her. He would fuck her first, fuck her and then let her go. That seemed the best idea. Fuck her, he thought, fuck her! He would take back what she had stolen, and then they would be quits. He gave chase in the silence of the forest. Only the noise of their feet thudding through the leaves could be heard. But he was tired and maybe fucking her was not such a good idea. He did not feel like it. He was surprised he even thought of it in the first place.

Out of the shadow loomed a temple. Saleem had not expected to see such a place here. It was far too north for this sort of thing. He stopped and pressed his face up against the warm irongate and looked in. He began wrenching at the gate, pulling and pushing it until its hinges pulled away from the soft sandstone of the wall. With a final kick, the gate swung away on one side and allowed him to enter.

Inside he looked up at the temple wall and thought he could make out the same picture of the blue god that he had found upon his wall at home. Saleem put all thoughts of Amina aside. She was not worth the effort anyway and maybe he had done enough. That would be the last they saw of her. "Most convenient," he muttered to himself. And rather pleased that his plan had succeeded, he walked through the doorway into the main building and wandered through the empty rooms. Stale hot air wafted about his nostrils. Any altars and gods would have been taken away by the government years ago. But they could not take away the atmosphere of the place. Saleem never considered himself a superstitious man but there must have been a reason that fate had led him to this spot.

"Wife!" he cried out and heard his voice echoing back at him. "Mother of my child!"

What had she been doing on that road? he thought to himself.

"Why did you leave me like this?" he cried out.

Somehow he thought there might be a trace of Jamilla there: a slipper, a foot print, a hair, all might be present, for he knew she must have been here as a girl. This would be why a northern girl like her had been so keen on attending Castrol's temple. This would explain a few things about some of his wife's habits. And Sufiya for that matter. He must have passed that liking for northern girls onto his son. How apt for Amina to have led him here. She was a devil and he sensed this would be his death. Was he frightened of that? It was nonsense.

He began to look for any signs, the slightest hint, a smell, a shadow, he did not know what it might be that would let him know if this was real or supernatural or... He reached the back room and looked out of the window over a garden. The jungle pouring in through the gap in the garden wall, had covered paths and the overgrown flowerbeds. You can never hold it back, he thought. He had been watching the desert wipe out all trace of his village, his childhood, his life, for years. Here it was the jungle. It was the same thing. There was no turning it back wherever you were.

"Jamilla!" he cried out.

He remembered their first meeting. At a cousin's wedding he had caught a glimpse of this shy young girl and asked his mother who she was. That had been enough to set the ball rolling and within a year they were married.

The air began to chill and he gave a shiver. Somewhere, somehow, Jamilla was there. He could sense her presence. He had always known that one day a vision would be sent to him. It would redeem him, transform him, make sense of his life, and turn what others saw as a meaningless unwashed shambles, into someone noble. If the vision were to come now, it would be in the shape of his wife. If a devil were to destroy him, it would also come in the shape of his wife.

His prayer was not one of words. There were no words, as far as he knew. He knew Castrol's crazy father always had words he claimed were ancient but Saleem never believed him and was always surprised that the idiot survived with such thoughts. Words were pointless anyway. His prayer was one of feeling. His whole body vibrated to the frequency of his deepest longings and he did not know what they were. It was not true that he was empty, he thought, he was merely wordless and any god worth his salt would understand that.

Saleem sensed a presence. The chill in the air had a perfume about it. He opened his eyes, turned and caught a glimpse of blue. In the darkness he heard feet shuffling. He stepped forward.

"Jamilla?" he whispered, then moved towards the door.

A dark shadow moved outside the door. Devil or whatever, if it looked like his wife he wanted to see it. To risk damnation for a last glimpse...

"Who are you? What are you?" he asked and ran down the corridor knowing this to be foolish. But he could recall chasing his son around the rooms of his old house. The screams of delight and joy as the two had run through the empty stone floored rooms seemed such a long time ago. How did that time pass? What happened to it? What did it result in? What point had it all been?

He stopped and looked into one of the large side rooms. There was nothing there but shadows cast by the swaying branches of the trees outside the window. He listened and heard the sounds again: whimpering, cries, and something harsher. Through the window he looked and down beside the gate he saw something, two people, maybe one, on the floor, but he could not make out what it was that he was really seeing.

He ran back through the dark corridor, down the cold stone steps through the door to the outside world where he found Shoes, half-naked, wrestling with someone, something... Amina.

Shoes looked up into Saleem's eyes and grinned, his hands fixed about Amina's throat. Her eyes showed only the whites, as if in ecstasy.

Shoe's grip tightened further and her eyes began to have the pop-eyed dead black look of a startled chicken. Saleem felt his heart beat faster and faster. Suddenly it stopped as Shoes and Amina went limp. Saleem watched the two separate. There was a last twitch and then nothing. All he could hear was the wind whistling through the carved panels that let the cool air into the temple. All he could see as he fell was a swirl of leaves, sky, branches, soil...

As the blood began to flow through his brain and his heart began to beat once more, Saleem thought maybe there had been some transfiguration of his soul and he was in another world. Jamilla then would ride up on a white horse and call to him. But the numbness subsided and he knew a moment of transfiguration had not come. He was still in Daoistan, and still the same, and his wife was nowhere to be seen. Instead, he crawled to his knees and he found a dead girl before him and an idiot boy grinning and putting his pants back on. Maybe the hand of god, through this boy, had reached out and struck this devil down? Saleem began wringing his hands. He had to do something. He could not leave things like this. Should he run away? Where to? He did not know.

"She's nothing!" he heard Shoes say. "Nothing!"

The boy ran off through the gate and Saleem crawled over to look at Amina. He took her by her arms and dragged her out of the courtyard up into the undergrowth. She had to be hidden, he thought, she had to be covered up. Saleem began grabbing at branches and leaves and the mulch of the earth. The more he scooped with his bare hands, the more the branches scratched, entangled themselves about his arms, his legs, his hair. Handful upon handful he covered Amina until no more of her could be seen. There she would lie, he thought, and here her spirit would roam seeking revenge. He was more frightened of that than anything any law could do to him. No-one would miss her though. She was crazy. She had drifted away from her people and appeared like a devil, transformed, to prey upon his family for some evil purpose. He had had to stop her, he knew that now. His prayer had been answered in this form. She was a sacrifice he had to make to the blue god. If it had not been her, he would have had to sacrifice

169

himself. Yet her crazy spirit would not take that for an answer. No, he was doomed to be haunted by it for the rest of his life.

"Jamilla!" he cried out as the moon appeared from behind a cloud.

All around, the jungle lit up. A snake slithered across the leaves for cover, leaving bare earth where it went, as if it had written a passage from a holy book.

These are crazy thoughts, Saleem said to himself as he stared back towards the road. "Most crazy," he said.

***

Adam sat waiting in the run down, airconditionless office. Some files lay piled upon the regulation desk and a regulation tin wastebasket full of mouldering mango stones and melon skins sitting beneath it. The door snapped open and an army officer entered. Adam half stood from his seat.

"No no," said the officer, "Sit sit."

He was a young man with an officious but courteous manner, dressed in a smart uniform. He took his seat, sniffed the air, looked beneath the desk then gave out a shout that made Adam jump. Another soldier immediately entered. The officer held up the offending bin and the soldier took it, stood to attention, tried to salute and then turned and left. The officer shook his head.

"These people," he said, "They have no idea."

Then he sat back down again.

"Well," he said, sifting through the files on the desk.

"Ahaa," he said, finding the appropriate file.

"Hmmm," he said as he sifted through the notes, nodding and tutting to himself.

"I think," said Adam, "There has been an injustice here."

The officer gave a maybe sort of expression. His chin was clean shaven and his hair neatly shorn up to the top of his head where a greasy lock hung down into his eyes. Every so often he flicked the lock back.

"This will take some time to process," said the officer, "And there is a price for speeding up the process. That is the way it is. You can either wait your turn or jump the queue. But to do that others must be compensated."

"I understand," said Adam.

"And this boy is not lily white," said the officer, "If he is released into your custody then you must guarantee he will not break the law and will not leave the country. The courts may not make their decision in the boy's favour."

"I think the courts can be persuaded," said Adam.

The officer nodded. "Yes," he said, "They can be persuaded. A good lawyer can make them do anything. It is not justice, just sharp practice."

"This time it will be justice," said Adam.

"Maybe," said the officer, "And maybe the case will never get to court. Amnesties and changing circumstances may well solve all their problems."

"I'm sure there will be changing circumstances," said Adam, picking up from the floor the plastic carrier bag he had brought with him. The officer nodded then slammed shut the file and gestured Adam to follow him.

At the door the officer waited for a moment, coughed slightly and held out his hand. Adam delved into the bag and pulled out a box containing a new mobile telephone. He also handed over an envelope to the officer, that was quickly slipped into his inside pocket.

"Give my regards to Rashid," said the officer, examining the colourful red, blue and green box, "He was at school with my brother you know."

"No, I didn't know," said Adam.

"All the instructions are in here are they?"

"Oh yes. And a spare set of batteries."

The officer nodded and then opened the door and led the way with Adam following. They passed down a long corridor, the grey breezeblock naked on the walls, then onto the concrete steps that wound down towards the courtyard.

"They failed to put lifts in this place," said the officer. "Can you imagine planning an eight-story building without lifts? Just what is in the mind of some of these people? Climbing these stairs will either kill us or make us all very fit."

Outside in the courtyard Sufiya's brother stood shivering, shoeless, grasping the top of his beltless pyjama pants with his handcuffed hands. When Adam and the officer arrived, the officer nodded to a couple of troopers who unlocked the handcuffs and stood back.

"All yours," said the officer to Adam and then walked briskly away with his troopers, flapping the file at the side of his legs. One of the troopers began to punch out the numbers on his mobile phone and the telephone the other trooper had in his pocket suddenly began to ring. They found this very amusing.

Joseph looked suspiciously at Adam. He had hunched shoulders, wary eyes, a shaved head. Adam pulled out from the plastic carrier bag some shoes and a change of clothes that were immediately snatched at and changed into.

"Hurry up," said Adam. "Let's get out of here."

Joseph had the look of Sufiya in his face but there the resemblance ended. His body was the grey emaciated body of someone who had been locked in darkness for a long time. With his shoes loosely hanging on his feet, he quickly shuffled towards the gate. The barrier rose up, powered by a single soldier carelessly chatting on a mobile-phone to someone. Joseph passed through with Adam ushering him along, half-fearful that the barrier would drop with them the wrong side.

Across the road by the ditch, Amina's rented car waited for them. On seeing it Joseph's face lit up into a broad grin. He stretched and glanced up at the sun then casually crossed the road to the car, which he walked around, patting the roof, kicking the tyres, saying, "Not bad, not bad, it must be true that you are a rich man with influence."

Adam saw no reason to tell him otherwise. "Just get in," he said, unlocking the doors.

Driving back towards the village, Joseph played with the tape deck. One hand pressed the buttons and the other rifled through a stack of tapes he found.

"Does this thing have a microphone?" asked Joseph.

"No no," said Adam, "It merely plays back."

"But it would be a very useful thing to have a microphone," said Joseph, "Then we could all sing along."

Joseph sat back and dismantled one of the cassette boxes in search of a sheet of the lyrics.

"I have sung all the songs I know," said Joseph in the front seat, turning up the volume on the radio.

"That girl has sexy pants," sang the male singer, "Don't you think she has sexy pants?"

"Our people are making stupid lyrics," said Joseph, "They are not ones you can sing without all the technology to cover them up. I passed my time singing all the old songs and they have real lyrics. You can sing them without any instruments."

"Then you don't need a microphone," said Adam, honking the horn at some straying sheep. They bounced out of his way. He liked the way they bounced. If only the rest of the world behaved like that. Blaaap on the horn and booing, away they bounce.

"I like the microphone," said Joseph, "I want to sing stupid songs! The stupider the better!" yelled Joseph, becoming excited. "With flashing lights. And little bowls of peanuts on the table whilst you are doing the singing. And drinks that glow in the dark! And the Keff girls with lycra dresses..."

"I take it you are glad to be free," said Adam as he accelerated and turned down the road towards the village. The question is, he thought to himself, whether or not he could trust Joseph to look after Amina. Another question was whether he wanted anyone to look after her at all. There were certain disadvantages to all the present options available.

On arrival, Sufiya rushed forward to greet her brother. They hugged, then turned to face their father, who was dressed in his best suit and cap looking very stern. Adam wondered about that suit. It looked suspiciously like his own. Sufiya could not have given it to her father? Surely she would not have done that? As he climbed from the car, Adam exchanged a glance with Sufiya but nothing in her expression gave away a thing. A subtle war had no doubt broken out between them. How long would this go on? Forever? Others he knew had wives with whom they silently struggled. Nothing was said but always the atmosphere prevailed. Was that to be his lot now, forever?

Adam watched as Joseph lowered himself before his father, who placed his callused hand upon his shaved head, then scrubbed it fiercely and pushed him away, tears in his eyes. It was a sentimental relationship with no criticism on either part. Unlike his own with Saleem. Much in Sufiya's family was spoken in their silences. As if to prove the point, Sufiya nodded to Joseph to acknowledge the two Aunts darkly waiting in the background.

"Aunties!" he said, "I am back."

The Aunts stood up tall and waited for Joseph to bow his head. When he did so they went back inside their houses. That was the future, thought Adam, a constant silent battle.

"Well I can see they are happy to see me," said Joseph.

"I think," said Sufiya, "They thought they might be going to inherit the farm."

Her father unsteadily held up the bottle he had behind his back and made it clear that he expected everyone to follow him indoors to drink to freedom. Why, thought Adam, does he never speak? He could remember when he did speak, so when did he lose the power? That too was the future, the reduction of intimacy to so little. When battles no longer matter, all that is left is the doubt they were worth fighting in the first place. Talking of which, Adam noticed that his own father was missing. And where was Amina, his momentary cure and humiliation?

"I don't know," said Sufiya, "He is your father. And she was your friend. Maybe they have run off together!"

There was that look again. He was sure she hated him. "I do this for your brother," he said through gritted teeth, "And you still insult me!"

Not that Adam could think why his saving her brother should stop her feeling the way she must be feeling towards him. He did not blame her.

Joseph took his sister's hand and started to follow his father back indoors.

"Wait!" demanded Adam, "We must find my father. He must join us."

There was no response. His alarm did not communicate. Why they could not understand him, he did not know. Sufiya's family was always like that.

Adam walked out of the compound and began calling to the children. He was surprised to find Joseph joining him. If anyone it should have been Sufiya as it really was no business of Joseph. He resented him for his show of concern.

"There is no danger for your father," Joseph said. "Surely he is too old for the soldiers to bother picking him up?"

Adam, irritated, ignored Joseph and began walking through the village questioning anyone that came within shouting range. He questioned some of the children that now gathered around. They pointed up vaguely into the hills but could give no definite directions. He tried to discover how they looked, was anyone else with them, were they smiling? Joking? But no-one could say until he came across the boy he knew as Shoes. The boy's mud streaked face was cracked by a grin. He knew everything, he told Adam, and offered to take him into the hills.

"That's the only place anyone could have gone," he kept saying.

"Then take us now!"

Shoes ran on ahead as Adam followed and shouted at Joseph to stay behind to explain to Sufiya what he was doing. Adam was prepared to follow Shoes all night if he had to. His father could have easily got himself into some sort of trouble. A stupid remark to a soldier, an ill considered spit in the wrong direction, could all have ended up with his father's arrest. It was not inconceivable that the authorities took his father in exchange for Joseph: a kind of warped quid pro quo that ensured Adam would never think he could win in any situation without their blessing.

Amidst the trees leading up the mountainside, Shoes led the way along the narrow dirt path, pointing out where army patrols always passed. Above them a jet screeched.

"They will not shoot," said Shoes, as Adam ducked down in fear. "They are not there to shoot anyone at the moment."

"And when they are?" asked Adam. "How will you know?"

"We won't know," said Shoes with a nervous giggle. "We'll be dead."

Adam decided not to go into partnership with Shoes. As a male model he was far too short. And there was a sly nastiness about him that conveyed itself within the waddling walk, the constant nose picking, the shifty grin and black specs of pupils in his blood-shot eyes. How Adam could have mistaken him for muscular handsome ordinariness, fit to promote the shoes sensation of the century, he could not even begin to understand.

Darkness fell rapidly now. They seemed to have been walking for hours. Adam put the sense of time down to the disagreeable nature of his companion, for it was less than an hour all told. Yet the village was gone and only the trees and the path could be seen and the racket of insects heard. This might have been a million years in the past or the future, for all the recognisable environment he found himself in. The enclosure of plants and dark greenery startled his desert born eyes. His father could easily have become lost in here, he thought and he too might easily be lost, led to what by Shoes? Murder by Sufiya, by some trick of her murderous brother, or brooding father who had feigned his senility and now waited at the end of the trail to murder him for the betrayal of his daughter...

Shoes let out a whoop. He had seen something and rushed ahead. Adam, startled from his interior monologue, ran, kicking his way through the thick undergrowth. He was determined not to be left behind. It could be a trick. It could be a joke. There could be a comedy taking place with him at its centre, the star, and after the event he would replay it for his child: the day he lost his father. The day his father, like a child, wandered away from the safety of the home and had to be hunted down... Let that be a warning never to stray so far...

Shoes looked very pleased with himself as he stood beside the unshaven, unwashed Saleem.

"I could smell him!" announced Shoes with a giggle.

Adam approached his father. The old man looked older. His eyes were blood-shot and unfocussed. He had last seen his father in such a state when his mother died.

"Where's Amina?" asked Adam, unsure what his first question should be.

Saleem made no movement, no sound.

"Your father went a bit crazy," said Shoes. "Ha haa. We'd better bury it. Hide it well."

Adam did not know what Shoes was talking about. He could not see what Shoes apparently could see. Maybe Shoe's familiarity with the surroundings made him a better judge of disturbance. Whatever it was, Shoe's strange comments made Adam clamber over a lightening struck tree that had fallen onto the walls of an old temple. For a moment he propped himself against the tree and looked around, but he was not sure what he was supposed to be looking for. But there was something not quite right. He still could not register what it was, but then the shape leapt out at him. How he could have missed it he did not know. It was Amina. She was stuffed under the roots. Ants were swarming over her body. There was no doubt that she was dead. And in death there seemed to be little of her. She hardly filled up any space at all. It was barely her. What had happened? What had his father done? How had he reduced her to this?

"Look what he has done!" said Shoes. "Look at the mess he has made. Well she is nothing though. So don't you worry. It is for the best."

Shoes began picking up small twigs then discarded them in favour of large damp branches that he greeted with a groan of disapproval. Nothing seemed to be suitable for his mysterious ends. But he settled for throwing a couple of branches across Amina and then emptied the lighter fuel from his cigarette lighter over her. But he hesitated to set it alight.

"Your father will say all sorts of things," said Shoes, "But tell him not to say anything. Tell him that. He says nothing and he is safe."

Adam tried to think what this meant. His father had killed her, of that he was sure. For what reason, he was not too sure, but could guess it was his father's warped attempt to solve Adam's problem with his wife. Though it was too late now since the damage had been done. Could he forgive him anyway? No. It was unforgivable. Was it excusable? No. Maybe it was an accident though...

"Have you got her credit cards," Adam called after his father, "If anyone spends her credit cards they'll know where to look for her. Just throw them away. Burn everything. Burn everything!"

That was it. Burn everything. The solution. Then nothing would exist, all would be wiped clean. And maybe he could forget what his father had done. He could have easily forgotten Amina anyway. Tomorrow if she had lived he would have sent her on her way with Joseph and no doubt seen no more of her. Perhaps within a few seconds of seeing her, when he had returned that evening, he would have found her a different girl from the one he had ten erotic unconsummated minutes with the night before. And that would have ended the spell, if she wanted it ended. If...

Saleem was walking down the hill and Adam ran after him, grabbed his shoulder, swung him round and shoved him, sending him sprawling to the ground. Saleem lay on the ground motionless. He did not look at Adam, but kept his head turned away. If he was ashamed, thought Adam, then what happened here was something far worse than he could imagine. He would not examine Amina further. He would not think of her anymore. To do so might reveal truths about his father; about his mother. For a fleeting moment he saw his father killing his mother. Then killing him.

"I'm your father," shouted Saleem, "Don't you forget that! Your mother would not want you to forget it!"

With a whoop Shoes managed to get a blaze going. He shouted out and yelped excitedly, dancing about the crackling smoky flames.

"That crazy old bastard eh?" he shouted. "I always knew it you know. We knew it from the start."

Adam watched as Saleem blinked from the smoke. His eyes watered as a cloud of smoke billowed across his face leaving black streaks of soot. The eyes fixed upon Adam's and seem to be playing a part of an absurd grin.

"Smoky!" said Saleem. "Most inconvenient."

CHAPTER NINE

Adam and Saleem were silent and sullen as they joined Sufiya and her family. They had freshened up, changed clothes, even spoken a few civil words to each other. Not a direct word was uttered about what might have or might not have happened, though Saleem had shaken his head and said, "It is best not to say anything until I know what others are saying." This struck Adam as uncharacteristically shrewd, but then for murder to be hidden, shrewdness was called for. There would be an explanation, he assumed, and one day it would be forthcoming.

That night they sat at the table listening to Joseph explain how he survived his ordeal. Though Adam could not concentrate. He merely contemplated his father's missing few hours and the absence of Amina and how neither seemed strange nor suspicious. Saleem had been notorious for his eccentric coming and going ever since he was a young man, and Amina was unknown by Joseph, unwanted by Sufiya, and unnoticed by her father.

But all did notice, or feign more interest in or fear of, the noises they could hear coming from the village as trucks rumbled and gun shots rang out. Joseph, halfway through a bottle of The Spirit Of Daoistan went pale and rushed to the door to see what was happening. Saleem made it seem the worst thing that could be happening. He said how they would be coming to return all to prison, so that they could ransom them again. Adam concurred and there was no time to lose in escaping from such a situation.

"They will pick me up again," said Joseph, casting a nervy glance from the door towards the army making its unexpected swoop. "This is how they took me last time. That's how they will work. They take your money, let me go and then pick me up again!"

"Yes," said Saleem, "That is how they work."

"Dealing with the likes of Rashid," said Adam, casting a harsh look at Sufiya, "Is going to get us all in trouble eventually."

179

Adam glanced at his father and trembled at his own hypocrisy. "Go and get your things," he ordered Saleem, "Go on!"

Saleem slunk away like a scolded dog. Adam sensed the resentment but he was saving the man, he was taking him away from those who might wish to harm him. He now longed for the days when he took water to his father's home, where they grumbled and fought over nothing, and where neither lived in the same world. He should have realised that when he first felt a glimmer of understanding of his father, a glimmer of appreciation, that only disaster could follow for they were not supposed to live in a state of understanding. The world was too small for both to be of like minds.

Joseph returned indoors and nervously paced the room. He announced that he did not care to stay there even if the land needed tending and his father refused to move. He did not care. He would leave it to whoever took it. As the son he would still have a claim. He would be able get it all back no matter what the Aunts did or their sons with their treacherous thieving wives and ignorant brats who had been after the farm for years. No, he did not care.

"That's settled," said Adam, "Sufiya! Get our things..."

There was that look from Sufiya again. He wished he knew what it meant. Contempt? Love? Indifference?

"And my father?" she asked.

There had been no intention of bringing her father back to Number 3 New Town. He would not come, Adam was sure. But how does one ask such a man? He would say, if he said anything, that he did not want to go anywhere, but if pressed he would agree to whatever you told him to say.

"It's best to leave him in familiar surroundings," said Adam, thinking that a good enough reason to leave the old man. "We can always return later to get him, if we have to," he added, covering himself. Later when they had all gathered their belongings, Adam went to hurry his father along and discovered him sitting on the bed in his room, doing nothing but stare at the wall before him.

"Get up," said Adam, "We're going."

"It was not me," said Saleem.

"Whoever it was," said Adam, "Doesn't matter. We're leaving here now before anyone comes asking questions."

Saleem nodded and picked up his suitcase.

"It was that boy," he explained. "It'll be my word against his. But it might have been me that they all saw."

Adam did not know what to make of Saleem's statement. It seemed to contain many contradictory elements, but he did not want to press his father any closer on the issue. Whatever Saleem might say, Adam thought, it was better not to know any more. After all, maybe what had happened was a good thing for him. Amina was the sort of girl to turn up again and again and that would make life more complicated than it needed to be. It was a chapter closed and now there were more pressing things to consider. At least he could pretend for the moment that there were.

Hurriedly Suffiya, Adam, Joseph and Saleem threw their luggage into Amina's car, explained to Sufiya's father that they would have to go and then left him in the hands of the Aunts who darkly waited by the door. They waved as Adam started the engine and pulled out of the compound onto the road. Adam glanced into his mirror and at the end of the Village he could see four or five soldiers gathered about the Banyan tree. He hoped the car would not draw attention to itself but if it did, as a black Mercedes, it might fool someone into thinking the car contained government officials. It would be dangerous stopping such a car. As the soldiers faded into the darkness, Adam braced himself for a long dark night of driving. He was already tired, but this was the best thing to do. The further away he would be from his father's crime, the better.

Through the night they drove, the headlights powerfully guiding them along the narrow mountain roads until they found themselves back on the highway, where once again the military convoys were lined up, the troops asleep on the road beside their vehicles. None stirred, though Adam felt that one honk of the horn, one screech of a tyre, one crunch of a gear would awaken the whole army and they would be found in their midst, within all their gun-sights.

By the time they reached the central plains, the troops had disappeared. Adam relaxed and let go of the mad chase that had run through his mind with slips and diversions, with twists and turns and threats from gun-wielding psychotics, all of whom he tried to imagine himself gunning down, outwitting, or at their mercy. He would be rescued by the sudden appearance of Joseph with his gun or even Sufiya hurling a skilfully aimed stone that distracted the enemy sufficiently to allow Adam a quick kick to the groin and a reversal of fortunes. All this faded back into the film from whence it had come. The Lady Banditress, his mother, digging her spurs into the side of her squealing rearing horse, crying "Adios Amigo," and galloping into the sunset to live another day, and right another wrong. His eyes red, his brain fried, Adam gripped the steering wheel and ploughed on through the nightmare.

Early in the morning, waking from his sleep, Joseph attempted to engage everyone in singing various idiotic tunes he had learnt from the radio. Sufiya and Adam were obliged to join in otherwise they would prove themselves old fashioned, un-cool, not with it sufficiently, so explained Joseph. Saleem, of course, was excused all participation because he had supposedly had a funny turn and become disoriented and lost while walking. It was a sign of his age, so Adam pronounced, and believed it. For it was all a sign of Saleem's age. The third stage of man was not the final wisdom that comes with long experience and hard earned ability, but a disintegration of the components of one's mind. Some parts died, others lost contact with each other, and those over-used became stuck in repeating loops of disordered behaviour. Just as one got it together, it fell spectacularly apart. Never would there be a time to rest. Never would there be a time to bask in the glow of satisfaction from a job well done. It would all become a time for desperately trying to hold together the little strength of character one had managed to gather. Now was that noble? Was that right? Was that fair? Should one despair for this future? Should one escape through an early death? To burn out, to go slowly, to simply take it as it comes, were all solutions Adam contemplated as he drove on, but he came to no conclusion. Nothing, it seemed, amounted to much in the end, but he would continue out of habit if nothing else. If you fell, so what? If you rose to the top of the heap, so what? It was better to be rich than poor. It was better to live a long life than a short one. It was better, but so what? Then it dawned on him: So what so what? To be better was enough, was all that mattered. And whatever he thought was best for himself, was best. Not what others thought was best for him, not what wiser, greater, cleverer people thought was best for him, but simply what he thought was best. Because so what? He could be happy with that, he told himself. Getting away with it was all that mattered.

They arrived home and although Adam had not been away from his home for long, there had been great changes. When he drove the Mercedes along the newly tarmacked road out of the desert, Adam and Sufiya saw that the old village looked green. A spray of water filled the air as sprinklers watered newly laid out lawns. It looked like an advertisement from a magazine.

Adam could not resist stopping beside his father's old home. Some workmen were unrolling a perimeter fence and stapling it onto posts, but as yet anyone stopping on the highway could walk in unchallenged. The old well was visible again. The sand dune had disappeared. The ramp where the camels used to walk, lowering and raising leather water buckets, was in the process of being restored.

Adam stepped from the car, stretched, yawned and then climbed up the camel ramp to look over the rebuilt garden wall. A fountain, as yet without water, stood at the centre of newly dug in topsoil. Here and there trees and shrubs were already in position and growing. Green netting covered various squares ready for seeding. Sufiya, now beside him, said, "It would seem that the desert has been turned back."

Adam contemplated the new construction for a moment. The desert was still there but it was less intrusive. It was under control. One day it would break through again but for the time being, there it was, pushed back in favour of greenery and a few dollars. This western science, thought Adam, it might be able to push back that craziness that his father had succumbed to. Maybe it would go on forever and one could glide into a nice sort of unassailable stasis. And then the moon girls would come and massage away all pain.

When they returned to the car, Joseph, oblivious to the significance of this place, impatiently stood by the door, drumming on the car rooftop asking when they could get something to eat and where on earth was this big apartment store that Adam was supposed to own?

Adam slipped the car into gear and drove them past a hoarding declaring the site of The Emperor's Palace Casino. Steel pylons were being delivered to form the giant frame. The desert was being levelled out. The dunes were being replaced with lorries, bulldozers, and workmen's huts. As they approached the town, various hoardings outlined how the new map of the area would look: at various intersections, blocks of greenery-strewn buildings were to sprout up and turn the town into a latter day Babylon.

The car slipped into the main thoroughfare, busy with trucks and lorries tearing holes in the badly-made road. Here and there a motorcyclist whizzed along, weaving in and out of the damaged road surface. Then, the car continued past Castrol's, past Omar's office, and down the road to Adam's shop, which did not look that impressive to Joseph.

When Adam and Sufiya climbed out of the car, they found half the graveyard was smoothed over and parked with big-wheeled dumpers and scrapers. The newer section where Adam's mother was buried seemed left intact but Adam was certain that his grandparents had been buried where the trucks were.

They collected their luggage then unlocked the shop door. Entering, they felt as though everything had been rearranged. It was an immediate sensation. There was a smell of disturbance. Adam dropped his bag and ran to the bedroom. Some of the drawers were open and the contents neatly placed in piles on the floor. Sufiya found the kitchen equally upset. Nothing had been taken, there was no sign of frantic ransacking, merely systematic searching through their belongings and a failure to replace everything back exactly as they were.

"Is it a robbery?" asked Joseph.

Adam shook his head. He did not know what it meant. He would deal with that later. In the meantime he wanted to eat and do nothing but sit on the roof watching the red glow of dust that filled the sky. No parrots squawked because the trees had all been destroyed. No insects rattled. A deathly silence filled the air and Adam took Sufiya's hand and they kept the silence.

"This looks a very boring sort of place," said Joseph looking out from the roof.

***

The next morning came with the starting up of the construction vehicles. Jackhammers began their thudding. Motorcycles started roaring one way then another. Dust filled the air, not the grit of flying wind-blown sand that scraped the face and penetrated doors and windows alike, but a vague white fume of dust that turned the sun red and dried the inside of the nose.

Over breakfast Adam tried to list what he had to do. Mostly he had to get himself another truck.

"Do we need a truck?" asked Sufiya, "Maybe a van or just a car would do. Do you have to take that car back?"

Adam planned to go and set fire to it somewhere, but then thought maybe just changing the number plates would be enough. Surely nobody would come looking for it here? They would merely think that the car had been whisked over the country's border by some gypsy con-artist.

"And will you be going to work today?" Sufiya asked Saleem.

Saleem, unshaven and red-eyed, wearing his pyjamas, entered the kitchen and sat at the table. But he ate nothing and made no sound.

"You are very quiet," said Sufiya. "You are not still brooding over that stupid girl that Adam brought with him?"

Her brother's eyes widened and he quickly exchanged glances with Adam. Adam braced himself for some tirade, some exposure of his folly, some demand for explanations and excuses but it was not forthcoming. Instead Sufiya piped up with an explanation.

"She helped Adam when he was beaten up in the capital during the coup," she explained, "So we had to put up with her. But she was not a suitable person and well, there had been some unpleasantness when she was dancing at the hotel."

"A dancer!" said Joseph, tutting his disapproval of such a creature, his eyes wide. "They sow what they reap."

"Well it was not ideal having a girl like that around but she had helped Adam and so it was only right to extend our hospitality to her. However, the ungrateful thing just disappeared. She did not steal anything luckily but with these gypsies you never can tell."

Adam wondered how much Sufiya knew, how much she had guessed, why he was forgiven, was he forgiven? Either way he was sure that the incident was now officially in the past. She would mention it no more, though maybe would think of it and bring it up in defence as needs be. But as a constant source of pain, of reproach, Amina was to fade away. The crisis was over.

Adam could go about his business without worry. He could enjoy driving about town in the Mercedes. It would be safe, he thought, if he was brazen. If not, then it would arouse suspicion. Someone somewhere would report him. But as a brazen symbol of his success in the city, who would be any the wiser? Only Rashid knew otherwise, but he would not say anything. There would be no profit in that, not yet anyway. So when Adam arrived at the Hotel, he walked arrogantly through the foyer and down the colonnade towards his shop. Beside him walked Joseph, his eyes wide with wonder, so interpreted Adam, who showed him about, explained the rules, and threw impressive figures at him about how many guests checked in and out and how much money they each carried and spent on the complex.

When Adam found his shop-counter had been stripped of merchandise and there was no sign of his name, he explained this away as a temporary measure because they were about to upgrade the whole facility. Perhaps Joseph even believed him. There was no reason he should not since the boy had no knowledge of how these things operated, but Adam began to feel increasingly uncertain about his position. He took a deep breath, marched to Rashid's office, and rapped on the door. After a moment Rashid called out and Adam, with a quick glance at Joseph staring at his own reflection in the marble floor, pushed the door open.

Rashid had his head down as if busy at some very important work on his desk. Then he looked up and after a slight scowl, there was a smile.

"Aaah," he said, "Adam, yes come in!"

Rashid casually propped himself on the corner of his desk as he kicked his chair forward for Adam to sit down.

"You seem to have been gone a long time," he said, "I closed the counter down and sold off the stock. I've got some new cheaper stuff, better quality, coming in. And I've got a designer working on a new look. We checked out your shop in town as well. All those scruffy cardboard boxes will have to go. And I can see I'm going to have to bring your accounting system right up to date."

Rashid leaned forward a little and lowered his voice to a whisper.

"And I've dealt with that business between you and Omar," he added.

The audacity of Rashid stunned Adam. The man was brazen! He robs you and declares it the greatest favour ever done.

"Lots of things have been happening whilst you've been away," continued Rashid, "And lots of rumours. The military crack-down in the north has led to many people asking all sorts of questions. I know that this does not really apply to you. Sometimes families are best kept at a distance but the drug barons of the north are a major problem and as a party member I have to keep an eye on anyone with even the remotest connection . . . You do understand?"

"I have no such connections," blurted out Adam, shaking and wondering if he should punch Rashid. He wanted to punch someone but there would be a price to pay and he could not risk it. So he smiled, much to his shame.

"Good good," said Rashid, "However, I just think you should understand that Omar is now Regional Commander of the Police. Someone in the Capital had the bright idea of upgrading him. I believe he is even going to have several constables under him. In short, he is now not a man to get on the wrong side of. Understand what I'm saying?"

"What are you saying?" said Adam, his face glowing red as he tried to keep control.

"How was the journey to the big city?" asked Rashid, ignoring Adam's question. "Was it a great success or what?"

Adam contained himself. It must have been obvious to Rashid that Adam was fuming, that he was shaking and clenching his fists. But Rashid showed no sign of being anything but relaxed.

"I learnt a few things," mumbled Adam, "And will develop a suitable strategy to account for the prevailing on-the-ground situation."

That was not bad, thought Adam. He controlled himself well there and found the right sort of business type phrase. He hoped it would impress, though why he should impress this fraud and cheat he did not know.

"I did warn you," said Rashid, "You're not a businessman. You're a shopkeeper. Not a bad shop keeper. But essentially a shopkeeper. You have a talent with the customers. Stick to it. Mind, I think this partnership thing is stretching the meaning of the word."

"What?"

Adam dumbly stiffened.

"You have no capital Adam! Your stock was worthless. The property is rented from the state. You are lucky to have done so well, but I cannot call you a partner, can I? You're an employee!"

"You don't think employing someone with my family background will cause you any problems?" asked Adam bitterly.

"No, no," replied Rashid with a friendly smile and a welcoming hand gesture, "I need a good shopkeeper, someone with the old-fashioned sense of service. You could be most useful. But let us be realistic here..."

"Realistic?" There was a shriek in Adam's voice.

"How's your wife's brother?" asked Rashid, changing the subject, "I bet he's glad to be out of prison now?"

"I'm not just a shop keeper!" squeaked Adam, "I'm a businessman!"

Rashid shrugged and shook his head. "It's up to you," he said, "As your friend I have done the best I could do. You're going to lose the shop as a matter of course. The government wants the land for redevelopment. So, hesitate to take my offer, and you won't even be a shopkeeper. Now if you'll excuse me, I've somewhere to go."

Rashid stood up and opened his door to usher Adam out. Through the open door Adam could see Joseph lounging against one of the pillars in the foyer. Adam shot a glance at him and he immediately stood up straight.

"My wife's brother," explained Adam to Rashid, who remained impassive at the introduction.

"Nice suit," said Joseph, gangly and awkwardly offering his hand to be shaken. Rashid hesitated then let Joseph grasp it tight and pat him on the shoulder. "Great suit," he said with a wink.

"You should thank Rashid," said Adam, "He helped obtain your release."

"That's real good of you," said Joseph. "Nice to know a bit of bribery and corruption can swing it in your own favour now and again."

"There was no bribery or corruption," said Rashid, shrinking form the unwanted contact, "Just a little push in the direction of justice."

"Of course," said Joseph, "Justice was done. As usual. But if there were any real justice, I'd be a guest here and not... what is it you're offering? A security guard? Better than nothing I suppose. A temporary job though. I've got plans."

"Very good," said Rashid hurrying away across the marble floor of the foyer.

"I want to be a big shot like my brother-in-law," shouted Joseph with a wave, "Then we'll all be partners, huh?"

Rashid quickly walked passed the bar, into the restaurant and out of Adam's sight.

"Did I say something?" asked Joseph.

"No," said Adam, "I think he likes you. I could tell immediately."

***

Omar had a couple of phone calls that morning; one from Rashid demanding he find out more about that thug that Adam had brought back with him and another from the military police up north. There had apparently been a bit of ethnic conflict there, and gypsies were victims yet again. Some youth had been caught trying to use stolen credit cards in the Karaoke store. Under interrogation he had passed on a bizarre garbled tale of how he found the cards and that he was a freedom fighter trained by some old man who had driven off in a wedding car. The upshot of this being the discovery of the charred remains of a girl near where the cards were supposedly found and the mention of a name: Hacheem, Jaleem, Saleem?

Omar stifled a little laugh and immediately regained his composure. This was serious. It was deadly. He lowered his voice and muttered: "Terrible. Appalling. These gypsies are being blamed for everything when it is only a minority that are trouble makers." Such compassion could only improve his position in the world. Omar the compassionate, the just, the swift, and no more Omar the fat. But when he put the phone back he gave out a whoop and almost leapt to his feet. That would have been carrying things a bit too far, but he considered it a suitable action that he would achieve mentally if not physically.

There was no time to lose though. He stood up, fetched his uniform, and covered his naked body. Maybe, spending the mornings naked in his office was not the sort of thing a man of his stature should do nowadays. Who knows who might drop in when he least expected them? Nonetheless, it was hot, and so staying naked until he had to move beyond the door was a reasonably reasonable thing to habitually and boldly and a whole host of other adverbs do.

When he arrived at Adam's shop, for there was no other place for him to go right that moment, he marched in, with his uniform impeccable, his back straight, and his gun conspicuously by his hand. He gave it a tap with his one unbitten fingernail and Sufiya, who was sitting behind the counter while her brother amused

189

himself shooting at stones at the back of the house, glared at him. With every gun-shot of the brother, Omar nervously patted his gun and tried to convey a strut about the shop. He succeeded only in knocking a tray of old coins onto the floor and fell to picking them up. Then decided that was not his business so he ignored them and crunched over them with his boots.

"Well," said Omar, eventually, stifling a few apologies for the coins, "You're back."

Another gun-shot rang out with an accompanying ricochet but Omar managed to avoid looking behind him or otherwise flinching. Sufiya still glared at him, her eyes, he could swear, unblinking.

"I suppose you must have heard how things have changed around here," he mused, as he stumbled on a pile of coins and slapped a steadying hand into a pile of incense burners that clattered and crashed, "And er, congratulations on the coming birth. You jumped to the wrong conclusions about me you know."

Omar waited for Sufiya to say something like, "Is that so?" thus opening up a way of explaining himself. But all she did was silently glare. Omar thought he should glare back and so stood his ground and tapped on his holster until finally she spoke.

"Adam was going to go to you," said Suffiya, "Because when we returned from our trip we found that someone had been searching through the house."

"Anything stolen?" asked Omar, genuinely feeling that he should help, even though it had been him that had been rummaging about. He was careful not to take anything. He merely wanted to check there were no stolen goods, no incriminating paper work, no pictures of him in compromising positions, or whatever he thought might do him harm. On reflection he did not think his search had been a good idea. It was the kind of stupid act that had got him into trouble in the past. He wished he could avoid such things. Maybe from now on he would. He had been recognised after all and that gave him a certain position to maintain. From now on he would be very good.

"I see nothing wrong," said Omar, giving a quick glance about him. And then defining his new goodness as an attention to the facts of a case. "In fact I think you're making it all up." He was on a roll. He could feel his stature rising. "It is a serious offence wasting police time," he added. "You aren't wasting my time are you?"

Sufiya had that look again. It looked right through him, her brown eyes framed by her long black hair pulled severely behind her ears and over the back of her shoulders. A yellow silk scarf was wrapped around her neck and each end thrown over her shoulder to hang down her back.

"No," said Omar, "I thought not."

"What do you want?"

Working down from the neck, Omar discovered the fullness of Sufiya's breasts, and the freshness of her skin. There was no doubt, she was driving him insane. Her brother giggled hideously like some cackling donkey and shot off his gun. If Omar felt he was being driven insane, he felt certain that Sufiya's brother was insane. Ever since he had arrived, Omar had heard the idiot firing off his gun hour after hour. Castrol had called it public masturbation and for once Omar thought Castrol had got it right. Omar walked over to the back door and looked out at the boy. He reminded him of the two soldiers that had escorted him to the capital. Something in the northern air, or just plain in-breeding must produce such creatures.

"If I have any trouble from him I won't hesitate," he told Sufiya, patting his holster.

Sufiya sighed and looked out of the shop window and Omar could feel himself falling in love once again. The utmost contempt with which he was treated by this woman could mean nothing more than that he stood a good chance. Unfortunately she was pregnant so this was not a good time for such a venture and besides it would spoil his new image.

Omar tried to ignore her and set about the business that he had come for. He looked out the back door and saw that Saleem was sitting upon his haunches, miserably watching all the shooting.

"Saleem," shouted Omar, above another ricochet, "How's it going?"

Omar entered the courtyard and offered Saleem a cigarette. As he reached up to take it, Omar whispered to him, "I hope you didn't think this fellow would make life any easier for you, because I know someone here killed that girl and although I cannot really believe it was you or Adam, well, people have come forward. They have told the police. They have shown us where it happened. She was nothing, I know, but well, I am sure the people's court will take everything into consideration. Do you understand what I'm asking of you here?"

191

Omar felt relieved to get all that off his chest. It was not the subtlest of approaches but the reaction it got from Saleem suggested it was not a bad ploy, merely a very dangerous one.

Saleem threw his cigarette onto the floor, got up and snatched the rifle from Joseph. Omar froze as he stared down the barrel. Saleem fumbled with the rifle for a moment but then, much to Omar's relief, dropped it onto the floor and walked off towards the graveyard. Omar shook and found that sweat was squirting out of the pores on his forehead and under his arm. He would have to change his shirt if he wanted to go out later that day, he thought. Then he turned towards Sufiya and Joseph, who both stood by the door watching.

"See?" said Omar. "That is a sign!"

"Of what?" said Sufiya. "That you are a very rude man?"

Rude? Thought Omar. Rude? Him? And somehow to accuse a suspected murderer of the crime was to be no more than rude? Whatever he was, rude was not it. But the accusation penetrated to his soul. Its absurdity in the face of the enormity of the crime, in the face of the history of their relationship, in the face of the danger he was putting himself in with this nigh on psychotic bunch of characters, made him forget that he should maybe press home his case. But Saleem, he reasoned could wait. He had little evidence, other than a suspicion, which would have been enough at another time, but today was not enough. He began to giggle. And as he pushed between Sufiya and Joseph he howled with laughter.

"Rude?" he said to them in passing. "Rude!" The contempt, with which he had been treated, the lack of sensitivity to his lonely plight in this town, his adoration, his diffidence, was not even considered as worthy of a name. But this one moment of performing his duty, his genuine duty, was impolite.

He was howling with laughter as he marched off towards his car. "Rude!" he kept saying to himself as he crossed the dusty road, opened the car and climbed in. "Rude!" With a deep breath he recovered his composure only to find Adam staring through the window, rapping his knuckles on it.

"Don't do that," yelled Omar, lowering the window. "You'll stain the glass."

"Just keep away from my wife," muttered Adam.

"How is that nose of yours?" boomed Omar, screwing up his eyes to see what scars he might have left on Adam, "Still in one piece I see."

Omar tried to grab hold of Adam's nose and drag his head into the car where he would be able to tell him what the score was and how he wanted him and his nasty little family of degenerate donkey boy hill-billies out of the town and how he was going to make sure that his trading licence was revoked and that his father was imprisoned and that his brother was drafted into the army and that Sufiya was... The violent and very rude sexual acts that he had planned for her did not come to mind so easily, much to his surprise, but he put that down to the nobility of his nature...

But as he tried to grab Adam and mutilate him, Adam stepped back and was now holding onto to Omar's wrist and yanking it painfully up onto the roof of the car. As the pain began to increase, Omar found his mind strangely preoccupied with the thought that Adam had got the drop on him and might use this opportunity to do him extreme physical damage. If he had been Adam, he probably would have at least poked an eye out. And then most likely would have had to finish the job because the punishment for worse was much the same as for less. If punishment there would be! No-one would witness this, thought Omar. He could be dead meat right then and there.

"And don't park outside my shop," said Adam through gritted teeth, "Or someone is bound to do something to you when you least expect it."

"Do what?" asked Omar, squirming in pain, and the embarrassment of asking such a ridiculous question under the circumstances.

"You cannot look both ways at once," explained Adam, "I know people."

"What?" said Omar, the day turning stranger by the moment, "Rashid? Him? He's a nobody."

"You've pushed me too far," said Adam. "So don't make the mistake of thinking circumstances don't change."

"I've got witnesses. Don't you worry. We know," threatened Omar.

"Witnesses to what?"

"We know!" yelled Omar, wondering if this was the best of circumstances to be telling a man that he was about to make sure his father was to be hanged, but it was looking like Adam was incapable of breaking the law, no matter how ridiculous the law was.

"Yes. And maybe we know things as well," said Adam.

Omar could see Sufiya's brother by the shop door, his rifle casually slung over his shoulder. Now, he thought, now the bullet would come. "Bloody hillbillies," muttered Omar as Adam let go of his arm and let him drag it back inside the car. Omar quickly closed his window and pushed the gear stick quietly into place. The pleasures of a new car, he thought, are many. He flicked on the air-conditioning and then, without fear of stalling, he smoothly drove forward and away from Adam in what he hoped was a dignified unhurried four-wheel-automatically-geared fashion. When he was a sufficient distance away, he stopped and opened his window to shout, "We know that your father murdered that girl! We know! And I will be coming back to arrest him and all of you who try to stop me!" Omar quickly rolled the window up and accelerated away. There, thought Omar, let the money grubbing little weasel try to get out of that one.

***

Adam watched Omar dustily disappear into the distance. That had been one of those moments when he had a chance to gain his revenge but it would not be revenge. He was annoyed with him, but not angry. He had merely wanted to warn him off Sufiya and perhaps punch him on the nose, if he had the strength, the opportunity, the sudden influx of will, but he found he did not. Revenge was meaningless. But defence was everything. To harm someone and thus harm yourself was no cure for anything. But to make someone aware they could not harm you again, was to ever leave that person in fear of being harmed. So reasoned Adam. Though such reasoning felt of no importance as he listened to Sufiya's story of how Omar had come there making wild accusations about his father. What the man knew he could only guess, but a little knowledge in Omar's case was a dangerous thing.

When Adam finally found Saleem, he was sitting cross-legged upon the bulldozed spot where Jamilla's grave once used to be. The stones that had marked the spot, that had cracked in the heat and fallen over, that would have melted away to the rubble that characterised all the other graves, had been scraped into a heap and carted away to provide filler for a new road. The anonymity that was supposed to occur, was to happen just a little sooner than expected. And what did it matter?

"Maybe you should have stayed up north near the border," said Adam handing Saleem a bundle of money.

Saleem reached out and took the bundle. He held it in his lap and appeared to ignore it for a moment, then he rifled the money, though too quick to be counting. The face of the founder of the republic shimmered with each flick, and the numbers above his head jittered and jumped from high to low to high, racing through the numerals.

"You collect together some things," said Adam as matter-of-factly as he could manage, "And I'll drive you to the railway line."

"Where am I going?" asked Saleem.

This could be the last time that Adam saw his father, he thought. Or at least the last time he could talk to him. Not that he ever really talked to him. For what was there to say? What thoughts could they have had that were worth sharing that were not already known? Though Adam could not think of any worth knowing, he was sure there had been. But that was then, some time ago, maybe. He forgot. As everything would be forgotten. Get away with it and survive. Survive and get away with it. Try to make things better, for the moment at least. And this would be better...

"I suggest you go as far away as possible. Go to a city where you can get lost and maybe find a job of some sort. Telephone us when you want some more money. I'll try to get some to you. But just go."

"I won't even be able to sit beside my wife's grave," said Saleem.

"That's right," said Adam, "But then the alternative is being locked up by Omar."

"He's got nothing," said Saleem, "He cannot do anything."

"He can do even less with you not here."

Saleem sighed and tried to stand. Adam held out his hand but Saleem looked him in the eye and held it steady. Adam did not flinch. He waited with his hand held out. Saleem slapped it away and stood up without help.

"It was the boy that did it," he said, "It was nothing to do with me. You understand? Nothing to do with me."

"Nothing to do with you," said Adam, "The whole thing is a lie. They are all jealous of us, and trying to keep us down. That is what it is all about."

"Say it as if you mean it," said Saleem.

"I do."

And he did, for the moment, until doubt would again creep in. How could he have doubt about his own father? How could he not have doubt about him? That was how it had to be.

"So sure you've got it right," said Saleem, "Like my grandfather. Did I tell you about my grandfather having his mistress buried alive with him? I saw that. He was a great man. Like you'll be. But me, they strangled at birth."

Adam tried to take his father's hand but Saleem shook him away.

"It's too late for all that. There was never that much between us. That is why you don't believe me."

"I believe you."

"No you don't. Because we are strangers. Most confusing, don't you think?"

"No," said Adam, "We are not strangers."

Saleem waved the money before Adam's nose. "The bounty of the desert," he said, then spat on the floor. "I'll take it of course. Who knows what you might need where I'm going."

"I'll give you a lift!"

"No," said Saleem, "Don't be seen driving me away."

"It was an evil thing to do," shouted Adam, as Saleem walked away from him.

"I know," said Saleem, "But it happened. That is the way with evil things. They happen and we cannot control them, that's what makes them evil. And now I have to go. I have to be free of you. Free of your embarrassment and of my jealousy. Free to go wherever I find my inclination taking me."

Adam could not imagine his father with any inclination to go anywhere but he hoped that just this once he did. Something must stir in his imagination, some destination that he had always dreamt of, must lure him. The moon girls perhaps would rescue him. Some gypsy band would take him on board and escort him around the world. Or perhaps he would become a bandit in the hills, a terror and scourge of all hypocrisy: a rousing villainous climax to an indifferent life. Had it been so indifferent? Adam could not imagine.

"Goodbye," he shouted.

Inconvenient, thought Adam, most inconvenient.

***

Castrol, wearing his father's old red and green robes, marched towards the entrance of the temple. He paused a moment as a tour group, all cameras, handbags and burnt knees, climbed out of a mud spattered minibus and began photographing him. It was a toss of a coin as to whether he should hold his hand out and ask for a donation, but he decided that was undignified. With a slight bow of his head, now sprayed with 'Yes, Hair! The unique colouring agent,' he went inside.

It was a relief to get out of the harsh light and into the smoky incense-laden atmosphere of his temple. He paused before the great universal eye standing between two radial tyres decoratively filled with a spread of flowers and ferns. He bowed his head a second. Meanwhile, wandering about the place, various tourists flashed their cameras and pointed questioningly at the polished spark plugs, piston rings, and petrol caps on display upon the altar. Castrol continued on his way and whisked passed the tourists ignoring any questions they asked. He entered the room at the back where he had laid out a table, some chairs and a vacuum flask of hot tea. There he found a couple of ancient townswomen toothlessly gossiping with each other. They nodded to him, then wanted to know if he had heard from their dead husbands yet.

"This isn't like a telephone exchange," he said, amused at their audacity. He had only recently announced that he would start holding meetings.

"But," one of them said, holding out the reprint of the pamphlet his father had put all his religious beliefs in, "It says here that you are in contact with the dead."

"We are all in contact," he said. "What these meetings will be, will be an attempt to find a way of worshipping together in order to open our minds to . . ."

He was trying to remember what he used to hear his father saying. It had been such a long time ago.

"We are here to contemplate the infinite mystery, the unknowable, the thing that words cannot reach, that cannot be explained, where science cannot go, where we cannot see. And yet, it is part of us. And to contemplate it will help us judge all other things better. Everything will be put in perspective."

"I'd like to hear from my wife," said Saleem.

Castrol turned and found Saleem standing in the doorway. He looked strange. He was shaven for a start and his hair was oiled. The clothes he wore, although tight and a bit short, were clean. But something of another time hung about them. Even though pyjamas were just pyjamas with no particular difference from one year to the next, these looked out of season. Castrol nodded at him to sit with the two women.

"You can drink the tea," said Castrol pointing at the glasses and the vacuum flask.

The two women made a grab for the flask and poured some out into tiny cracked purple cups.

"I don't know how to do this," said Castrol, "There are only the three of us and I can remember my father dealing with twenty or thirty people. Maybe it only works with those numbers."

"My wife was hit by a truck. You fix trucks. Did you fix the truck that killed her? Did you get it on the road?" asked Saleem.

"I don't know," said Castrol, horrified to be asked such a question. "I fix a lot of trucks. What makes you think such a thing?"

"Nothing," said Saleem, "Except I've always been thinking it. I just never asked anyone, since no-one would have answered me."

Castrol poured himself a glass of tea and examined Saleem for any sign of anger, fear, or anything that might indicate he knew that it was Castrol that knocked Jamilla down. At least, Castrol feared he might have been the driver that did it. There had been blood splattered up the side of his truck the night she went missing and pieces of cloth snagged upon a few nails on the wood siding. Maybe it had really been a dog or a goat or some other animal he hit in the dark. The cloth was merely picked up on the wind. Besides, there had been nothing he could have done about it.

"Just tell me what Jamilla thinks," said Saleem. "What does she think about it all?"

There was no doubt about it, Saleem had finally cracked, thought Castrol. He has gone completely doolally.

"I suspect she does not think much about it," said Castrol, "But let me see if she comes in a dream."

"When will you have this dream?"

"Who can tell? These things happen or they don't. But I will tell you when it does."

Castrol tried to make out whether he had given a satisfactory answer or not. It was a very difficult skill being an intermediary between heaven and earth, but Castrol thought he had a calling. It was in the genes, he thought, like father, like son. And he suspected his mother had something to do with it as well, though all he recalled her saying about the matter is that his father was a lazy fool determined to get everyone in trouble with the authorities. But even she must have understood a little. And the skill, the main skill, the big skill was the skill in determining whether the people asking you questions about their dead, were crazy enough to believe everything you said. Then again there were degrees of craziness as well: the grief stricken moment, or the long brooding snapped forever kind. In his estimation, Saleem was snapped.

Saleem left the temple and Castrol thought he had better accompany him to the street. That had been something his father had been very strict about. One offered tea, one offered advice, and then one accompanied them to the door and offered one's hand as a final gesture. There was nothing worse than disappointing the really disturbed. They had a habit of turning up in the middle of the night with a noose in one hand and a burning torch in the other. But at the door Castrol looked for Saleem and could not see him. He had lost him. As if he was a ghost, thought Castrol, thinking that would be a nice story to tell. It gave his enterprise a touch of class. On the other hand the fact that the town bus was rumbling beside the stop and belching black fumes, indicated not so much ghostliness, as sudden bus chasing haste as Saleem turned out of the garage. For an old guy, he could get a lick on, thought Castrol.

***

EPILOGUE

A year later Castrol did have a dream and went to tell Sufiya about it. He would have gone to tell Saleem but the last anyone had seen of him was when he came to the temple asking those strange questions. After that he had disappeared, "Like a ghost," as Castrol delighted in telling the story and thus irritating Omar. There were also rumours of Saleem having raped and murdered some young girl and that he had always been up to those sorts of things. This was the reason why Omar had always gone about keeping an eye on all the young women of the district. Their safety had been of prime concern, because that Saleem had always been a strange one. Even the grandfather had buried some young girl alive before he had been hanged by the state for all sorts of crimes. And as for that brother of Sufiya's, well, he was not someone one would trust on a dark night. Adam too, for all his simple shopkeeper act, was just as tricky a character and definitely someone to keep on the right side of.

Still a dream was a dream and a promise a promise, and Castrol felt obliged to pass on his insight into the workings of the cosmos. When he entered Sufiya's shop, he was still stinking of 4-star from his delvings into the workings of another region of the cosmos. He felt very disconcerted by the screaming of Adam's baby.

"Stand back!" said Sufiya, "That stench is upsetting her!"

Castrol was even more disconcerted by the sound of gun-shots coming from the back of the house.

"Does your brother have to do that all the time?" he asked Sufiya.

"It helps him relax," she said, "Running the Karaoke Contest at the Hotel is a very stressful business. He's now thinking of setting up a night-club there. I think my brother will do well running a club. Especially with Adam and me doing the business side."

Another volley of shots rang out. Castrol understood what she meant. He thought he had better hurry up and deliver his message. It was too dangerous to be around these people for too long.

"Anyway, what do you want?" she asked.

"Is Adam here? It's about his mother . . ."

"He's at the hotel and most likely in the bar showing off the photographs he's taken."

"I must tell him my dream," insisted Castrol.

"Tell me. I'll get the message to him," said Sufiya, picking up the baby to give it a squeeze.

"Well, I dreamt his mother came back. She was riding this horse and was looking over the fence of a garden. And a child was there and I think you and Adam were there. And she asked, what happened to the money I lent you?"

"The dead come back to ask that sort of thing do they?"

"Well she did. And you said, in the dream that is, you and Adam said that it was all gone and that you couldn't afford to pay her anything."

"We have no debts," said Sufiya, with a tone of annoyance.

"This is just a dream," explained Castrol, "Jamilla then said, that she would never see you again."

"And that's what she said?"

"More or less."

"And what do you think it means?"

"I think this means she's alive. After all, whose body did they find in the desert? They didn't find it all did they? So, maybe she just walked off."

"And you saw this in a dream?"

"Yes!"

"It's a bit late isn't it? If you'd told Saleem earlier on it might have saved a lot of trouble for us all."

"Dreams are funny things. They happen when they happen. And perhaps this has happened now because Saleem has found her. And they are together. That's the message I feel I have to give. That Adam's father has found his mother. At least that's what I think it means."

Sufiya nodded and looked down at her daughter. "Well I don't know what it means. It probably means you shouldn't sniff that petrol of yours too much."

***

Omar drove his four-wheel drive over the dune to where the second phase of development had started. A couple of large-wheeled dumper trucks were already loading up sand, the vibrations and the fumes of their engines filling the air. Omar climbed out and approached the hard-hatted foreman who held out his hand to shake.

"It's over here," said the Foreman leading Omar to a sheet of blue tarpaulin. Omar pulled the sheet back. There were some bones with bits of flesh and clothing still on them. Animals had obviously made a feast of whoever it was. Omar covered the bones back over and began punching out the numbers on his mobile phone.

"I'll get Castrol to come and pick it up. There's not a lot of point in doing much of a search of the area. If there was an obvious gunshot or knife wound it'd be a different matter. Did you find anything on it?"

The Foreman pulled out a wad of bank notes.

"Mm," said Omar, taking them and putting them into his pocket. "Surprising that your men reported they found those."

"Not everyone's dishonest," said the Foreman.

"You must be paying them too much, that's all I can say."

Omar walked back towards his four-wheel drive. Even though there was dust and dead flies spattered up the doors, the chrome still glinted in the sun. It was beautiful. The Foreman followed behind.

"There's talk of a Karaoke competition," said the Foreman, "You going to enter?"

"Karaoke eh? Next we'll be having free elections."

"The money er, that will be taken care of?"

"Don't worry," said Omar, "I know who my friends are."

Omar started up the engine. The purr was music to his ears. The air conditioner cooled him. He put on his stereo cassette and the music began. He loved that tune. So sexy, so full of longing for passion, for life.

"Come on Come on Uh!" she sang.

It was not so much the song as the dance-number the singer performed on MTV. That was a work of art, thought Omar and when she comes to sing and dance at the opening of the Casino he will be in the front row in full uniform. That will surely impress her. He had already written thirty letters to the girl. He was her best fan, and told her so. He was sure that one look at his four-wheel drive would be all that was needed to show that he was good enough for her.

As he drove off, he waved to his friend, the Foreman. Not such a bad guy for a Westerner. He supposed he should do him a favour, like make sure building permits and the like went through without too much trouble. He had better check on anything outstanding before the man got the wrong idea.

Omar headed off on the day's tour of the shanties. They were springing up all round the town. People from the north were pouring into the area by the thousands. That would be more trouble. He hoped the government would send him the promised new recruits. He could not be expected to do everything!

THE END

ADVANCE RESPONSES

A breathless, Technicolor romp through something very like the modern, globalised world.'
 — Justin Hill, author of the *Washington Post* Book of the Year, *The Drink and Dream Teahouse*

Adam's Franchise is a cinematic, picaresque, family drama that reads like a comic tragedy. Adam's desire for modernity is contrasted against the traditional cultures of his widowed father and his wife's taciturn family. The events set in the fictional country of Daoistan that comprise the plot of this novel are amusing, slightly manic, and feel like escapades going awry. Adam's persistence in his desperate bid to be modern – he sets up a shop in a hotel, acquires a western suit, travels to the city to open a bank account – gives the story an intriguing energy. He proves a sympathetic character despite his many flaws, and he somehow succeeds in spite of himself, this protagonist who is fated to be thwarted at every turn. An enjoyable read, with a memorably mad cast of characters inhabiting a world that is slightly surreal, yet still dauntingly real.
 — Xu Xi, novelist, author of *That Man In Our Lives*

THE PUBLISHERS

Proverse Hong Kong (PVHK), founded by Gillian and Verner Bickley, is based in Hong Kong with long-term and developing regional and international connections.

Proverse has published novels, novellas, non-fiction (including autobiography and biography, history, memoirs, sport, travel narratives), single-author poetry collections, children's, young teens and academic books. Other interests include diaries, and academic works in the humanities, social sciences, cultural studies, linguistics and education. Some Proverse books have accompanying audio texts. Some are translated into Chinese.

We welcome authors who have a story to tell, wisdom, perceptions or information to convey, a person they want to memorialize, a neglect they want to remedy, a record they want to correct, a strong interest that they want to share, skills they want to teach, and who consciously seek to make a contribution to society in an informative, interesting and well-written way. Proverse works with texts by non-native-speaker writers of English as well as by native English-speaking writers.

The name, "Proverse", combines the words "prose" and "verse" and is pronounced accordingly.

THE INTERNATIONAL PROVERSE PRIZE
FOR UNPUBLISHED BOOK-LENGTH FICTION,
NON-FICTION OR POETRY

The Proverse Prize, an annual international competition for an unpublished single-author book-length work of fiction, non-fiction, or poetry, the original work of the entrant, submitted in English (unpublished translations welcomed) was established in January 2008. It is open to all who are at least eighteen on the date they sign the entry form and without restriction of nationality, residence or citizenship.

Founded by Gillian and Verner Bickley, the objectives of the prize are: to encourage excellence and / or excellence and usefulness in publishable written work in the English Language, which can, in varying degrees, "delight and instruct". Entries are invited from anywhere in the world.

The Prize
1) Publication by Proverse Hong Kong, with
2) Cash prize of HKD10,000 (HKD7.80 = approx. USD1.00)

Extent of the Manuscript: within the range of what is usual for the genre of the work submitted. However, it is advisable that novellas be in the range, 30,000 to 45,000 words; other fiction (e.g. novels, short-story collections) and non-fiction (e.g. autobiographies, biographies, diaries, letters, memoirs, essay collections, etc.) should be in the range, 75,000 to 100,000 words. Poetry collections should be in the range, 5,000 to 25,000 words. Other word-counts and mixed-genre submissions are not ruled out.

International Proverse Prize Annual Entry Deadlines (subject to confirmation and/or change)

Receipt of Entry Fees / Entry Forms begins	[Variable, no later than] 14 April
Deadline for receipt of Entry Fees / Entry Forms	31 May
Receipt of entered manuscripts begins	1 May
Deadline for receipt of entered manuscripts	30 June

**The above information is for guidance only.
More information, updated from time to time, is available on the Proverse website: proversepublishing.com**

**WINNERS OF THE PROVERSE PRIZE 2015
Gustav Preller and Lawrence Gray.**

**PREVIOUS WINNERS OF THE PROVERSE PRIZE
WHOSE ENTERED WORK HAS ALREADY BEEN
PUBLISHED BY PROVERSE HONG KONG**

**Rebecca Tomasis
Laura Solomon
Gillian Jones
David Diskin
Peter Gregoire
Sophronia Liu
Birgit Linder
James Mccarthy
Philip Chatting
Celia Claase**

THE INTERNATIONAL PROVERSE POETRY PRIZE
(SINGLE POEMS)

An annual international Proverse Poetry Prize (for single poems) was established in 2016. The international Proverse Poetry Prize is open to all who are at least eighteen years old whatever their residence, nationality or citizenship.

Single poems, submitted in English, are invited on (a) <u>any subject or theme, chosen by the writer</u> OR (b) <u>on a subject or theme selected by the organizers</u>.

Poems may be in any form, style or genre. Each poem should be no more than 30 lines.

Entries should previously be unpublished in any way (except in the case of unpublished translations into English of the entrant's own work already published in another language, providing the entrant holds the copyright).

**In 2016
cash prizes were offered as follows:
1st prize; USD100.00; 2nd prize: USD45.00;
3rd prizes (up to four winners): USD20.00.**

If there are enough good entries in any year, an anthology of prize-winners and selected other entries will be published.

In 2016, judging took place at the same time as the judging for the Proverse Prize for unpublished book-length fiction, non-fiction or poetry.

Judges: anonymous (as for the Proverse Prize for an unpublished book-length work).

Max number of entries per person: No maximum.

No poet may win more than one prize.

**The above information is for guidance only.
More information, updated from time to time, is available on
the Proverse website: proversepublishing.com**

FICTION PUBLISHED BY PROVERSE

Those who enjoy **Adam's Franchise** may also enjoy the following novels, novellas and short story collections (listed separately).

A Misted Mirror, by Gillian Jones. 2011.

A Painted Moment, by Jennifer Ching. 2010.

An Imitation of Life. 2nd ed, by Laura Solomon. 2013.

Article 109, by Peter Gregoire. 2012.

Bao Bao's odyssey: from Mao's Shanghai to capitalist Hong Kong, by Paul Ting. 2012.

Black Tortoise Winter, by Jan Pearson. 2016.

Bright Lights and White Nights, by Andrew Carter. 2015.

cemetery – miss you, by Jason S Polley. 2011.

Cop Show Heaven, by Lawrence Gray. 2015.

Curveball, by Gustav Preller. Scheduled November 2016.

Death Has a Thousand Doors, by Patricia W. Grey. 2011.

Hilary and David, by Laura Solomon. 2011.

HK Hollow, by Dragoş Ilca. Scheduled 2016/2017

Instant messages, by Laura Solomon. 2010.

Man's Last Song, by James Tam. 2013.

Mila the Magician by Zhang Jian (Catherine Chin). 2014 (English/Chinese bilingual edition).

Mishpacha – family, by Rebecca Tomasis. 2010.

Paranoia (the walk and talk with Angela), by Caleb Kavon. 2012.

Red Bird Summer, by Jan Pearson. 2014.

Revenge From Beyond, by Dennis Wong. 2011.

The Day They Came, by Gérard Louis Breissan. 2012.

The Devil You Know, by Peter Gregoire. 2014.

The Perilous Passage of Princess Petunia Peasant, by Victor E. Apps. 2014. (Young adult)

The Village in the Mountains, by David Diskin. 2012.

The Monkey in Me: Confusion, Love and Hope Under a Chinese Sky, by Caleb Kavon. 2009.

The Reluctant Terrorist: in Search of the Jizo, by Caleb Kavon. 2011.

Tiger Autumn, by Jan Pearson. 2015.

Tightrope!: a Bohemian tale, by Olga Walló. Translated from Czech by Johanna Pokorny, Veronika Revická & others. Poetry translated by Justin Quinn, Veronika Revická. Edited by Gillian Bickley & Olga Walló, with Verner Bickley. 2010.

University Days, by Laura Solomon. 2014.

Vera Magpie, by Laura Solomon. 2013.

SHORT STORY COLLECTIONS

Beyond Brightness, by Sanja Särman. Scheduled November 2016.

Odds and Sods, by Lawrence Gray. 2013.

The Snow Bridge and other Stories, by Philip Chatting. 2015.

The Shingle Bar Sea Monster and other stories, by Laura Solomon. 2012.

FICTION – CHINESE LANGUAGE

The Monkey in Me, by Caleb Kavon. Translated by Chapman Chen. 2010.

Tightrope! A Bohemian Tale, by Olga Walló. Translated by Chapman Chen. 2011. Chinese translation supported by the Ministry of Culture of the Czech Republic.

~~~

FIND OUT MORE ABOUT OUR AUTHORS BOOKS AND EVENTS

Visit our website:
http://www.proversepublishing.com

Visit our distributor's website: <www.chineseupress.com>

Follow us on Twitter
Follow news and conversation: twitter.com/Proversebooks>
OR
Copy and paste the following to your browser window and follow the instructions:
https://twitter.com/#!/ProverseBooks
"Like" us on www.facebook.com/ProversePress

Request our free E-Newsletter
Send your request to info@proversepublishing.com.

Availability
Most books are available in Hong Kong and world-wide from our Hong Kong based Distributor,
The Chinese University Press of Hong Kong,
The Chinese University of Hong Kong, Shatin, NT,
Hong Kong SAR, China.
Email: cup-bus@cuhk.edu.hk
Website: <www.chineseupress.com>.
All titles are available from Proverse Hong Kong
http://www.proversepublishing.com
and the Proverse Hong Kong UK-based Distributor.

We have **stock-holding retailers** in Hong Kong,
Singapore (Select Books),
Canada (Elizabeth Campbell Books),
Andorra (Llibreria La Puça, La Llibreria).
Orders can be made from bookshops in the UK and elsewhere.

Ebooks
Most of our titles are available also as Ebooks.